Charles M. Schulz

PEANUTS™

Special thanks to the Schulz family, everyone at Charles M. Schulz Creative Associates, and to Charles M. Schulz for his singular achievement in shaping these beloved characters.

Cover
Pencils by **Vicki Scott**
Inks by **Paige Braddock**
Colors by **Donna Almendrala**
Design by **Iain R. Morris**

Assistant Editor: **Alex Galer**
Editors: **Matt Gagnon & Shannon Watters**
Trade Designer: **Kelsey Dieterich**

For Charles M. Schulz Creative Associates
Creative Director: **Paige Braddock**
Managing Editor: **Alexis E. Fajardo**

ROSS RICHIE CEO & Founder • **JACK CUMMINS** President • **MARK SMYLIE** Chief Creative Officer • **MATT GAGNON** Editor-in-Chief • **FILIP SABLIK** VP of Publishing & Marketing • **STEPHEN CHRISTY** VP of Development
LANCE KREITER VP of Licensing & Merchandising • **PHIL BARBARO** VP of Finance • **BRYCE CARLSON** Managing Editor • **MEL CAYLO** Marketing Manager • **SCOTT NEWMAN** Production Design Manager • **DAFNA PLEBAN** Editor • **SHANNON WATTERS** Editor
ERIC HARBURN Editor • **REBECCA TAYLOR** Editor • **CHRIS ROSA** Assistant Editor • **ALEX GALER** Assistant Editor • **WHITNEY LEOPARD** Assistant Editor • **JASMINE AMIRI** Assistant Editor • **MIKE LOPEZ** Production Designer
HANNAH NANCE PARTLOW Production Designer • **DEVIN FUNCHES** E-Commerce & Inventory Coordinator • **BRIANNA HART** Executive Assistant • **AARON FERRARA** Operations Assistant • **JOSE MEZA** Sales Assistant

PEANUTS Volume Three, March 2014. Published by KaBOOM!, a division of Boom Entertainment, Inc. All contents, unless otherwise specified, Copyright © 2014 Peanuts Worldwide, LLC. Originally published in single magazine form as PEANUTS: Volume 2 No. 5-8. Copyright © 2013 Peanuts Worldwide, LLC. All rights reserved. KaBOOM!™ and the KaBOOM! logo are trademarks of Boom Entertainment, Inc., registered in various countries and categories. All characters, events, and institutions depicted herein are fictional. Any similarity between any of the names, characters, persons, events, and/or institutions in this publication to actual names, characters, and persons, whether living or dead, events, and/or institutions is unintended and purely coincidental. KaBOOM! does not read or accept unsolicited submissions of ideas, stories, or artwork.

A catalog record of this book is available from OCLC and from the KaBOOM! website, www.kaboom-studios.com, on the Librarians Page.

BOOM! Studios, 5670 Wilshire Boulevard, Suite 450, Los Angeles, CA 90036-5679. Printed in China. First Printing.
ISBN: 978-1-60886-357-0, eISBN: 978-1-61398-211-2

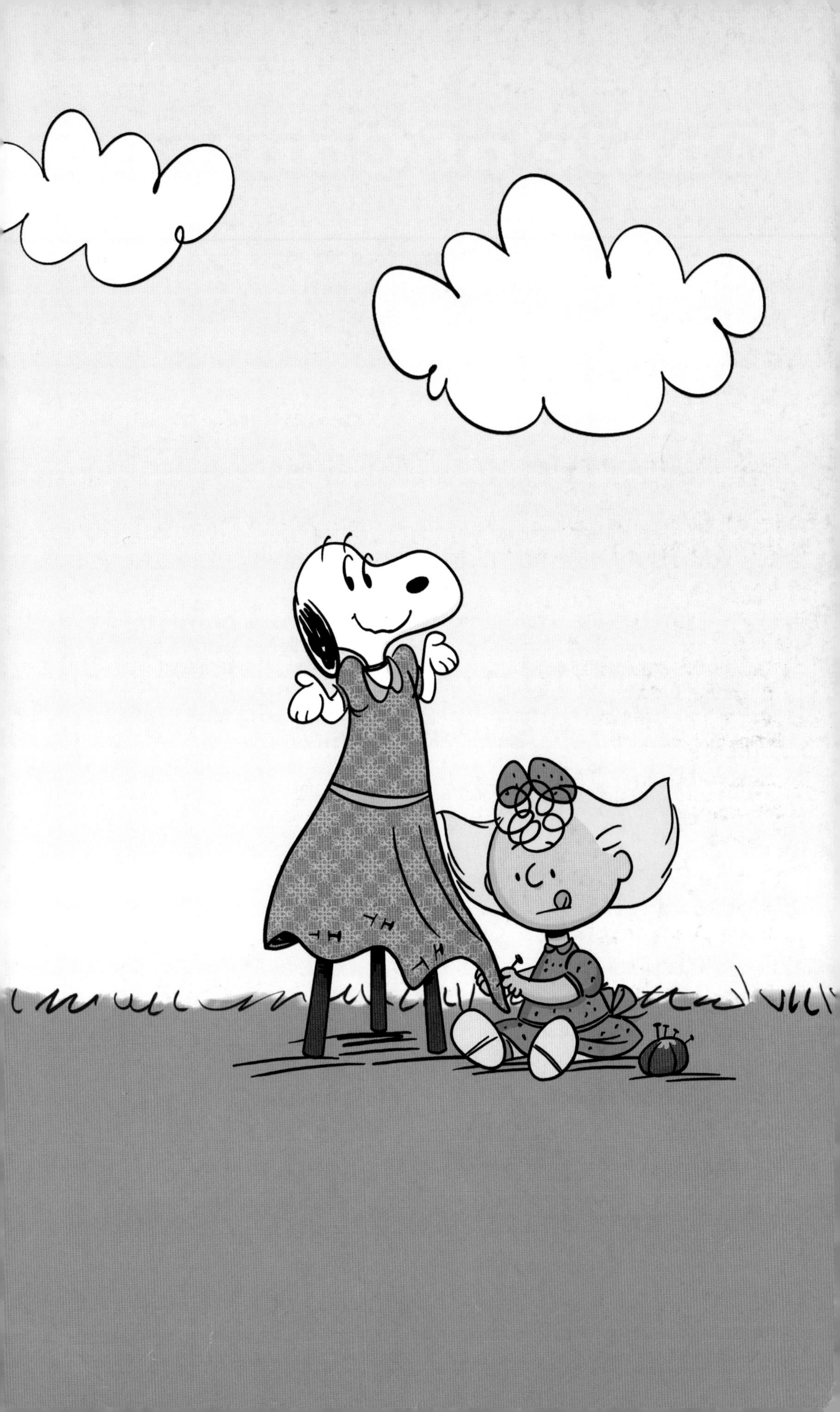

Table of Contents

Classic Peanuts Strips by
Charles M. Schulz
Colors by Justin Thompson & Art Roche

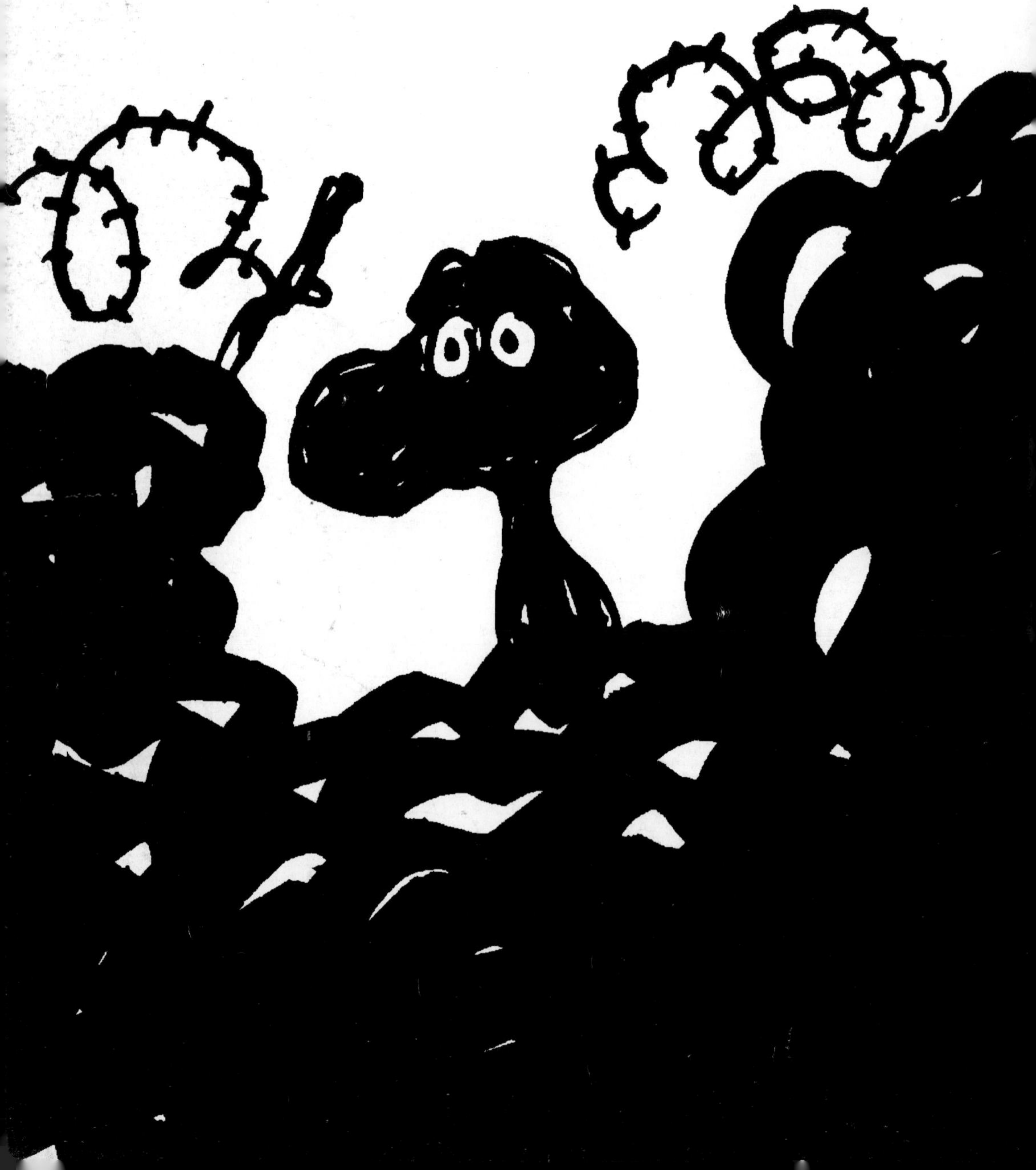

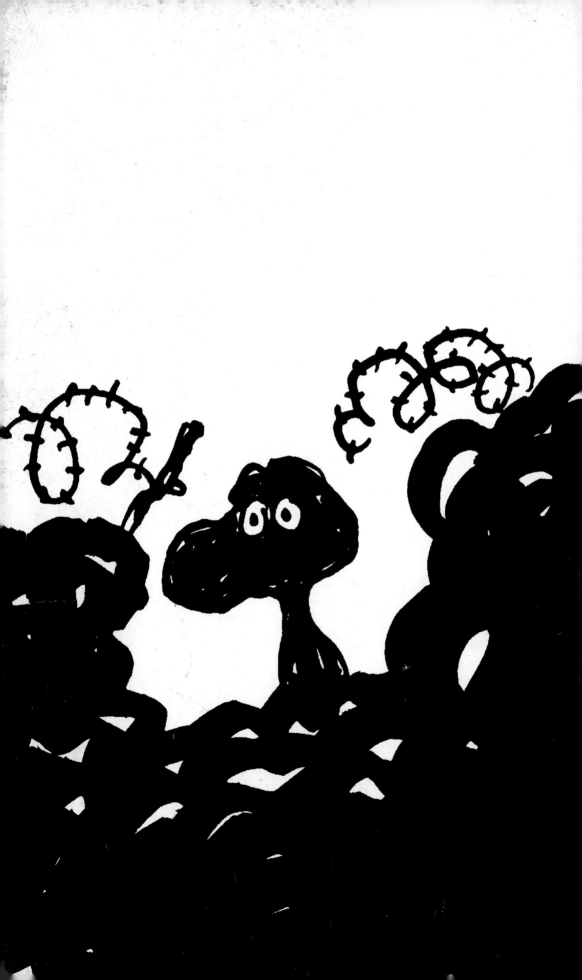

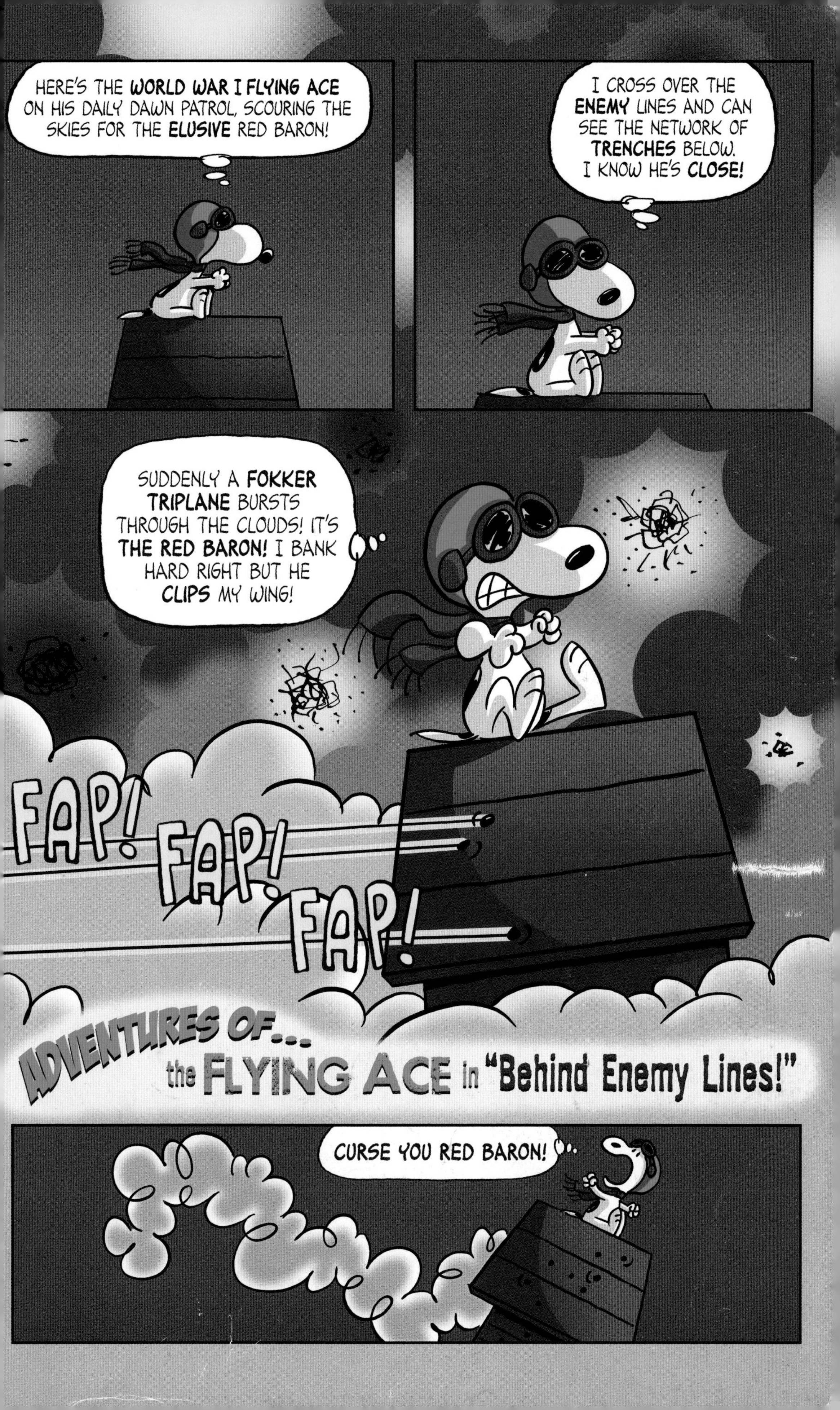
HERE'S THE WORLD WAR I FLYING ACE ON HIS DAILY DAWN PATROL, SCOURING THE SKIES FOR THE ELUSIVE RED BARON!
I CROSS OVER THE ENEMY LINES AND CAN SEE THE NETWORK OF TRENCHES BELOW. I KNOW HE'S CLOSE!
SUDDENLY A FOKKER TRIPLANE BURSTS THROUGH THE CLOUDS! IT'S THE RED BARON! I BANK HARD RIGHT BUT HE CLIPS MY WING!
FAP! FAP! FAP!
ADVENTURES OF... the FLYING ACE in "Behind Enemy Lines!"
CURSE YOU RED BARON!

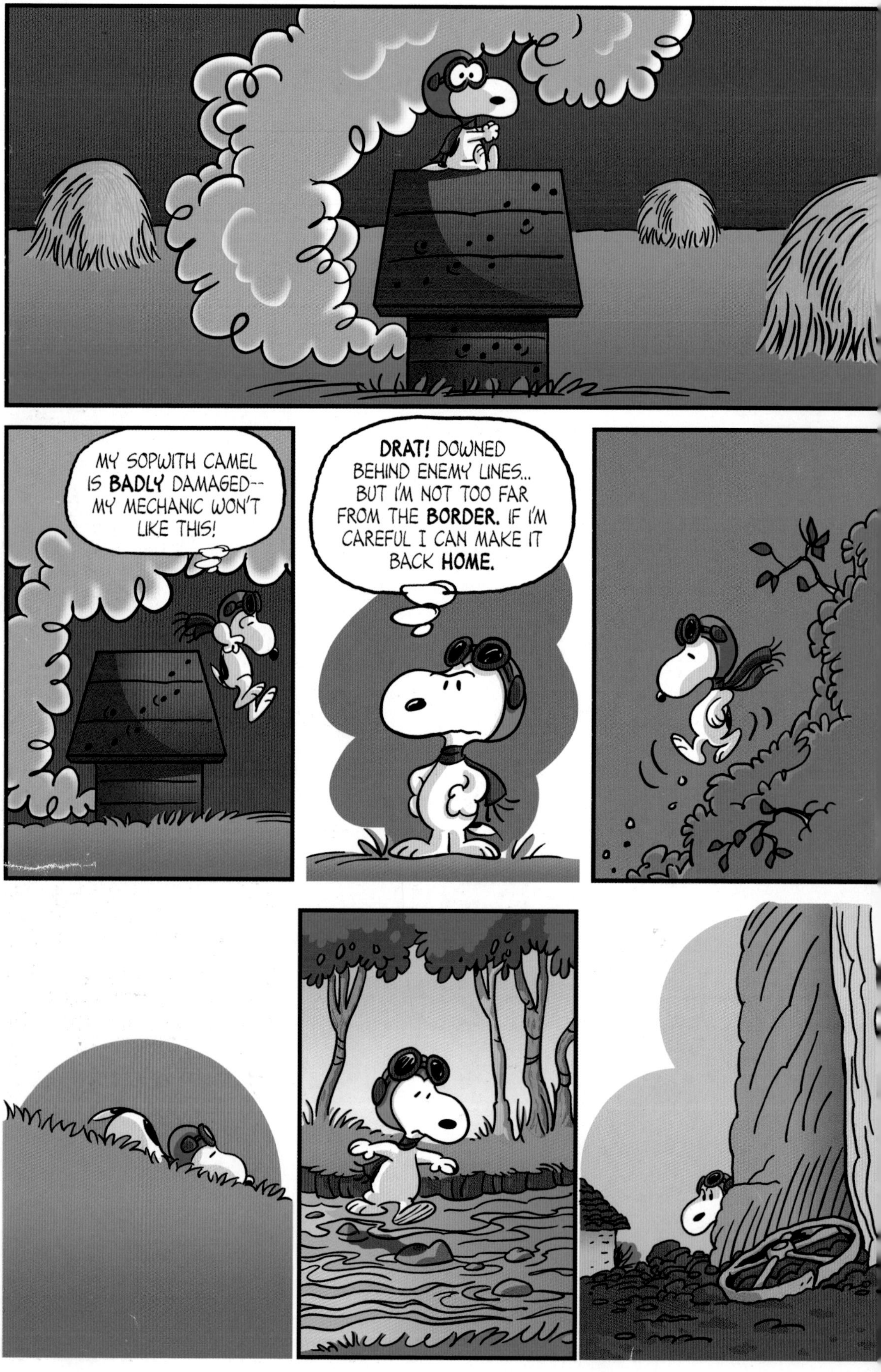
MY SOPWITH CAMEL IS BADLY DAMAGED-- MY MECHANIC WON'T LIKE THIS!
DRAT! DOWNED BEHIND ENEMY LINES... BUT I'M NOT TOO FAR FROM THE BORDER. IF I'M CAREFUL I CAN MAKE IT BACK HOME.

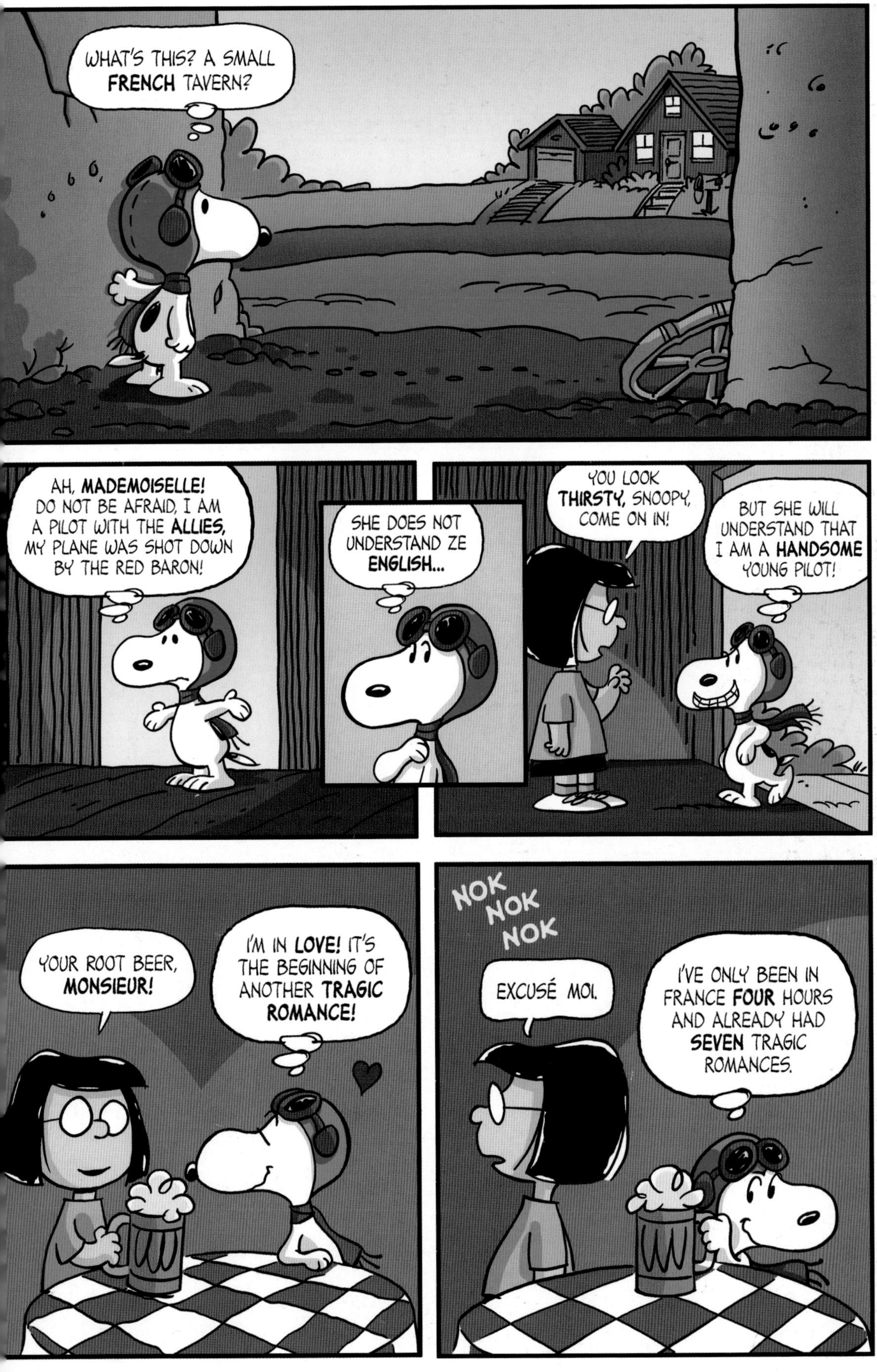
WHAT'S THIS? A SMALL FRENCH TAVERN?
AH, MADEMOISELLE! DO NOT BE AFRAID, I AM A PILOT WITH THE ALLIES, MY PLANE WAS SHOT DOWN BY THE RED BARON!
SHE DOES NOT UNDERSTAND ZE ENGLISH...
YOU LOOK THIRSTY, SNOOPY, COME ON IN!
BUT SHE WILL UNDERSTAND THAT I AM A HANDSOME YOUNG PILOT!
YOUR ROOT BEER, MONSIEUR!
I'M IN LOVE! IT'S THE BEGINNING OF ANOTHER TRAGIC ROMANCE!
NOK NOK NOK
EXCUSÉ MOI.
I'VE ONLY BEEN IN FRANCE FOUR HOURS AND ALREADY HAD SEVEN TRAGIC ROMANCES.

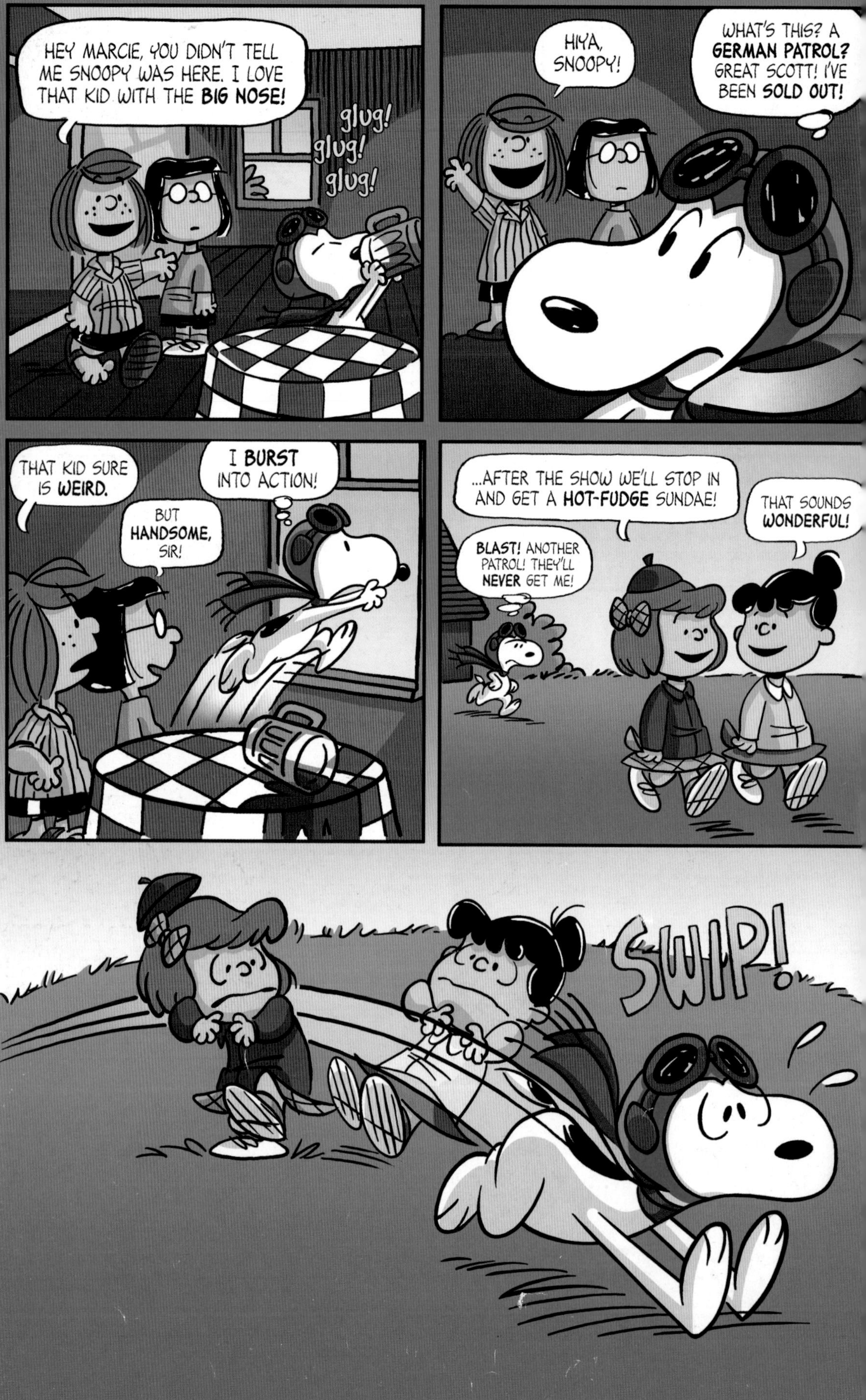
HEY MARCIE, YOU DIDN'T TELL ME SNOOPY WAS HERE. I LOVE THAT KID WITH THE BIG NOSE!
glug!
glug!
glug!
HIYA, SNOOPY!
WHAT'S THIS? A GERMAN PATROL? GREAT SCOTT! I'VE BEEN SOLD OUT!
THAT KID SURE IS WEIRD.
BUT HANDSOME, SIR!
I BURST INTO ACTION!
...AFTER THE SHOW WE'LL STOP IN AND GET A HOT-FUDGE SUNDAE!
THAT SOUNDS WONDERFUL!
BLAST! ANOTHER PATROL! THEY'LL NEVER GET ME!
SWIP!

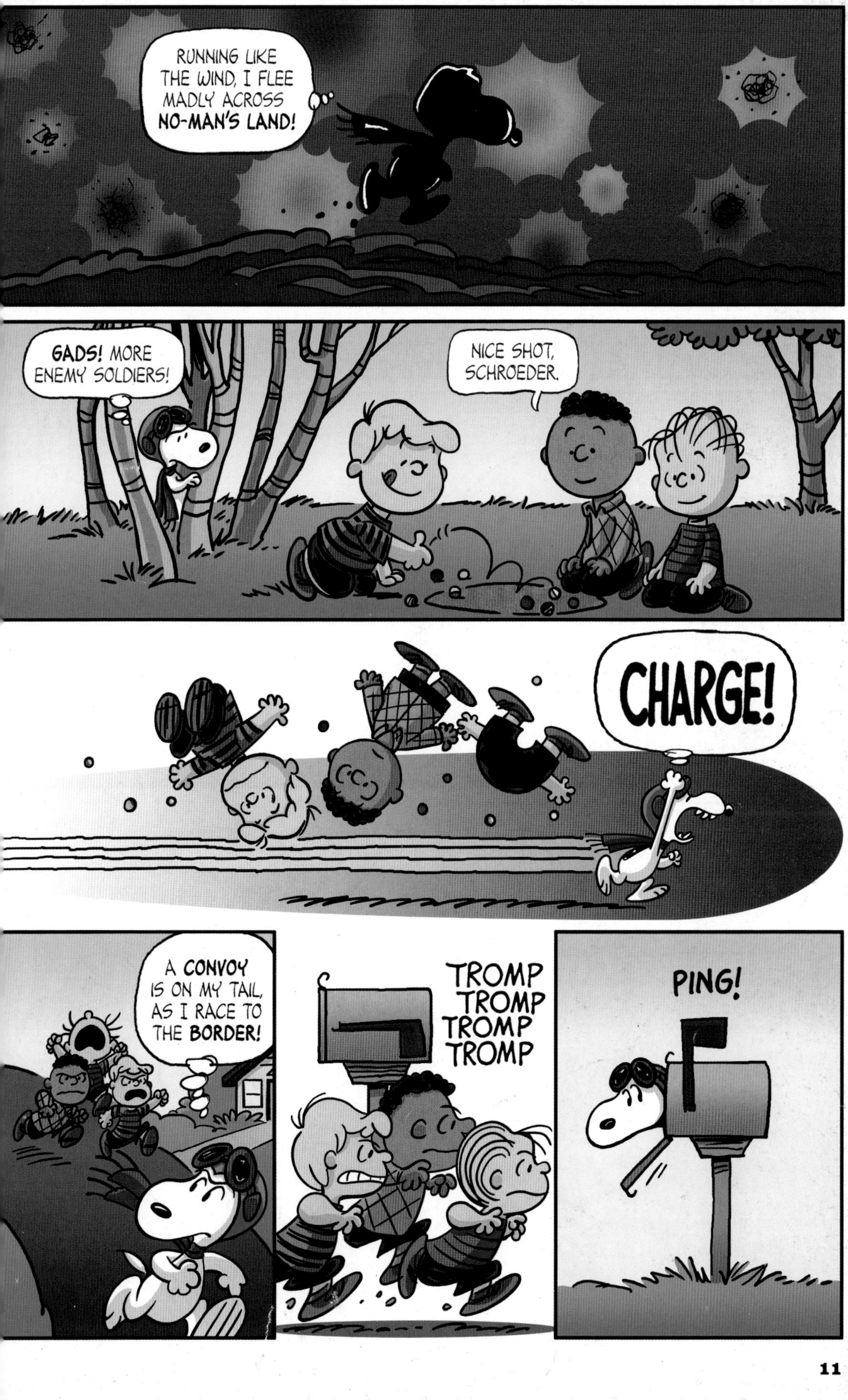
RUNNING LIKE THE WIND, I FLEE MADLY ACROSS NO-MAN'S LAND!
GADS! MORE ENEMY SOLDIERS!
NICE SHOT, SCHROEDER.
CHARGE!
A CONVOY IS ON MY TAIL, AS I RACE TO THE BORDER!
TROMP TROMP TROMP TROMP
PING!

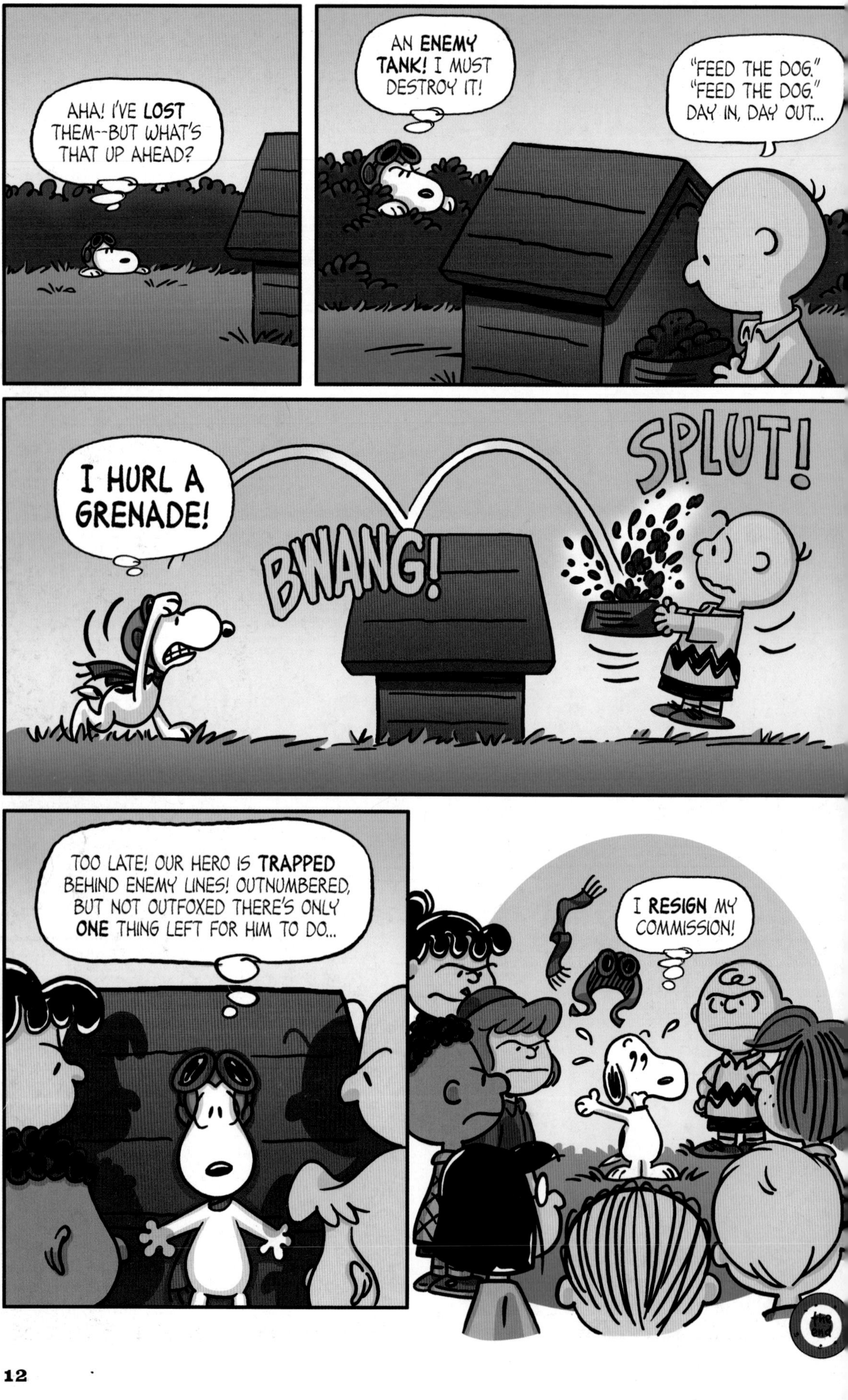
AHA! I'VE LOST THEM--BUT WHAT'S THAT UP AHEAD?
AN ENEMY TANK! I MUST DESTROY IT!
"FEED THE DOG." "FEED THE DOG." DAY IN, DAY OUT...
I HURL A GRENADE!
BWANG!
SPLUT!
TOO LATE! OUR HERO IS TRAPPED BEHIND ENEMY LINES! OUTNUMBERED, BUT NOT OUTFOXED THERE'S ONLY ONE THING LEFT FOR HIM TO DO...
I RESIGN MY COMMISSION!

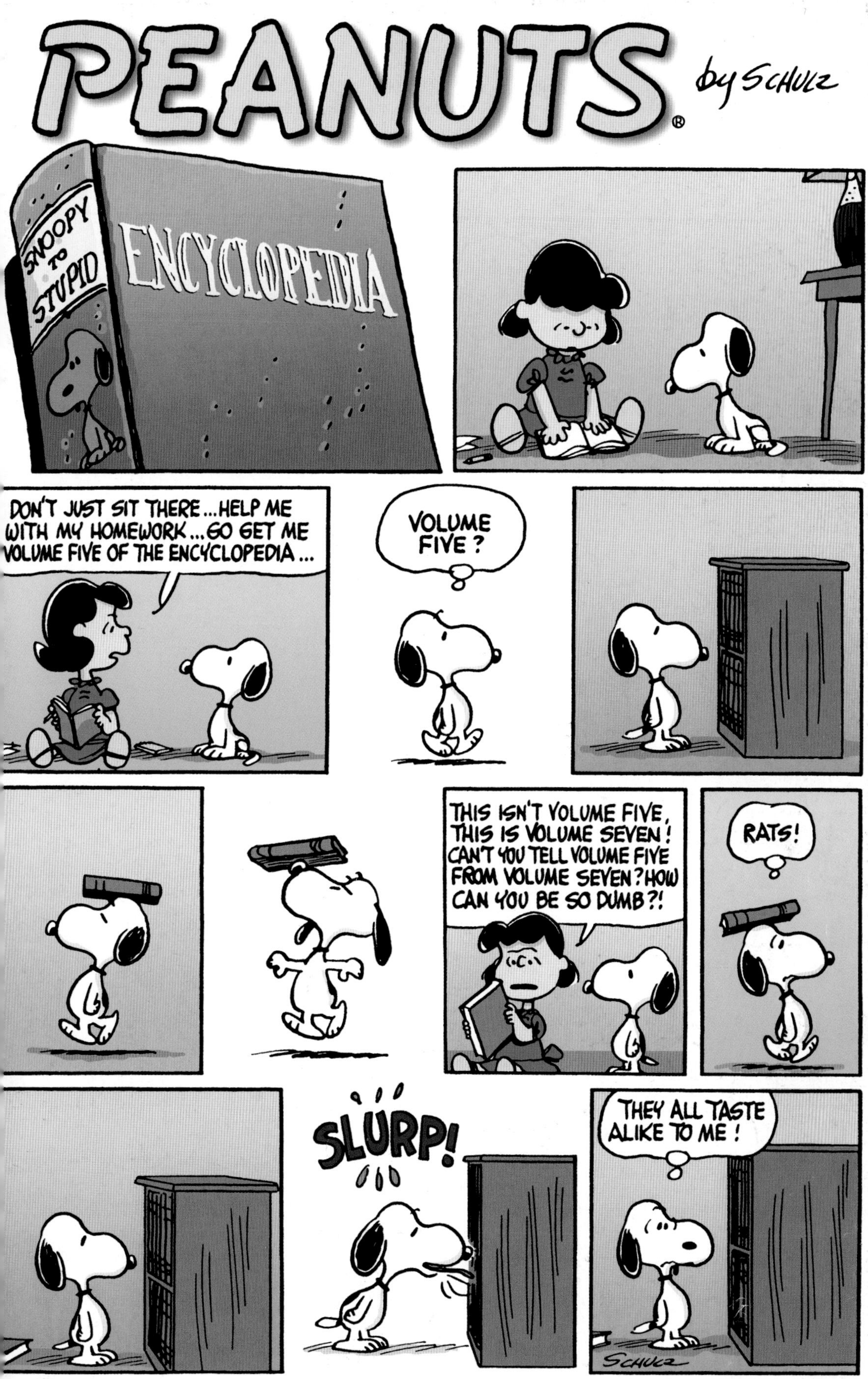

PEANUTS
by Schulz
SNOOPY TO STUPID
ENCYCLOPEDIA
DON'T JUST SIT THERE...HELP ME WITH MY HOMEWORK...GO GET ME VOLUME FIVE OF THE ENCYCLOPEDIA...
VOLUME FIVE?
THIS ISN'T VOLUME FIVE, THIS IS VOLUME SEVEN! CAN'T YOU TELL VOLUME FIVE FROM VOLUME SEVEN? HOW CAN YOU BE SO DUMB?!
RATS!
SLURP!
THEY ALL TASTE ALIKE TO ME!
SCHULZ

Crabby New Year

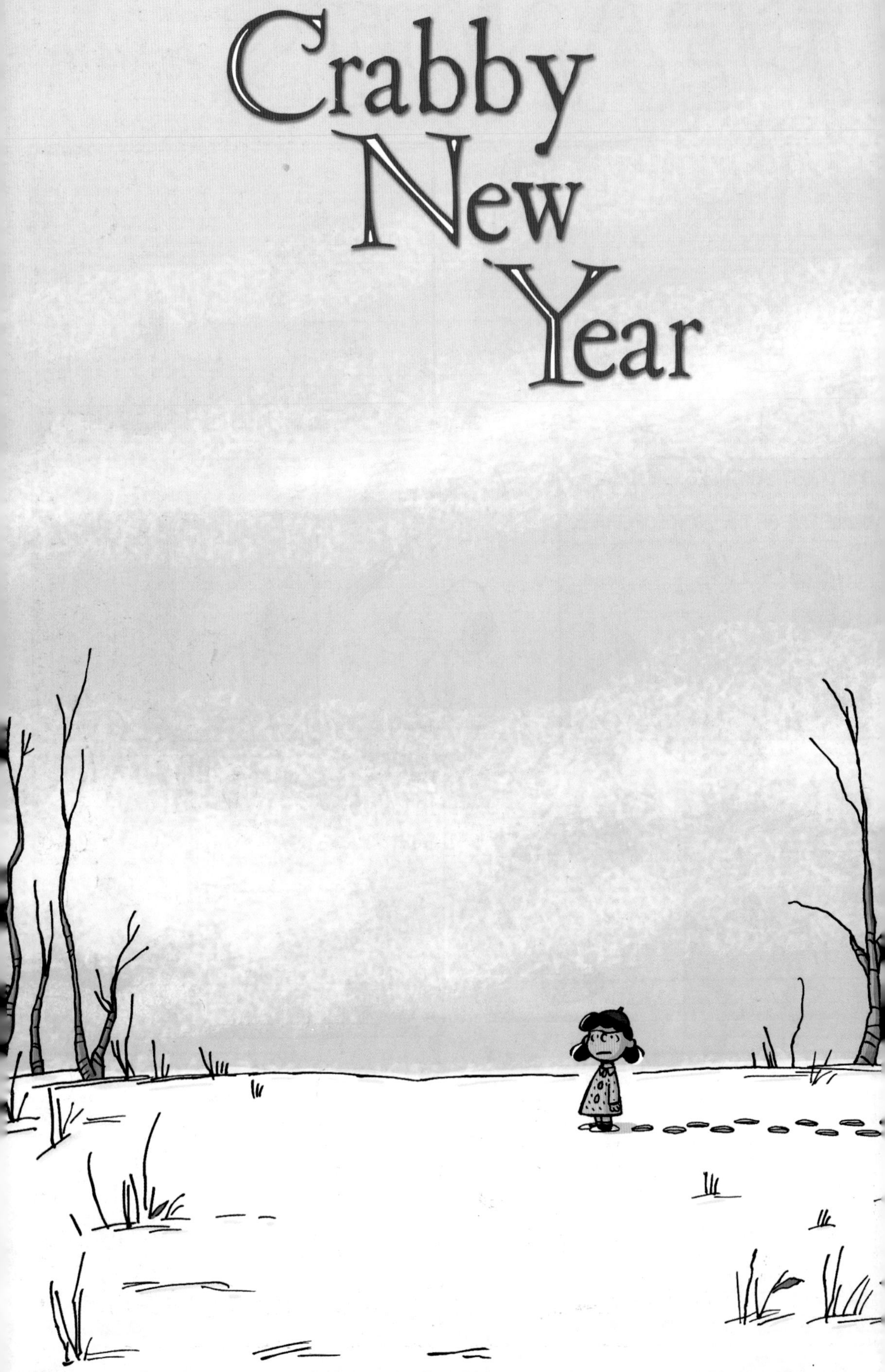

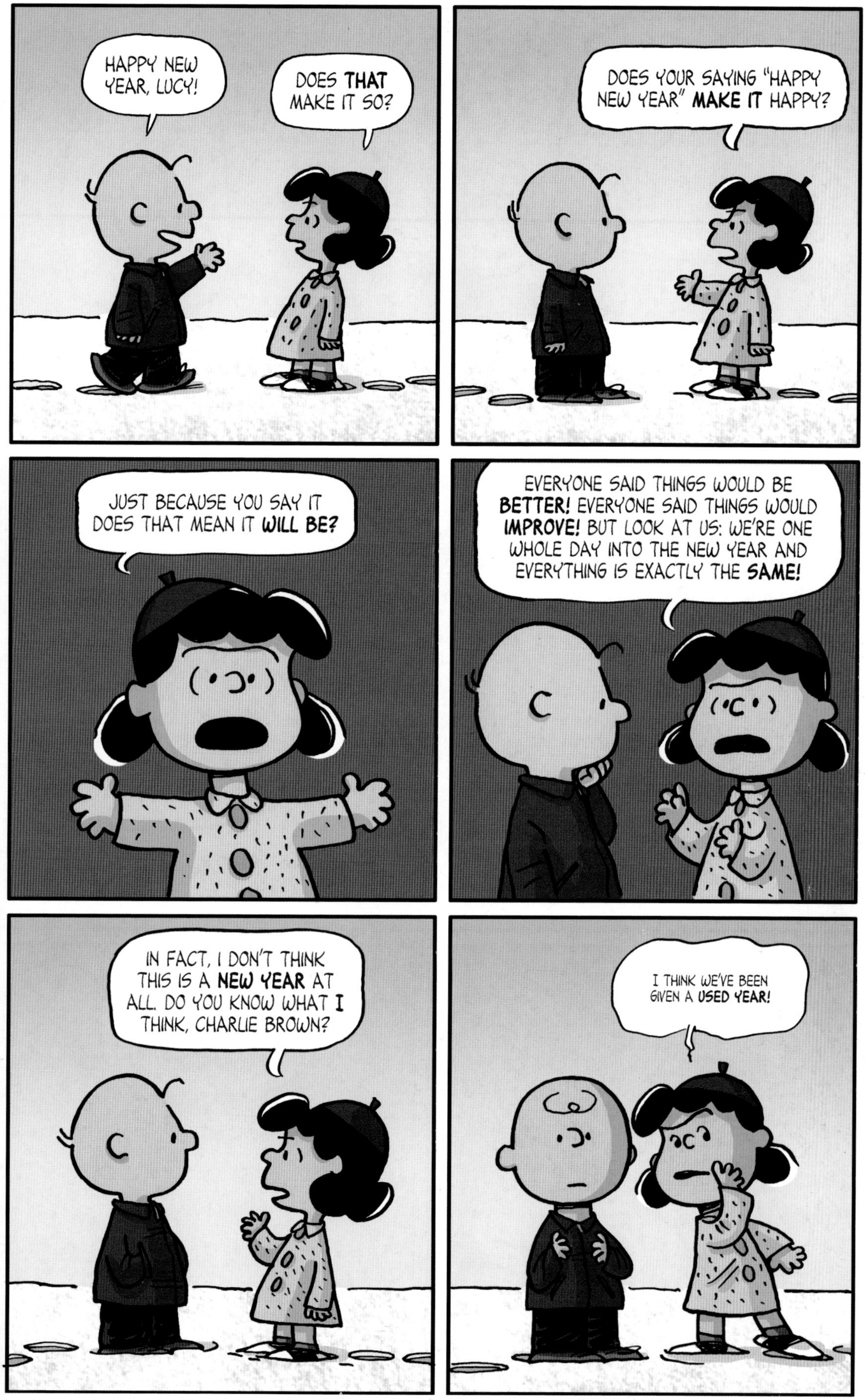
HAPPY NEW YEAR, LUCY!
DOES **THAT** MAKE IT SO?
DOES YOUR SAYING "HAPPY NEW YEAR" **MAKE IT** HAPPY?
JUST BECAUSE YOU SAY IT DOES THAT MEAN IT **WILL BE?**
EVERYONE SAID THINGS WOULD BE **BETTER!** EVERYONE SAID THINGS WOULD **IMPROVE!** BUT LOOK AT US: WE'RE ONE WHOLE DAY INTO THE NEW YEAR AND EVERYTHING IS EXACTLY THE **SAME!**
IN FACT, I DON'T THINK THIS IS A **NEW YEAR** AT ALL. DO YOU KNOW WHAT **I** THINK, CHARLIE BROWN?
I THINK WE'VE BEEN GIVEN A **USED YEAR!**

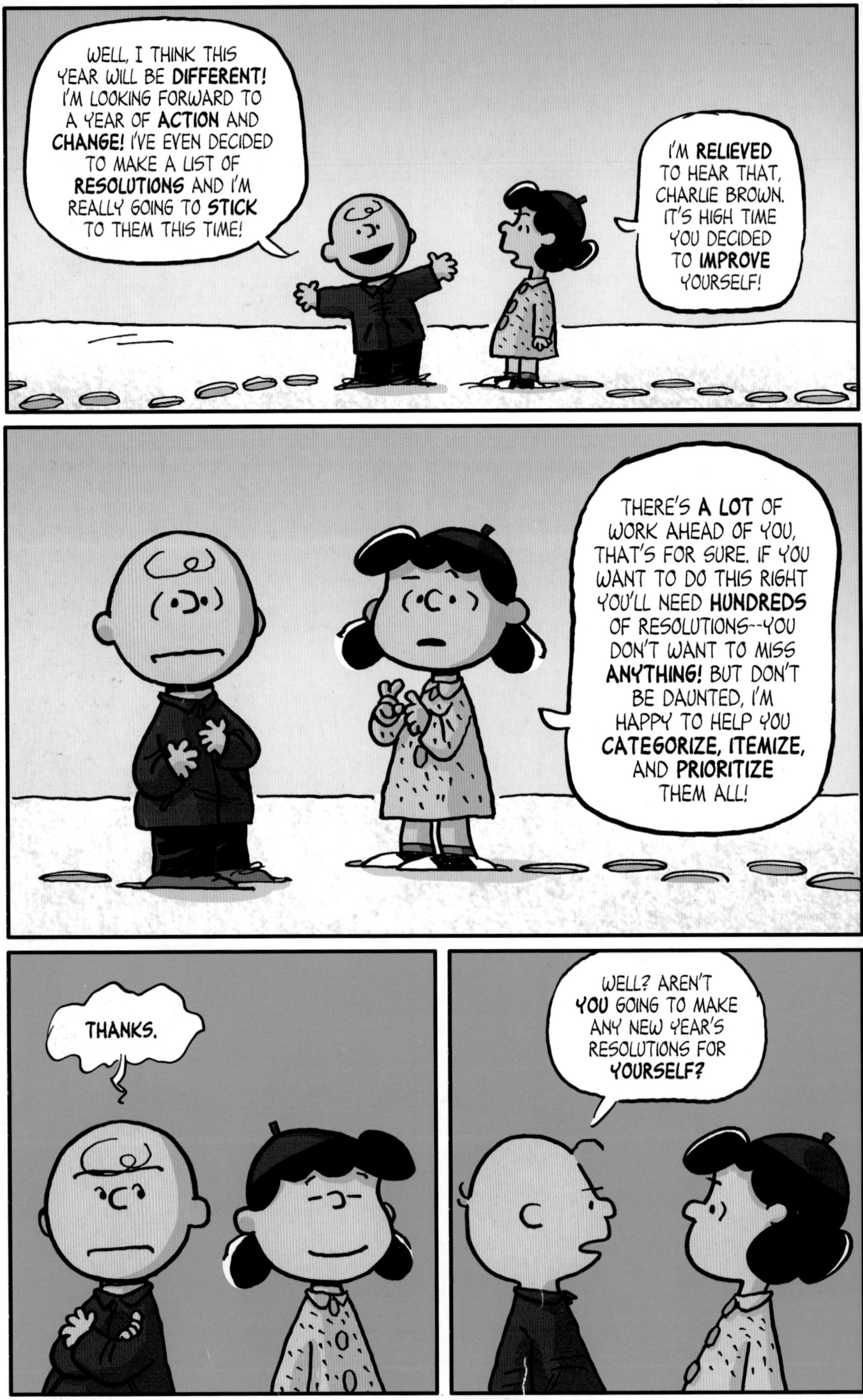
WELL, I THINK THIS YEAR WILL BE **DIFFERENT!** I'M LOOKING FORWARD TO A YEAR OF **ACTION** AND **CHANGE!** I'VE EVEN DECIDED TO MAKE A LIST OF **RESOLUTIONS** AND I'M REALLY GOING TO **STICK** TO THEM THIS TIME!
I'M **RELIEVED** TO HEAR THAT, CHARLIE BROWN. IT'S HIGH TIME YOU DECIDED TO **IMPROVE** YOURSELF!
THERE'S **A LOT** OF WORK AHEAD OF YOU, THAT'S FOR SURE. IF YOU WANT TO DO THIS RIGHT YOU'LL NEED **HUNDREDS** OF RESOLUTIONS--YOU DON'T WANT TO MISS **ANYTHING!** BUT DON'T BE DAUNTED, I'M HAPPY TO HELP YOU **CATEGORIZE, ITEMIZE,** AND **PRIORITIZE** THEM ALL!
THANKS.
WELL? AREN'T **YOU** GOING TO MAKE ANY NEW YEAR'S RESOLUTIONS FOR **YOURSELF?**

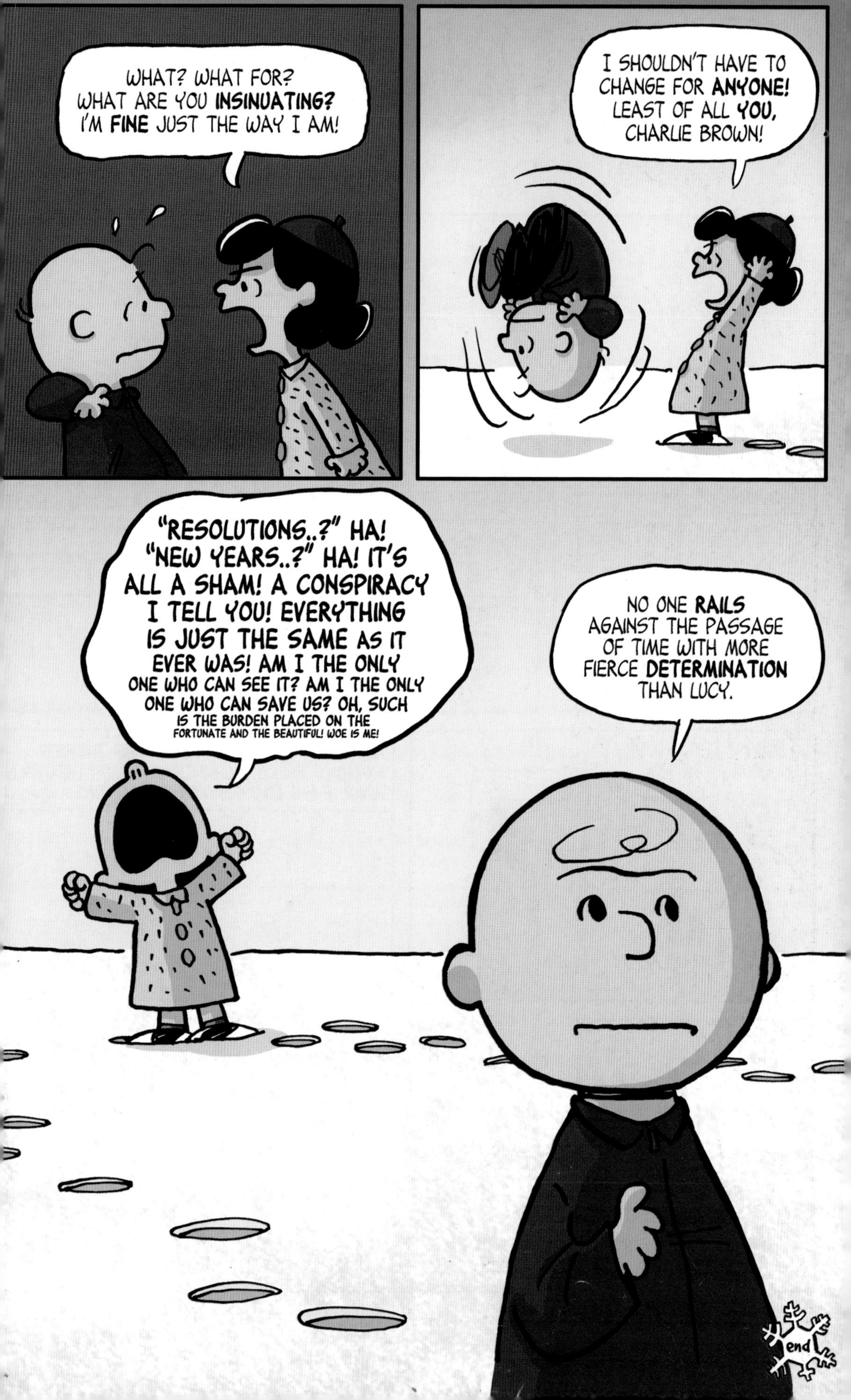
WHAT? WHAT FOR? WHAT ARE YOU **INSINUATING?** I'M **FINE** JUST THE WAY I AM!
I SHOULDN'T HAVE TO CHANGE FOR **ANYONE!** LEAST OF ALL **YOU,** CHARLIE BROWN!
"RESOLUTIONS..?" HA! "NEW YEARS..?" HA! IT'S ALL A SHAM! A CONSPIRACY I TELL YOU! EVERYTHING IS JUST THE SAME AS IT EVER WAS! AM I THE ONLY ONE WHO CAN SEE IT? AM I THE ONLY ONE WHO CAN SAVE US? OH, SUCH IS THE BURDEN PLACED ON THE FORTUNATE AND THE BEAUTIFUL! WOE IS ME!
NO ONE **RAILS** AGAINST THE PASSAGE OF TIME WITH MORE FIERCE **DETERMINATION** THAN LUCY.
end

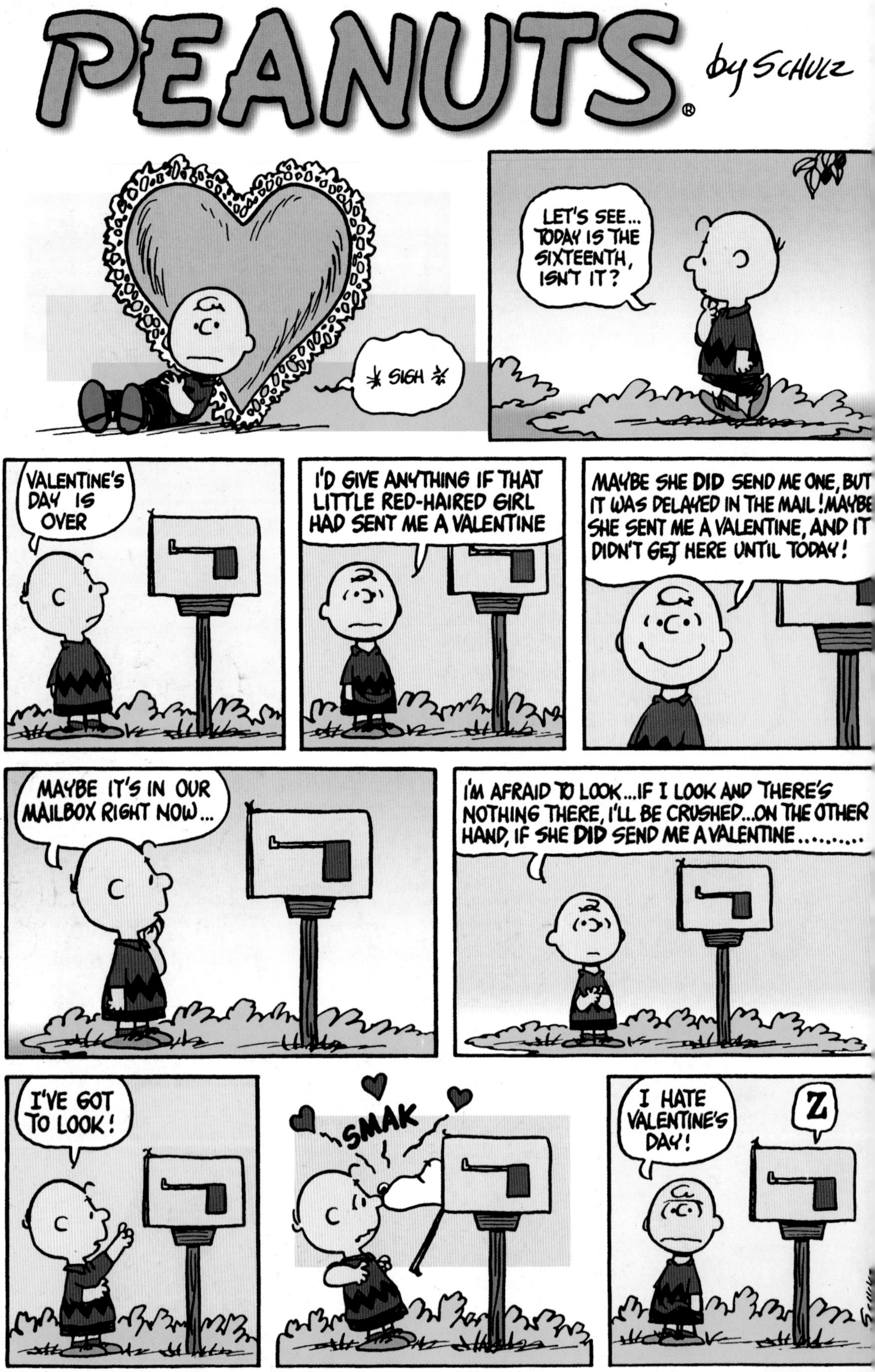
PEANUTS
by SCHULZ
SIGH
LET'S SEE... TODAY IS THE SIXTEENTH, ISN'T IT?
VALENTINE'S DAY IS OVER
I'D GIVE ANYTHING IF THAT LITTLE RED-HAIRED GIRL HAD SENT ME A VALENTINE
MAYBE SHE DID SEND ME ONE, BUT IT WAS DELAYED IN THE MAIL! MAYBE SHE SENT ME A VALENTINE, AND IT DIDN'T GET HERE UNTIL TODAY!
MAYBE IT'S IN OUR MAILBOX RIGHT NOW...
I'M AFRAID TO LOOK...IF I LOOK AND THERE'S NOTHING THERE, I'LL BE CRUSHED...ON THE OTHER HAND, IF SHE DID SEND ME A VALENTINE.........
I'VE GOT TO LOOK!
SMAK
I HATE VALENTINE'S DAY!
Z

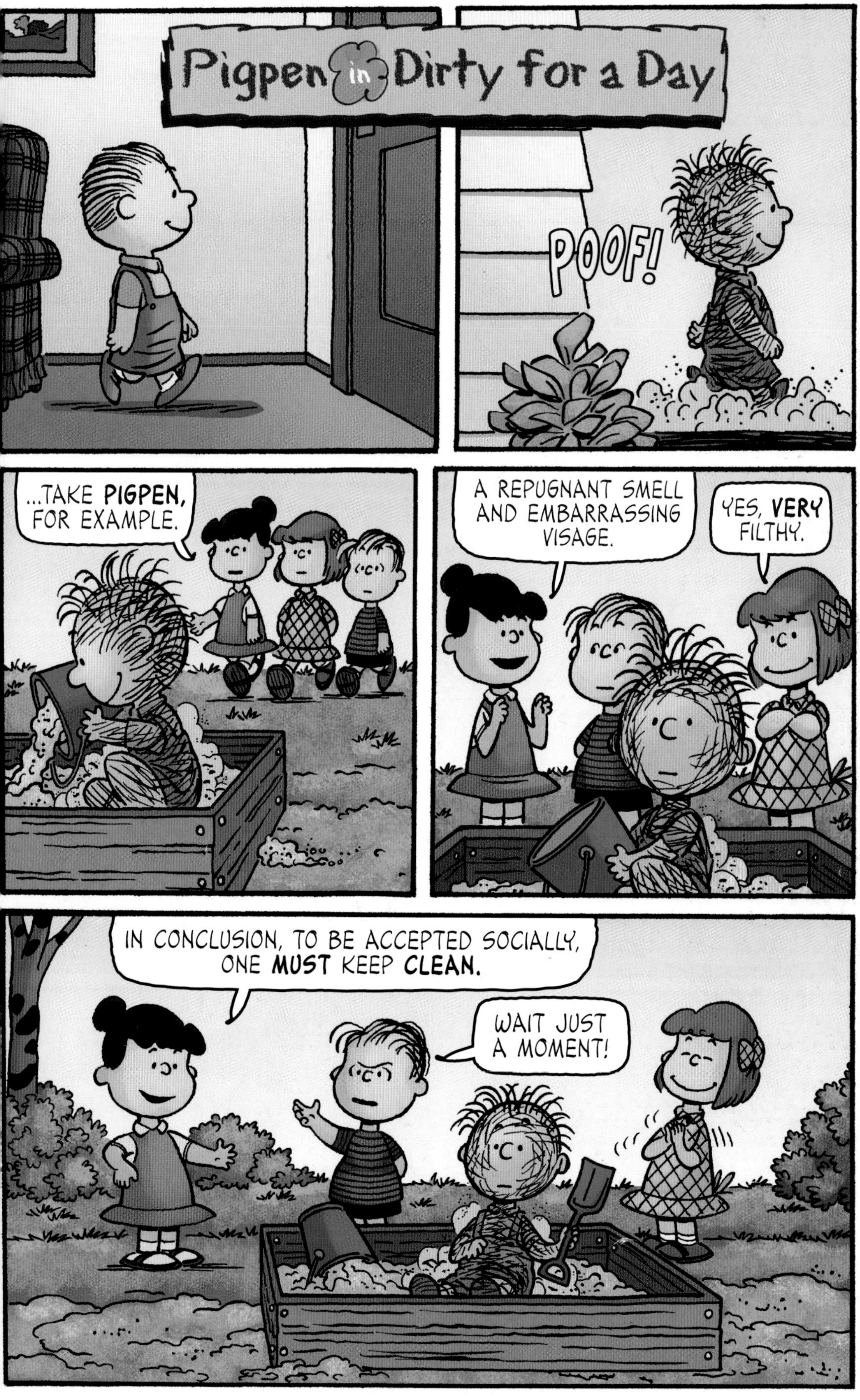
Pigpen in Dirty for a Day
POOF!
...TAKE PIGPEN, FOR EXAMPLE.
A REPUGNANT SMELL AND EMBARRASSING VISAGE.
YES, VERY FILTHY.
IN CONCLUSION, TO BE ACCEPTED SOCIALLY, ONE MUST KEEP CLEAN.
WAIT JUST A MOMENT!

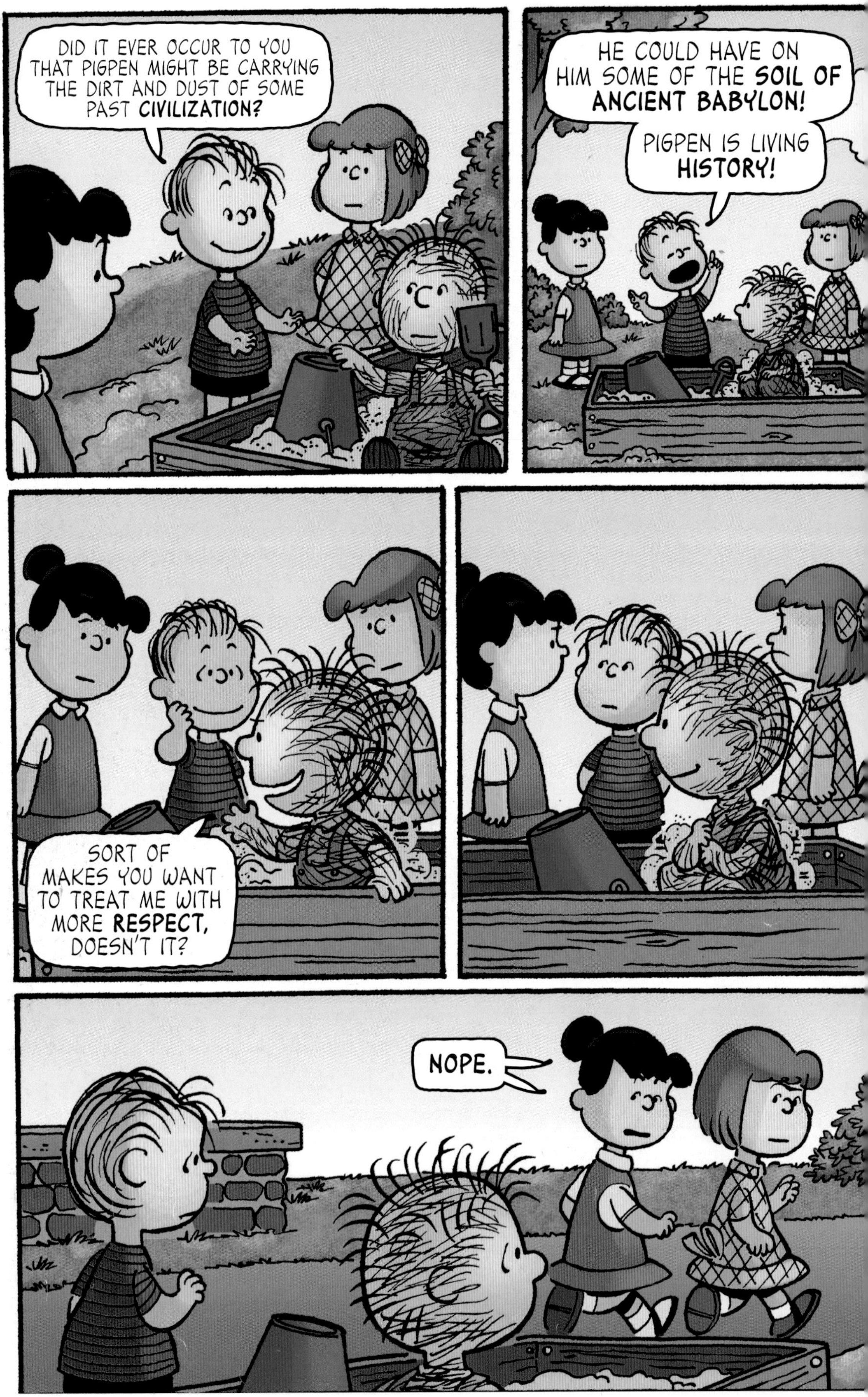

DID IT EVER OCCUR TO YOU THAT PIGPEN MIGHT BE CARRYING THE DIRT AND DUST OF SOME PAST CIVILIZATION?
HE COULD HAVE ON HIM SOME OF THE SOIL OF ANCIENT BABYLON!
PIGPEN IS LIVING HISTORY!
SORT OF MAKES YOU WANT TO TREAT ME WITH MORE RESPECT, DOESN'T IT?
NOPE.

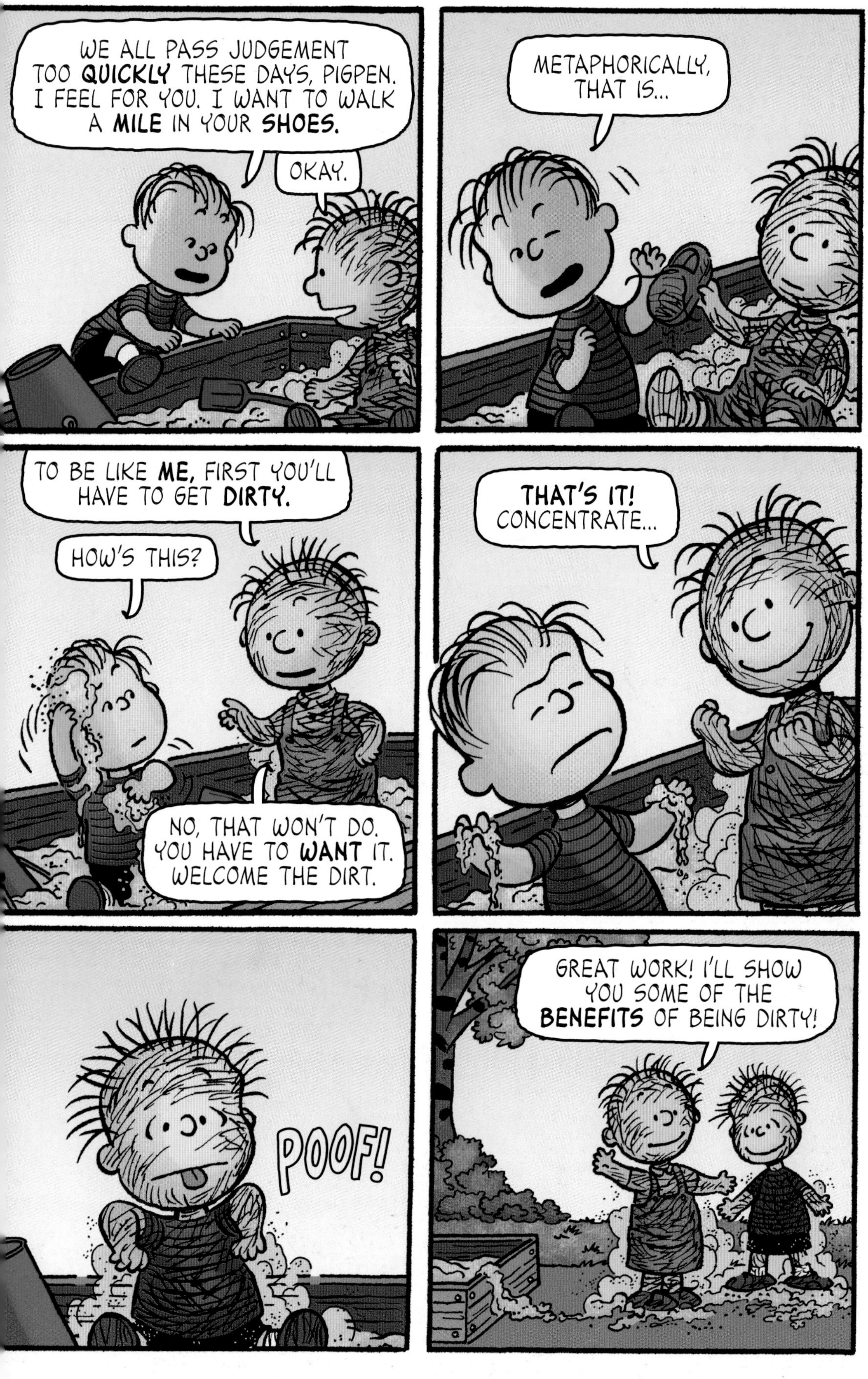
WE ALL PASS JUDGEMENT TOO QUICKLY THESE DAYS, PIGPEN. I FEEL FOR YOU. I WANT TO WALK A MILE IN YOUR SHOES.
OKAY.
METAPHORICALLY, THAT IS...
TO BE LIKE ME, FIRST YOU'LL HAVE TO GET DIRTY.
HOW'S THIS?
NO, THAT WON'T DO. YOU HAVE TO WANT IT. WELCOME THE DIRT.
THAT'S IT! CONCENTRATE...
POOF!
GREAT WORK! I'LL SHOW YOU SOME OF THE BENEFITS OF BEING DIRTY!

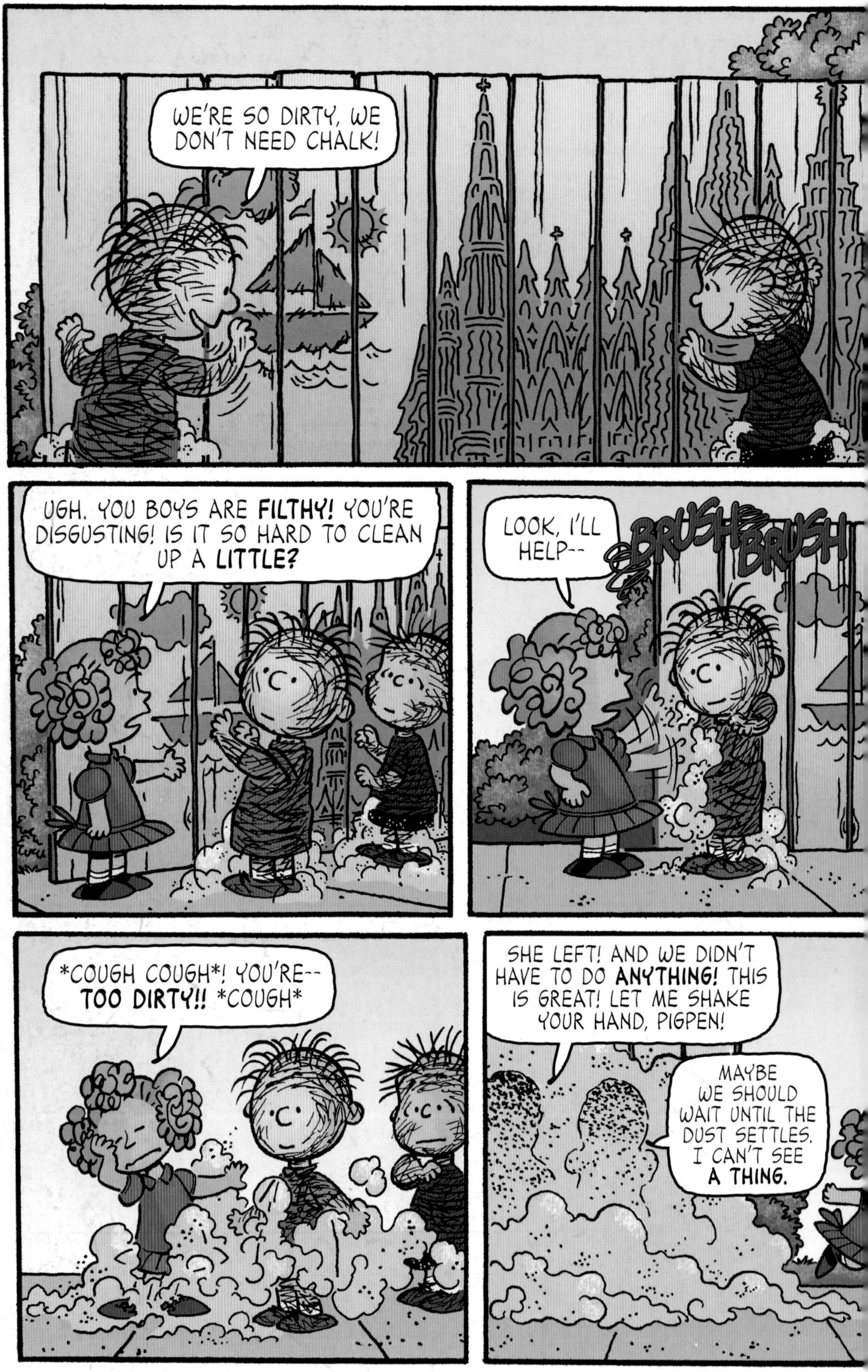
WE'RE SO DIRTY, WE DON'T NEED CHALK!
UGH. YOU BOYS ARE **FILTHY!** YOU'RE DISGUSTING! IS IT SO HARD TO CLEAN UP A **LITTLE?**
LOOK, I'LL HELP--
BRUSH BRUSH
COUGH COUGH! YOU'RE-- **TOO DIRTY!!** *COUGH*
SHE LEFT! AND WE DIDN'T HAVE TO DO **ANYTHING!** THIS IS GREAT! LET ME SHAKE YOUR HAND, PIGPEN!
MAYBE WE SHOULD WAIT UNTIL THE DUST SETTLES. I CAN'T SEE **A THING.**

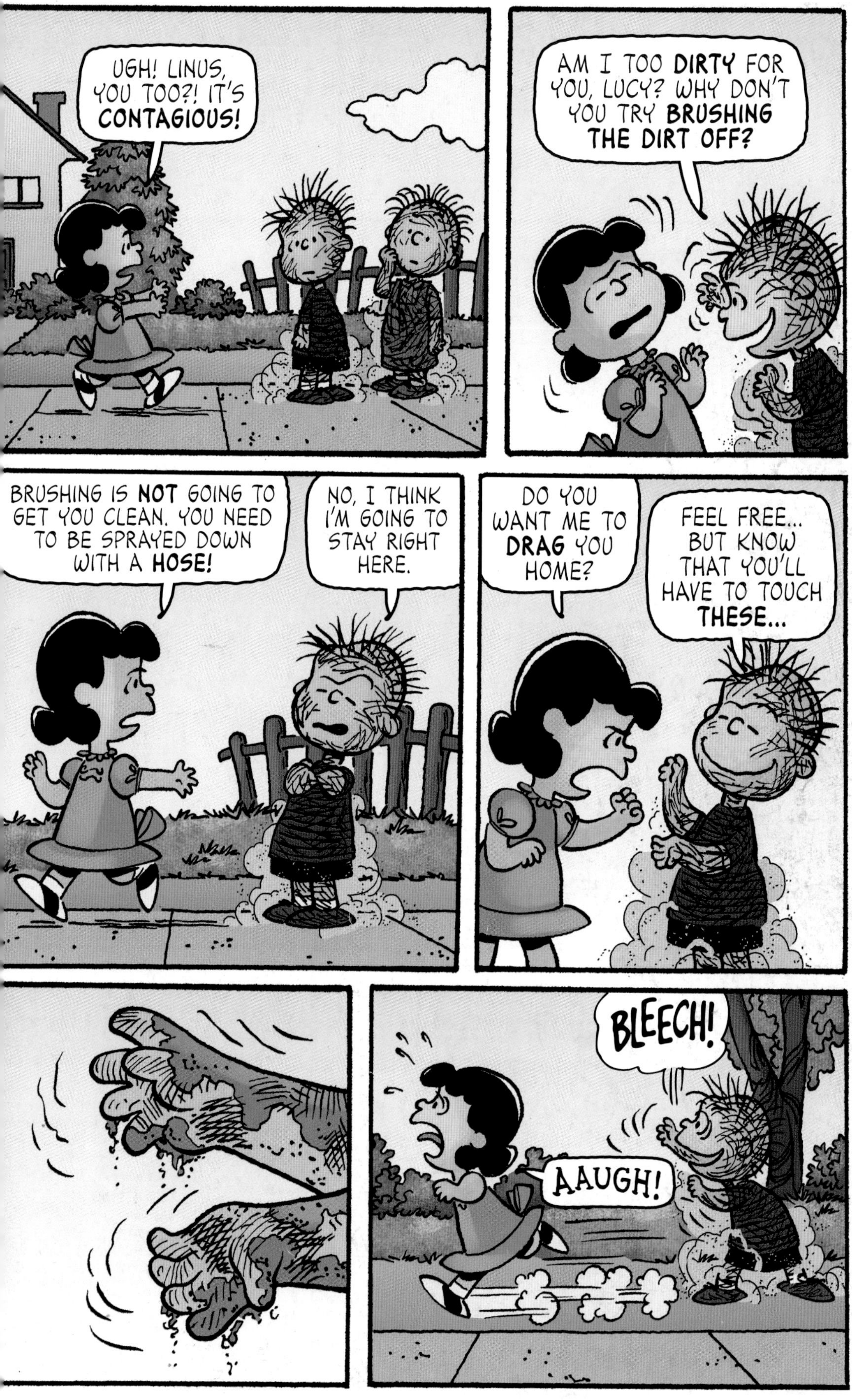
UGH! LINUS, YOU TOO?! IT'S CONTAGIOUS!
AM I TOO DIRTY FOR YOU, LUCY? WHY DON'T YOU TRY BRUSHING THE DIRT OFF?
BRUSHING IS NOT GOING TO GET YOU CLEAN. YOU NEED TO BE SPRAYED DOWN WITH A HOSE!
NO, I THINK I'M GOING TO STAY RIGHT HERE.
DO YOU WANT ME TO DRAG YOU HOME?
FEEL FREE... BUT KNOW THAT YOU'LL HAVE TO TOUCH THESE...
BLEECH!
AAUGH!

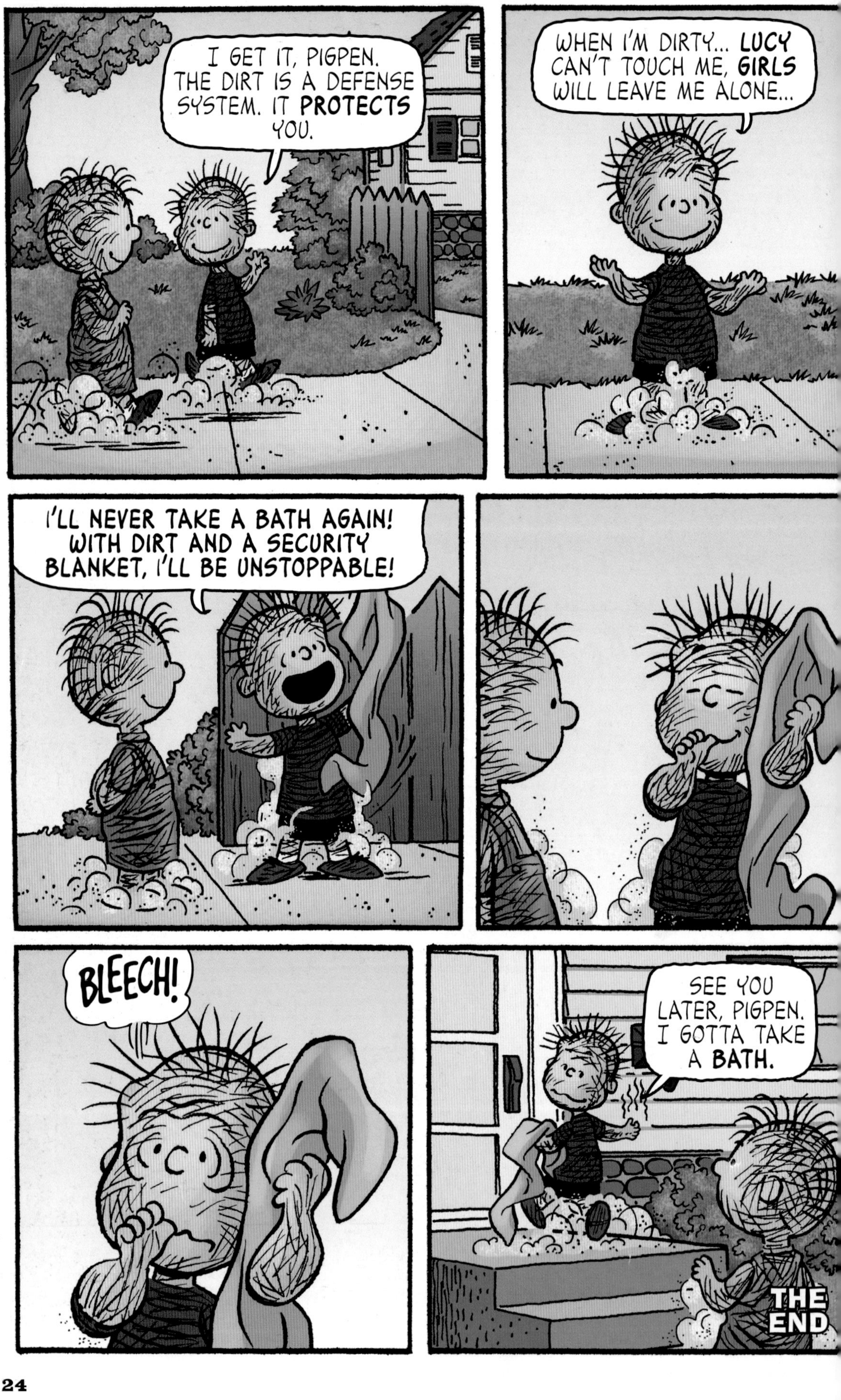
I GET IT, PIGPEN. THE DIRT IS A DEFENSE SYSTEM. IT **PROTECTS** YOU.
WHEN I'M DIRTY... **LUCY** CAN'T TOUCH ME, **GIRLS** WILL LEAVE ME ALONE...
I'LL NEVER TAKE A BATH AGAIN! WITH DIRT AND A SECURITY BLANKET, I'LL BE UNSTOPPABLE!
BLEECH!
SEE YOU LATER, PIGPEN. I GOTTA TAKE A **BATH**.
THE END

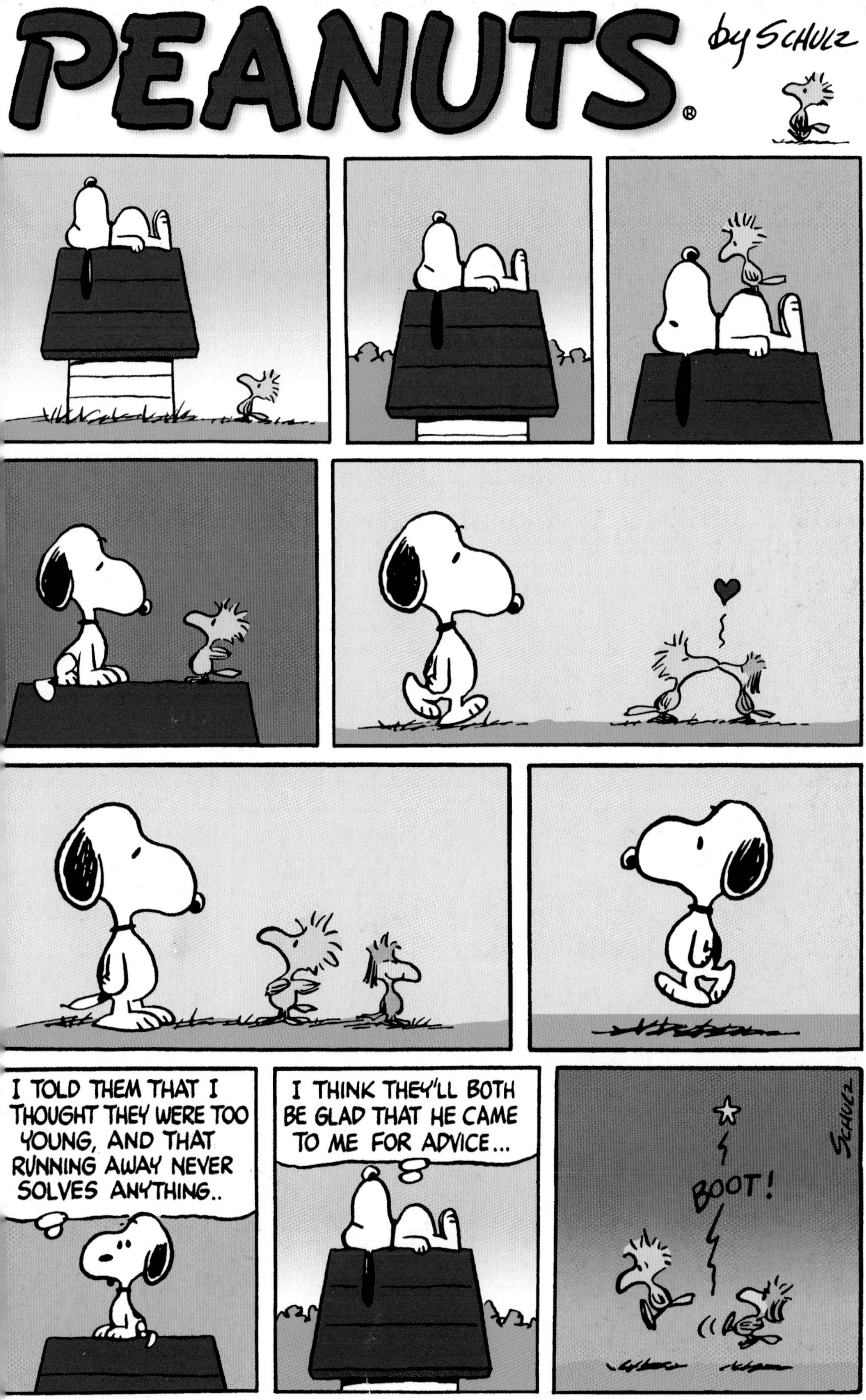
PEANUTS
by SCHULZ
I TOLD THEM THAT I THOUGHT THEY WERE TOO YOUNG, AND THAT RUNNING AWAY NEVER SOLVES ANYTHING..
I THINK THEY'LL BOTH BE GLAD THAT HE CAME TO ME FOR ADVICE...
BOOT!
SCHULZ

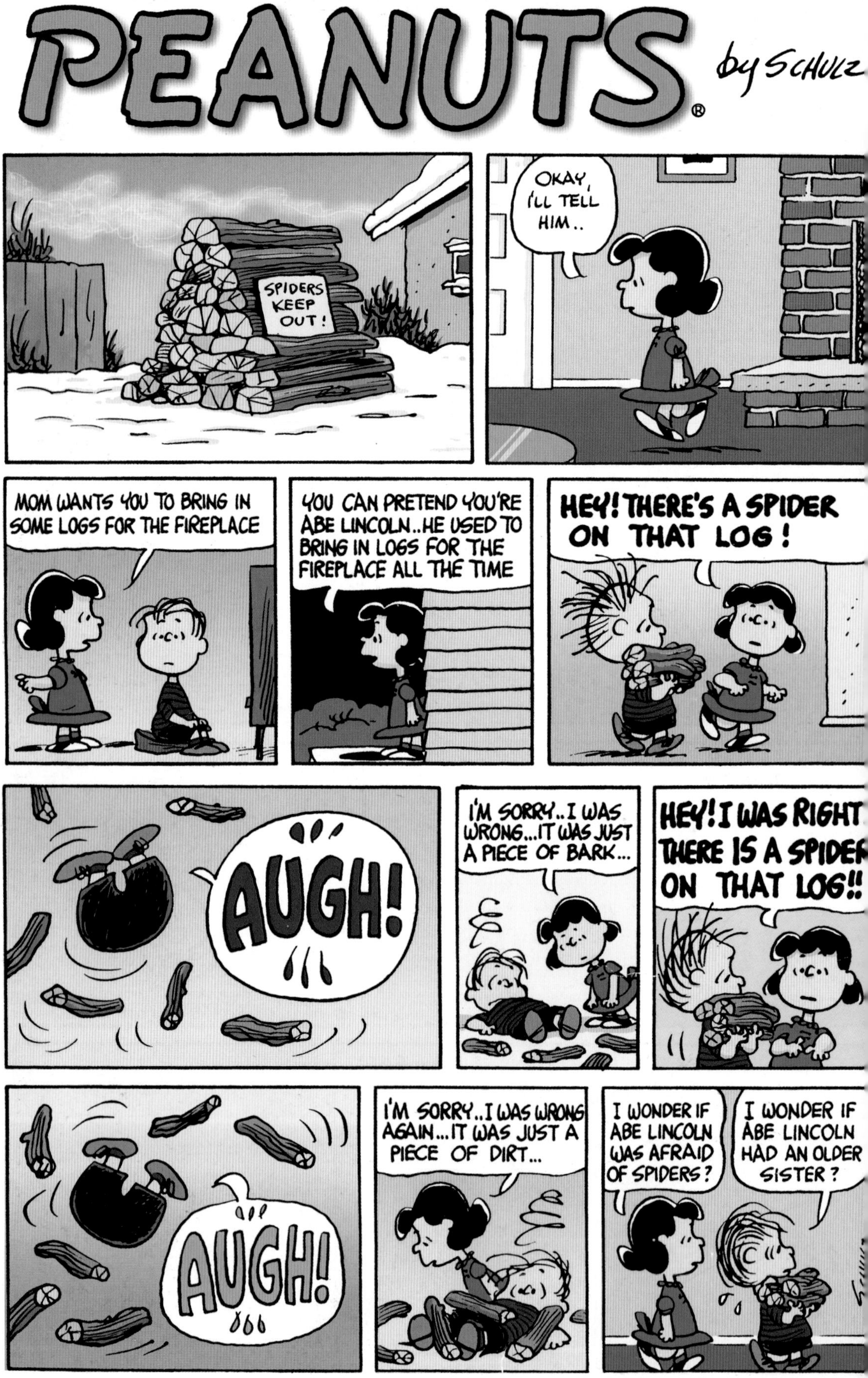
PEANUTS
by SCHULZ
SPIDERS KEEP OUT!
OKAY, I'LL TELL HIM..
MOM WANTS YOU TO BRING IN SOME LOGS FOR THE FIREPLACE
YOU CAN PRETEND YOU'RE ABE LINCOLN..HE USED TO BRING IN LOGS FOR THE FIREPLACE ALL THE TIME
HEY! THERE'S A SPIDER ON THAT LOG!
AUGH!
I'M SORRY..I WAS WRONG...IT WAS JUST A PIECE OF BARK...
HEY! I WAS RIGHT THERE IS A SPIDER ON THAT LOG!!
AUGH!
I'M SORRY..I WAS WRONG AGAIN...IT WAS JUST A PIECE OF DIRT...
I WONDER IF ABE LINCOLN WAS AFRAID OF SPIDERS?
I WONDER IF ABE LINCOLN HAD AN OLDER SISTER?

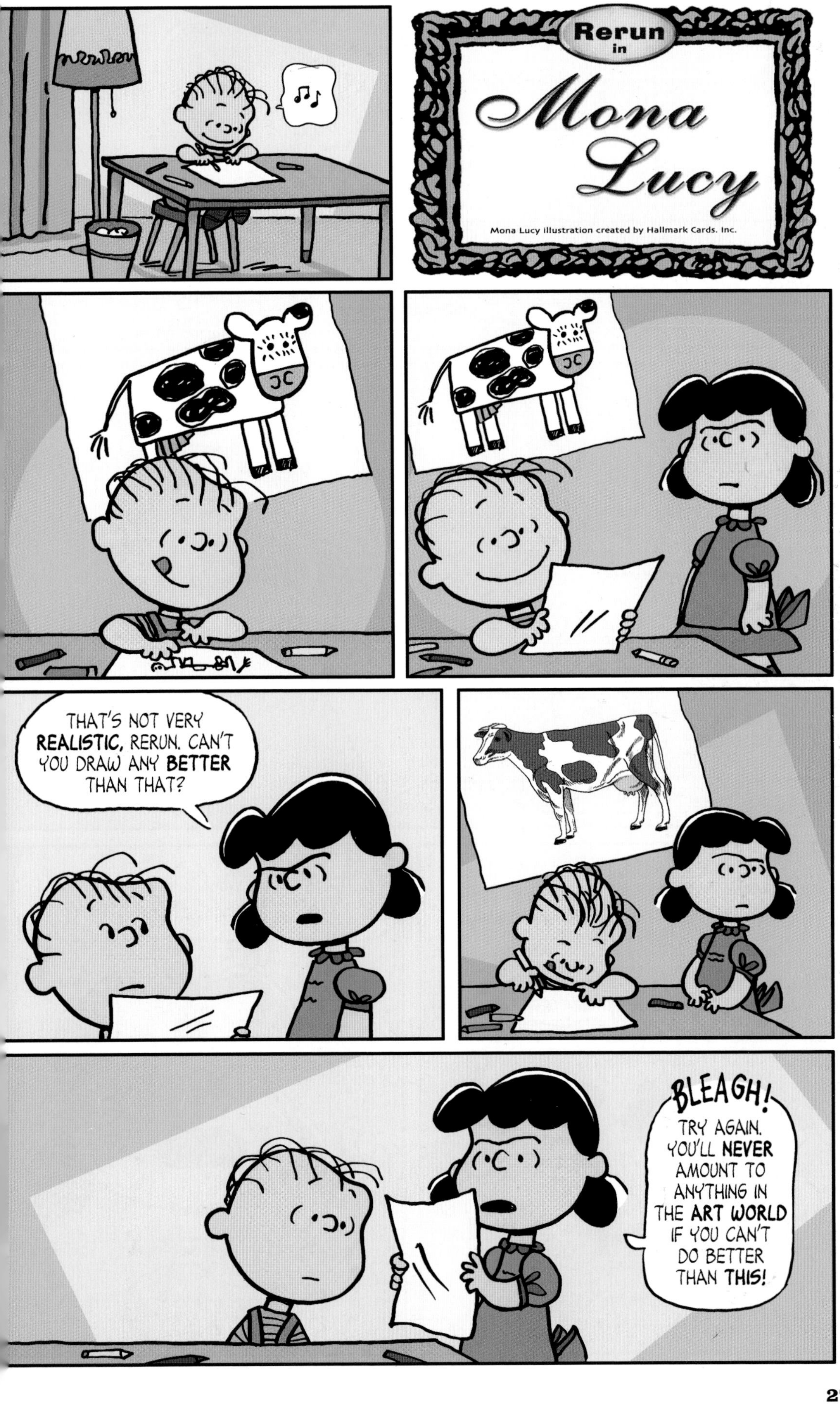
Rerun
in
Mona Lucy
Mona Lucy illustration created by Hallmark Cards. Inc.
THAT'S NOT VERY **REALISTIC**, RERUN. CAN'T YOU DRAW ANY **BETTER** THAN THAT?
BLEAGH!
TRY AGAIN. YOU'LL **NEVER** AMOUNT TO ANYTHING IN THE **ART WORLD** IF YOU CAN'T DO BETTER THAN **THIS!**

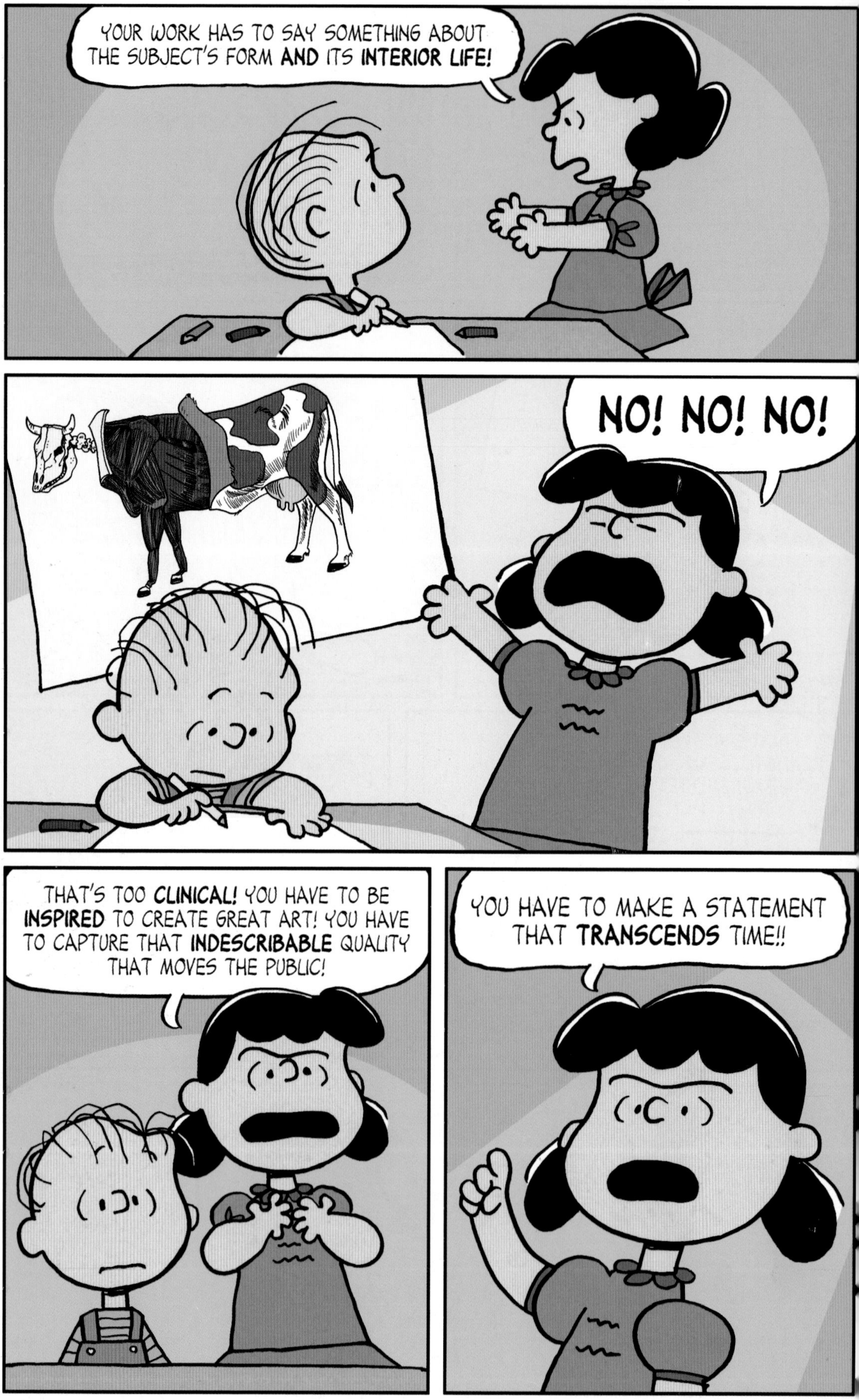

YOUR WORK HAS TO SAY SOMETHING ABOUT THE SUBJECT'S FORM **AND** ITS **INTERIOR LIFE!**
NO! NO! NO!
THAT'S TOO **CLINICAL!** YOU HAVE TO BE **INSPIRED** TO CREATE GREAT ART! YOU HAVE TO CAPTURE THAT **INDESCRIBABLE** QUALITY THAT MOVES THE PUBLIC!
YOU HAVE TO MAKE A STATEMENT THAT **TRANSCENDS** TIME!!

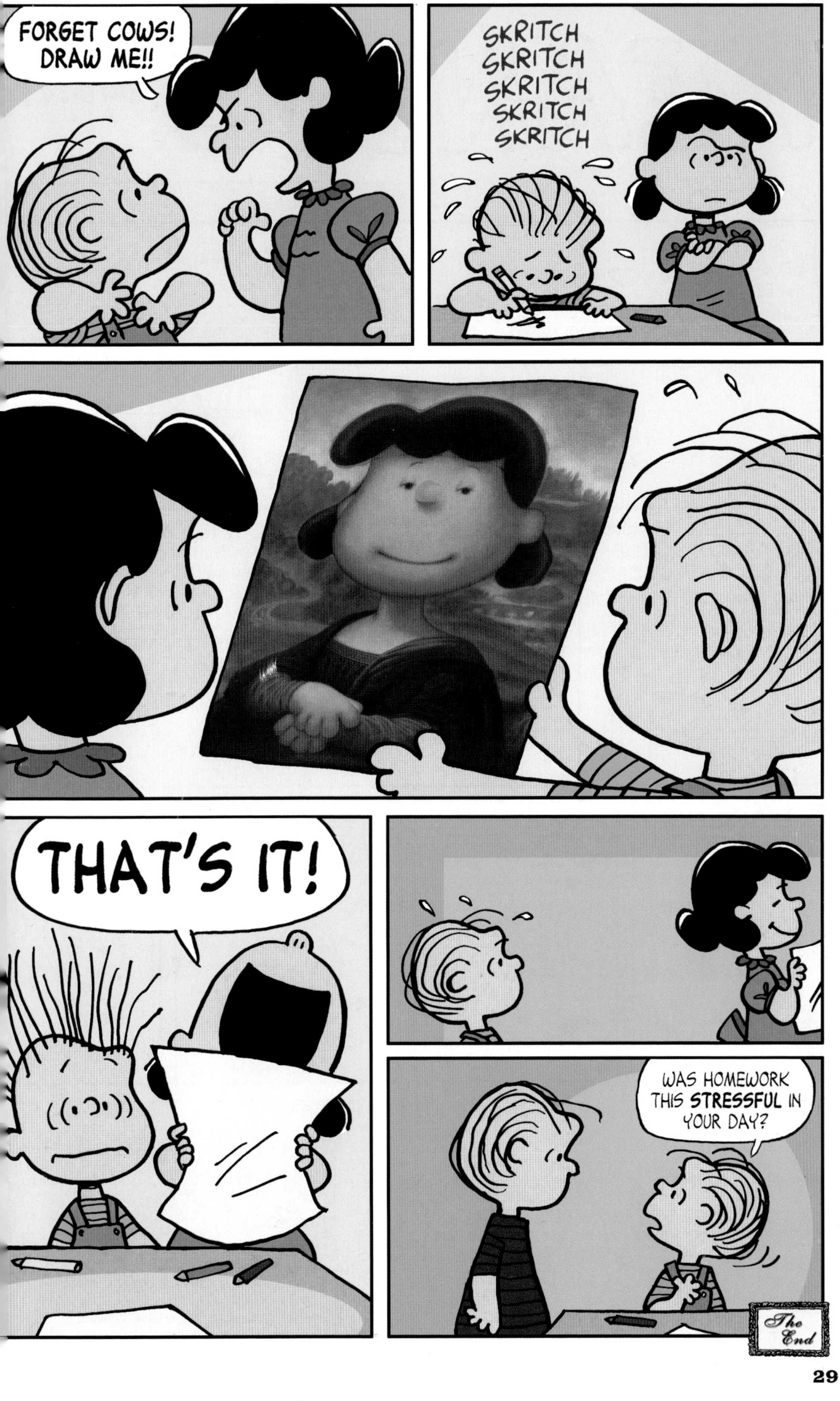
FORGET COWS! DRAW ME!!
SKRITCH SKRITCH SKRITCH SKRITCH SKRITCH
THAT'S IT!
WAS HOMEWORK THIS **STRESSFUL** IN YOUR DAY?
The End

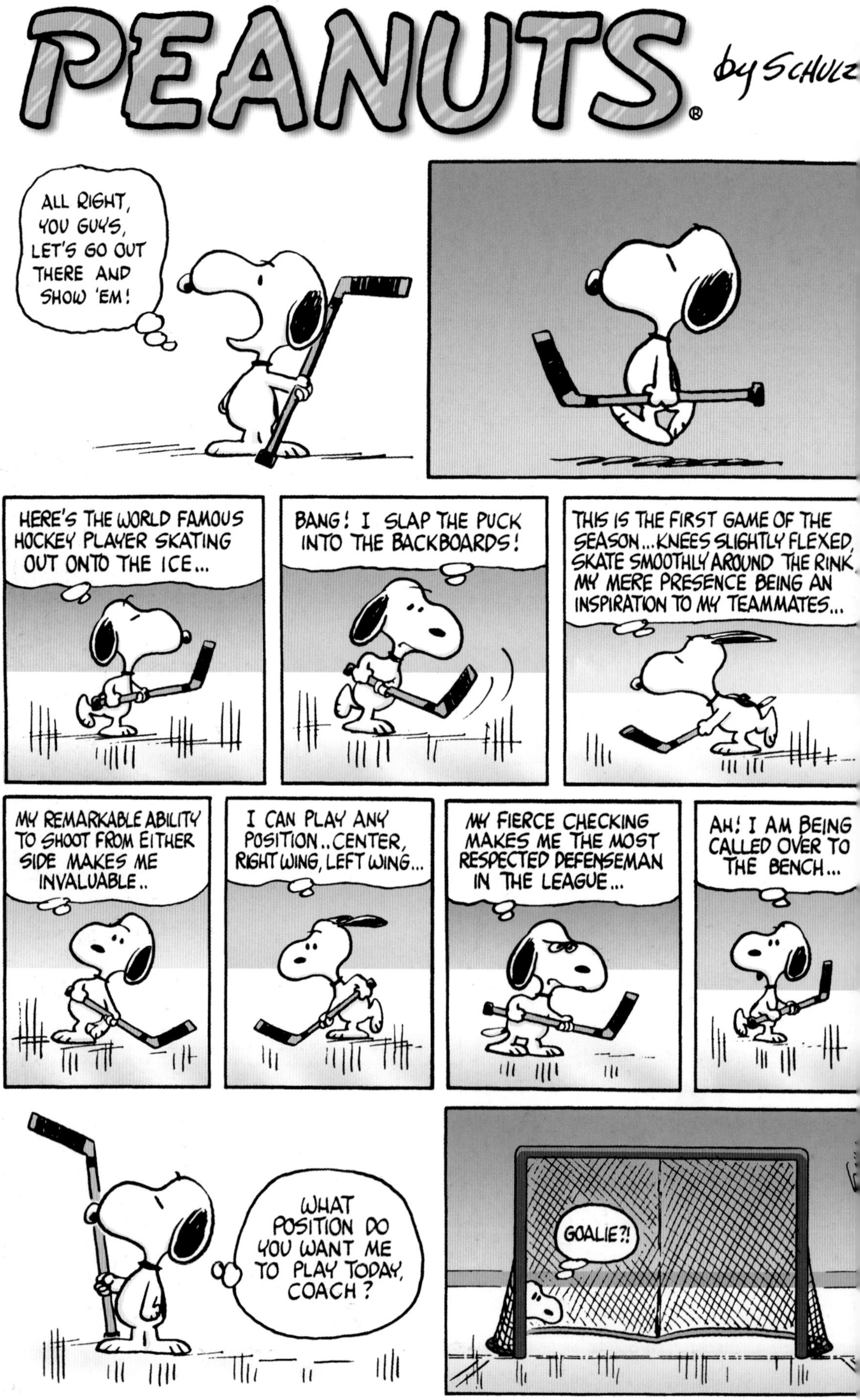
PEANUTS
by SCHULZ
ALL RIGHT, YOU GUYS, LET'S GO OUT THERE AND SHOW 'EM!
HERE'S THE WORLD FAMOUS HOCKEY PLAYER SKATING OUT ONTO THE ICE...
BANG! I SLAP THE PUCK INTO THE BACKBOARDS!
THIS IS THE FIRST GAME OF THE SEASON...KNEES SLIGHTLY FLEXED, SKATE SMOOTHLY AROUND THE RINK, MY MERE PRESENCE BEING AN INSPIRATION TO MY TEAMMATES...
MY REMARKABLE ABILITY TO SHOOT FROM EITHER SIDE MAKES ME INVALUABLE..
I CAN PLAY ANY POSITION..CENTER, RIGHT WING, LEFT WING...
MY FIERCE CHECKING MAKES ME THE MOST RESPECTED DEFENSEMAN IN THE LEAGUE...
AH! I AM BEING CALLED OVER TO THE BENCH...
WHAT POSITION DO YOU WANT ME TO PLAY TODAY, COACH?
GOALIE?!

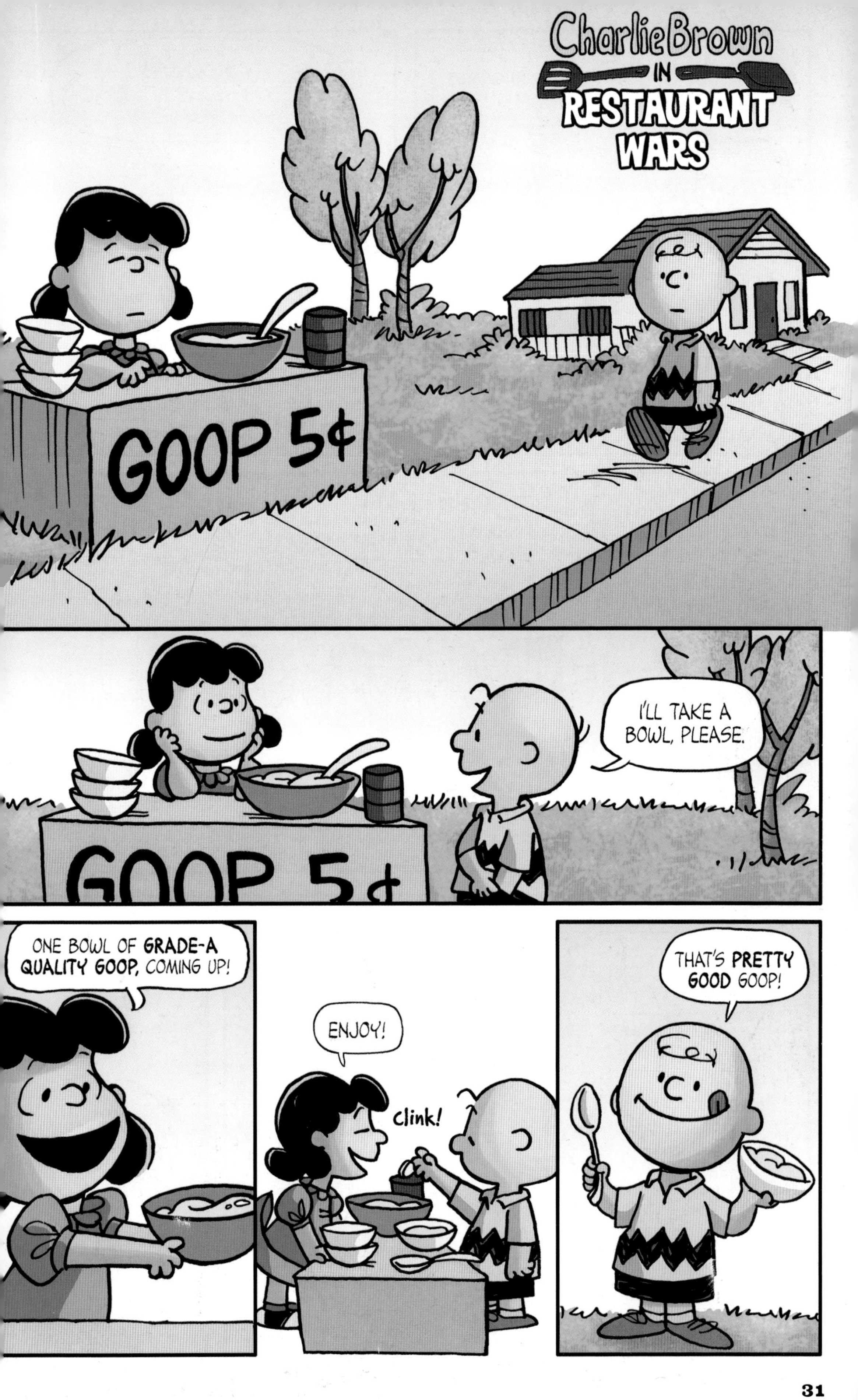

Charlie Brown IN RESTAURANT WARS
GOOP 5¢
I'LL TAKE A BOWL, PLEASE.
GOOP 5¢
ONE BOWL OF **GRADE-A QUALITY GOOP**, COMING UP!
ENJOY!
Clink!
THAT'S **PRETTY GOOD** GOOP!

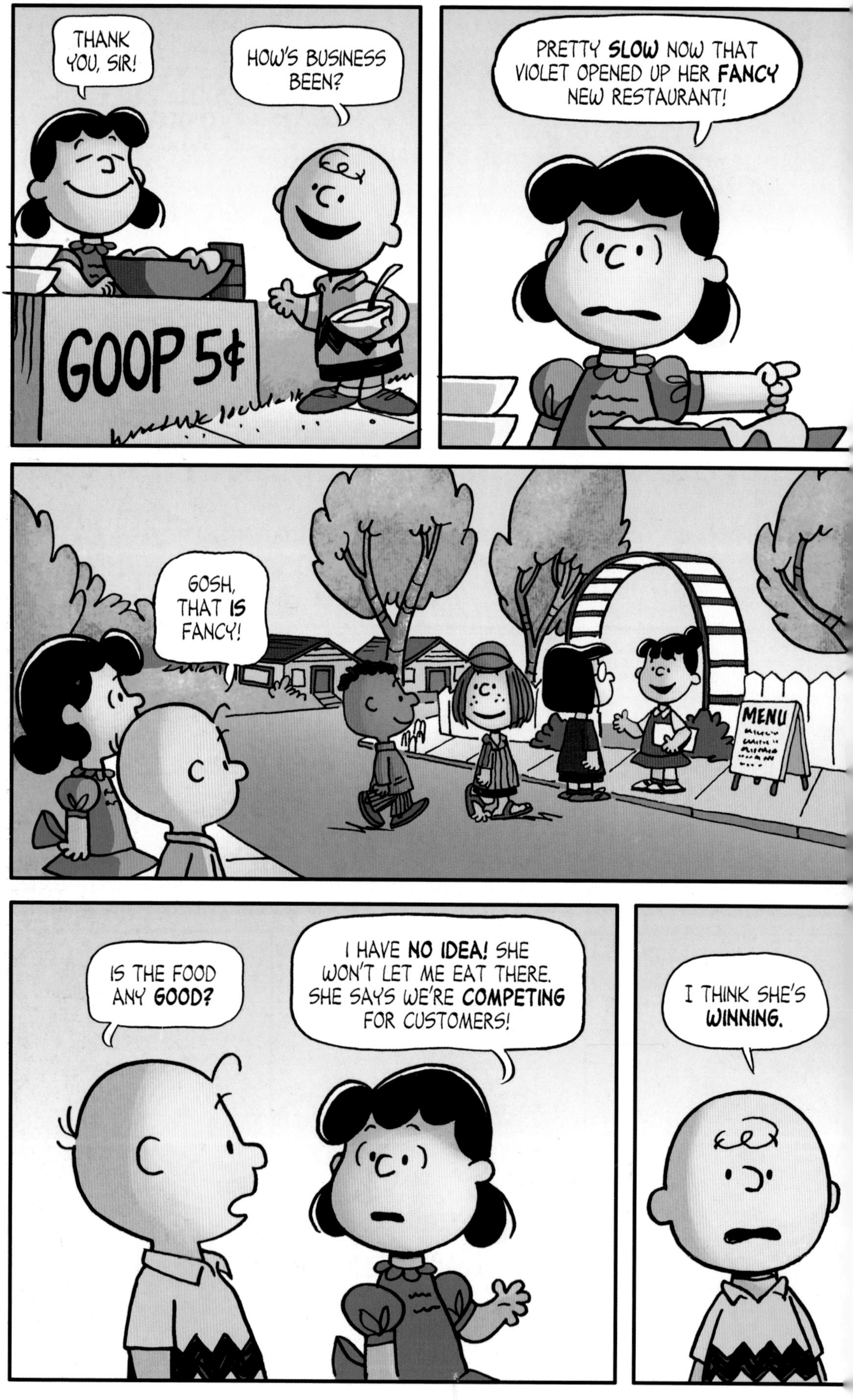
THANK YOU, SIR!
HOW'S BUSINESS BEEN?
GOOP 5¢
PRETTY SLOW NOW THAT VIOLET OPENED UP HER FANCY NEW RESTAURANT!
GOSH, THAT IS FANCY!
MENU
IS THE FOOD ANY GOOD?
I HAVE NO IDEA! SHE WON'T LET ME EAT THERE. SHE SAYS WE'RE COMPETING FOR CUSTOMERS!
I THINK SHE'S WINNING.

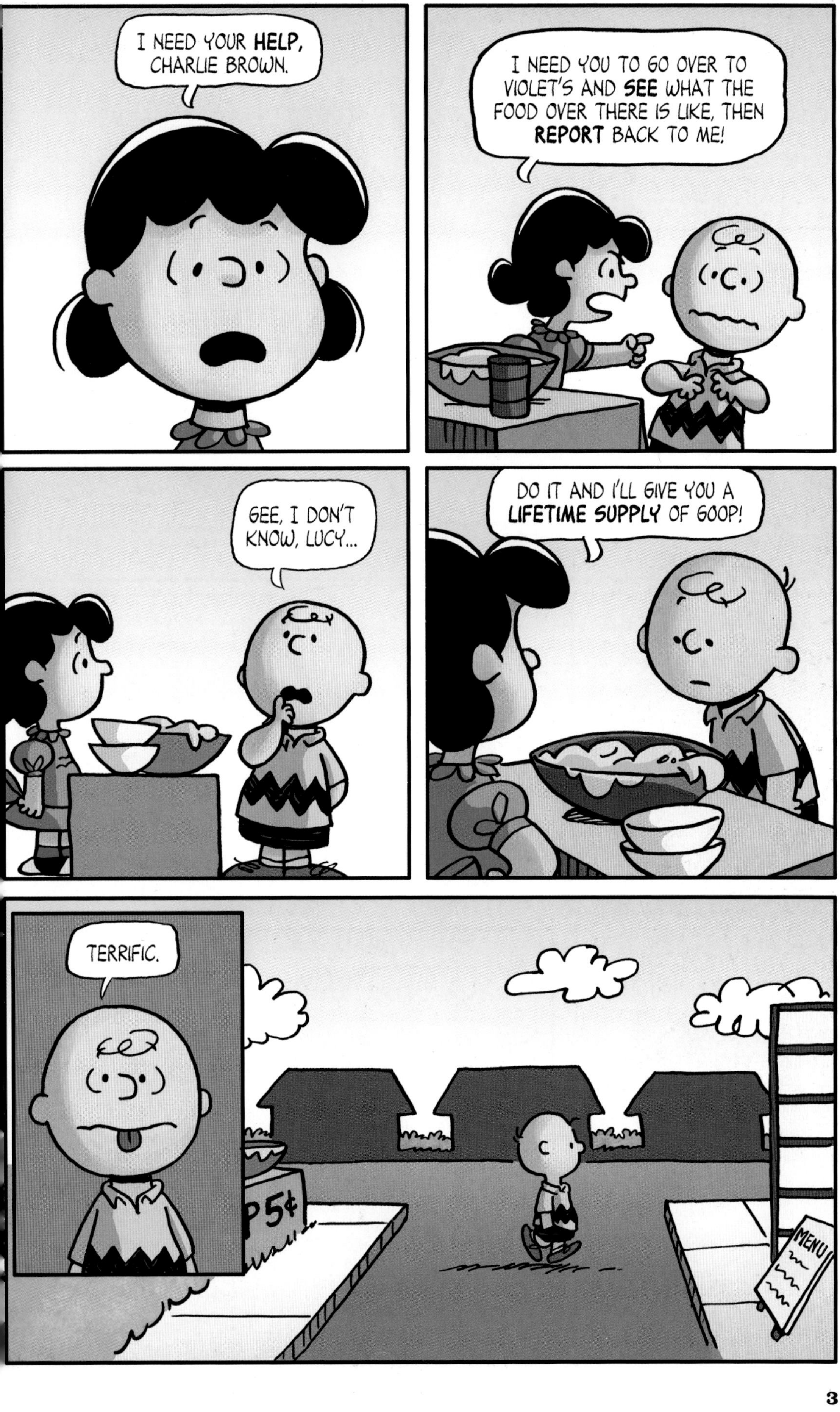
I NEED YOUR **HELP,** CHARLIE BROWN.
I NEED YOU TO GO OVER TO VIOLET'S AND **SEE** WHAT THE FOOD OVER THERE IS LIKE, THEN **REPORT** BACK TO ME!
GEE, I DON'T KNOW, LUCY...
DO IT AND I'LL GIVE YOU A **LIFETIME SUPPLY** OF GOOP!
TERRIFIC.
P 5¢
MENU

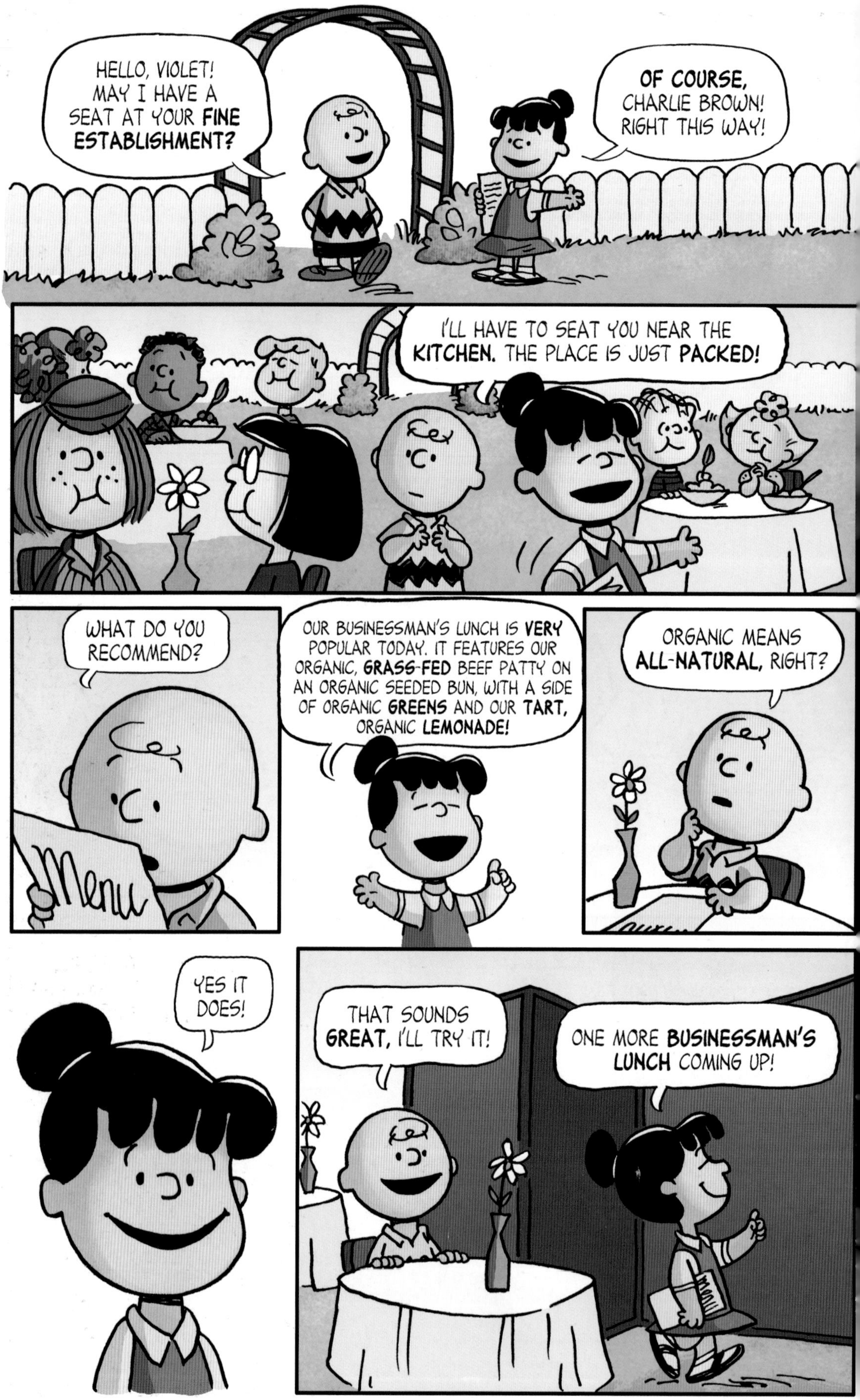
HELLO, VIOLET! MAY I HAVE A SEAT AT YOUR FINE ESTABLISHMENT?
OF COURSE, CHARLIE BROWN! RIGHT THIS WAY!
I'LL HAVE TO SEAT YOU NEAR THE KITCHEN. THE PLACE IS JUST PACKED!
WHAT DO YOU RECOMMEND?
Menu
OUR BUSINESSMAN'S LUNCH IS VERY POPULAR TODAY. IT FEATURES OUR ORGANIC, GRASS-FED BEEF PATTY ON AN ORGANIC SEEDED BUN, WITH A SIDE OF ORGANIC GREENS AND OUR TART, ORGANIC LEMONADE!
ORGANIC MEANS ALL-NATURAL, RIGHT?
YES IT DOES!
THAT SOUNDS GREAT, I'LL TRY IT!
ONE MORE BUSINESSMAN'S LUNCH COMING UP!

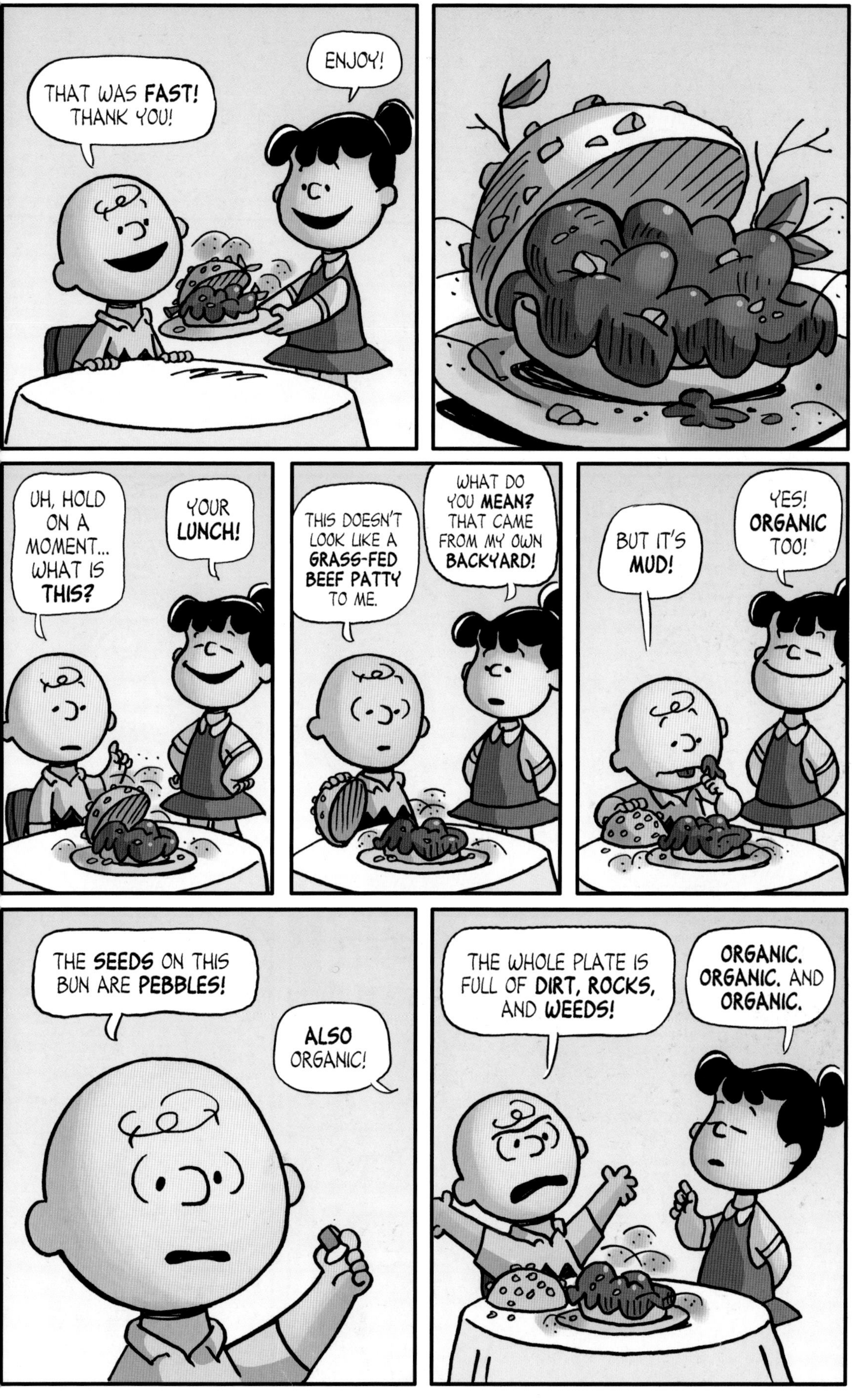

THAT WAS FAST! THANK YOU!
ENJOY!
UH, HOLD ON A MOMENT... WHAT IS THIS?
YOUR LUNCH!
THIS DOESN'T LOOK LIKE A GRASS-FED BEEF PATTY TO ME.
WHAT DO YOU MEAN? THAT CAME FROM MY OWN BACKYARD!
BUT IT'S MUD!
YES! ORGANIC TOO!
THE SEEDS ON THIS BUN ARE PEBBLES!
ALSO ORGANIC!
THE WHOLE PLATE IS FULL OF DIRT, ROCKS, AND WEEDS!
ORGANIC. ORGANIC. AND ORGANIC.

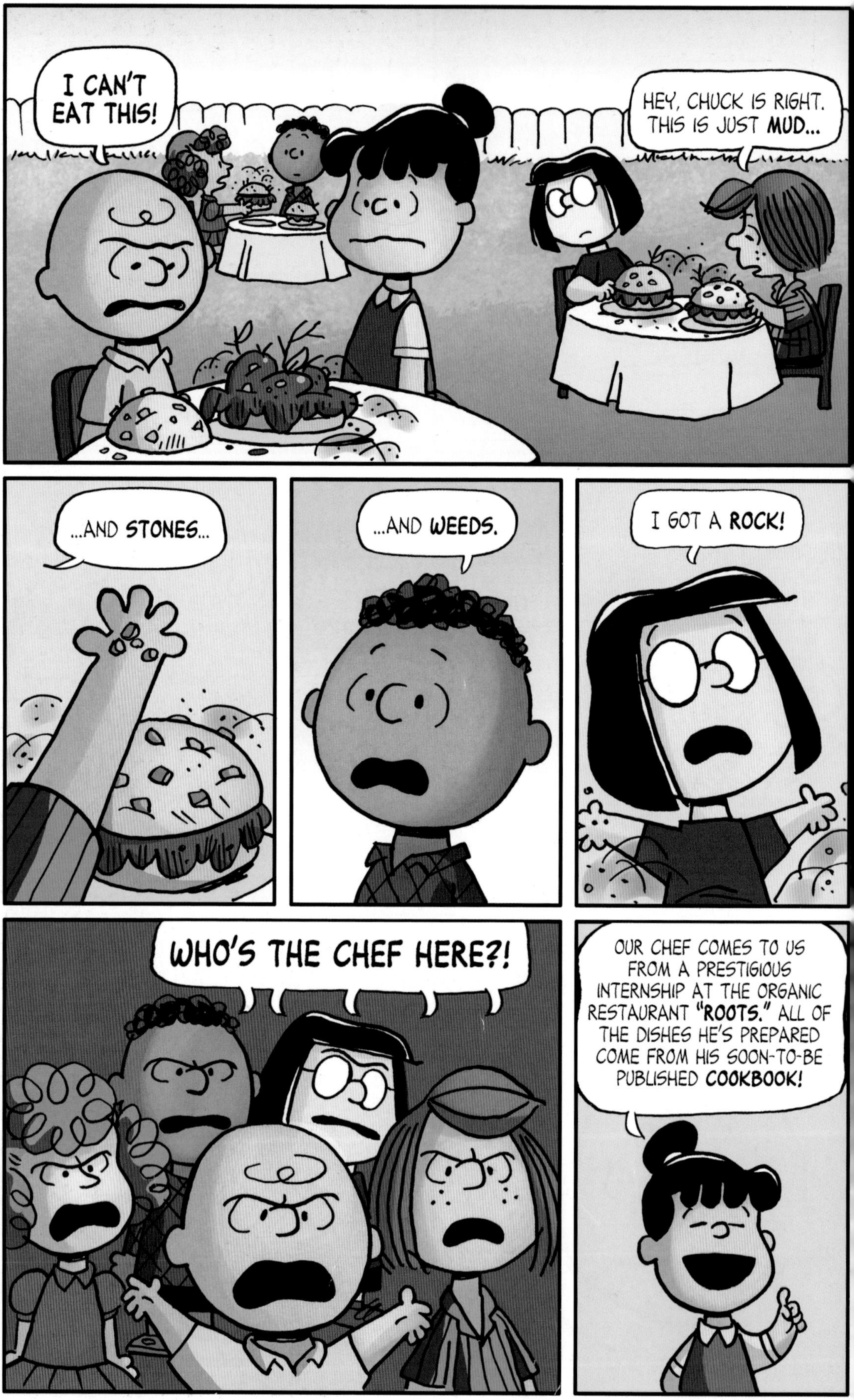
I CAN'T EAT THIS!
HEY, CHUCK IS RIGHT. THIS IS JUST MUD...
...AND STONES...
...AND WEEDS.
I GOT A ROCK!
WHO'S THE CHEF HERE?!
OUR CHEF COMES TO US FROM A PRESTIGIOUS INTERNSHIP AT THE ORGANIC RESTAURANT "ROOTS." ALL OF THE DISHES HE'S PREPARED COME FROM HIS SOON-TO-BE PUBLISHED COOKBOOK!

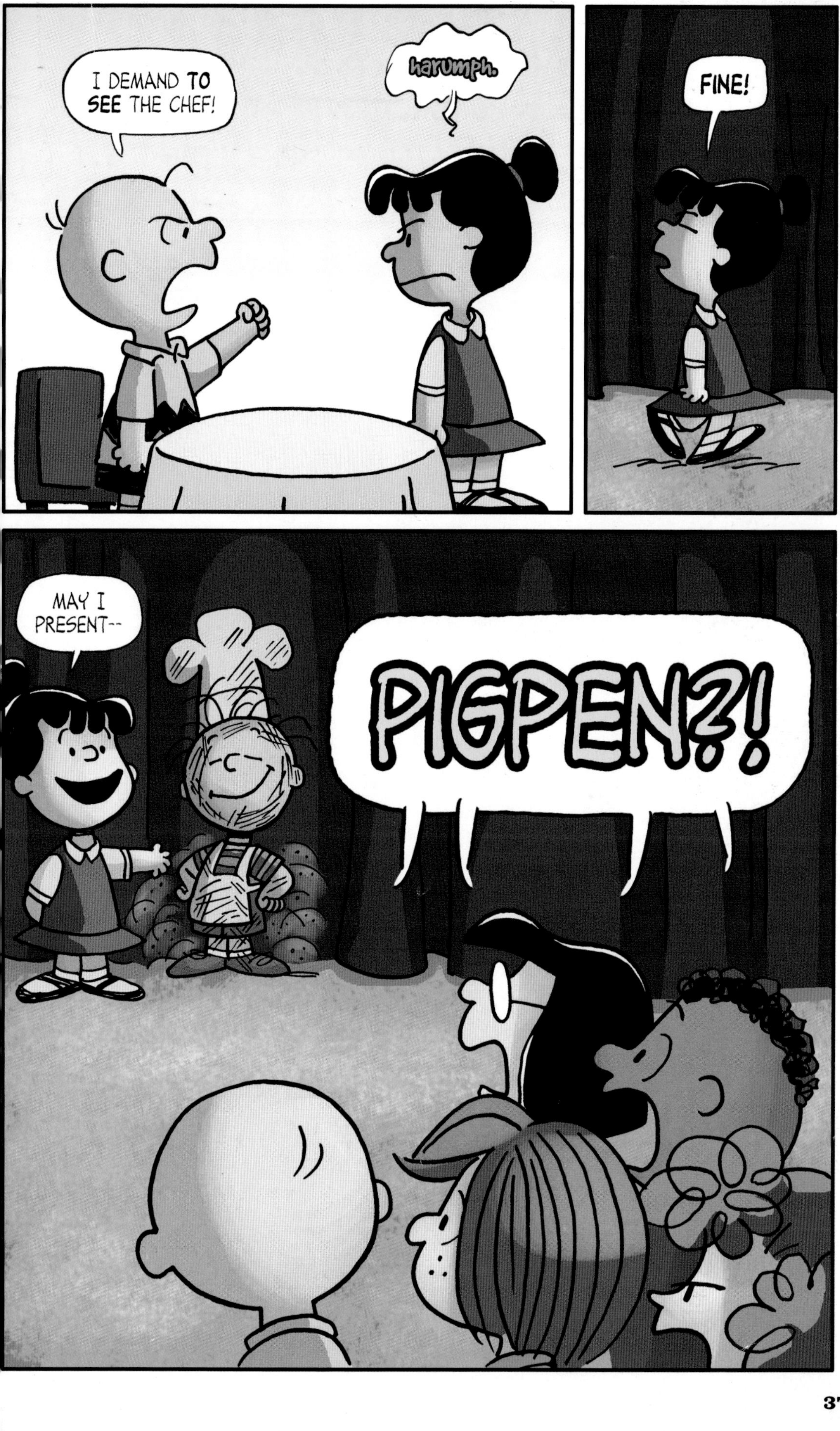

I DEMAND TO SEE THE CHEF!
harumph.
FINE!
MAY I PRESENT--
PIGPEN?!

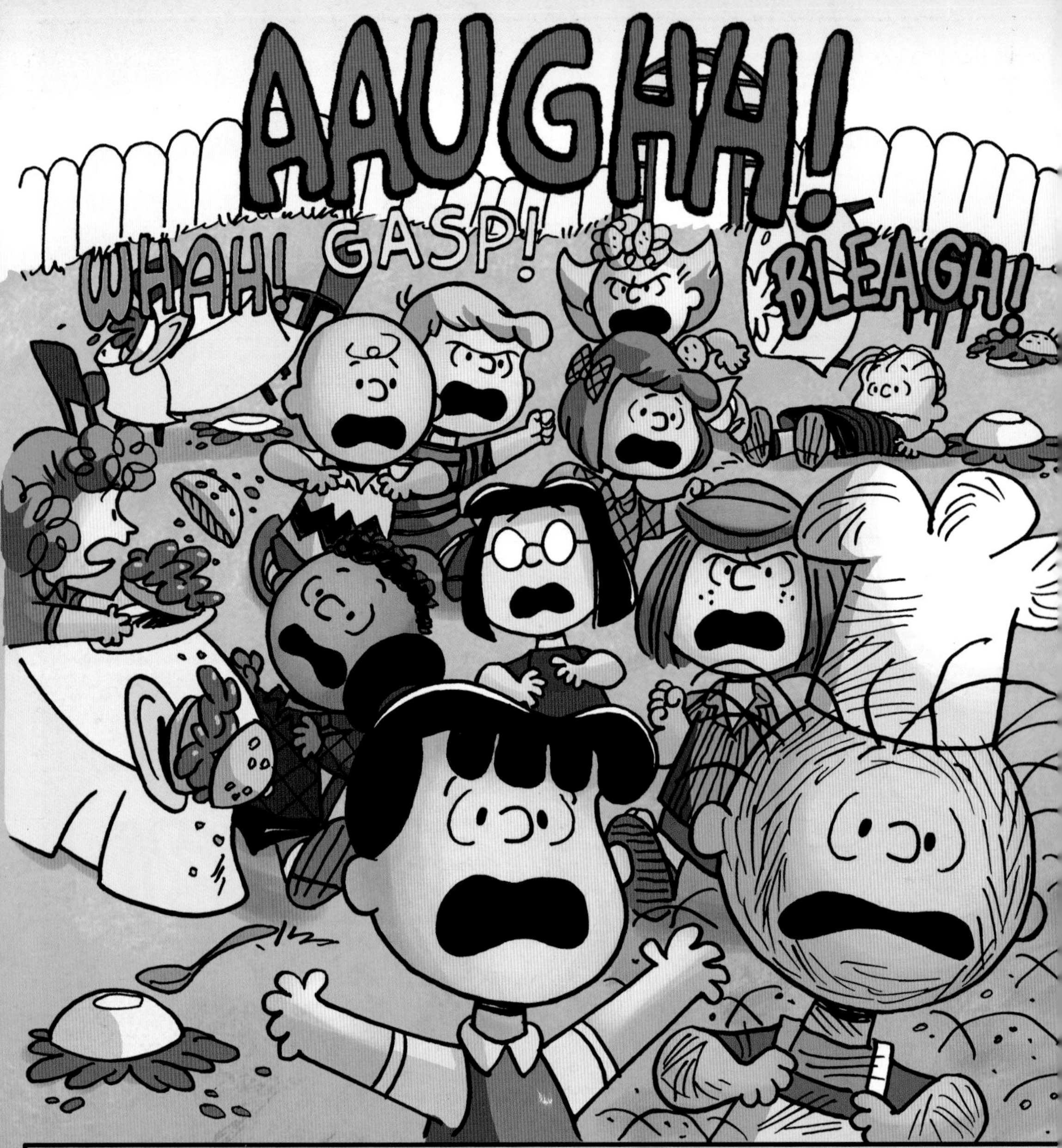
AAUGHH!
WHAH!
GASP!
BLEAGH!

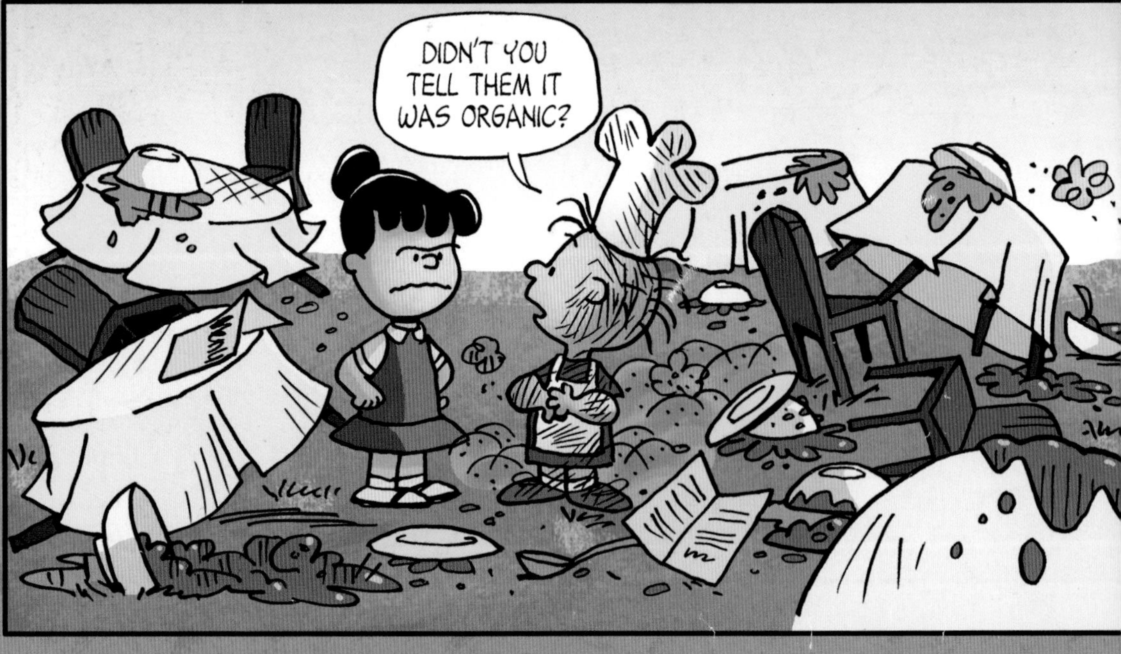
DIDN'T YOU TELL THEM IT WAS ORGANIC?

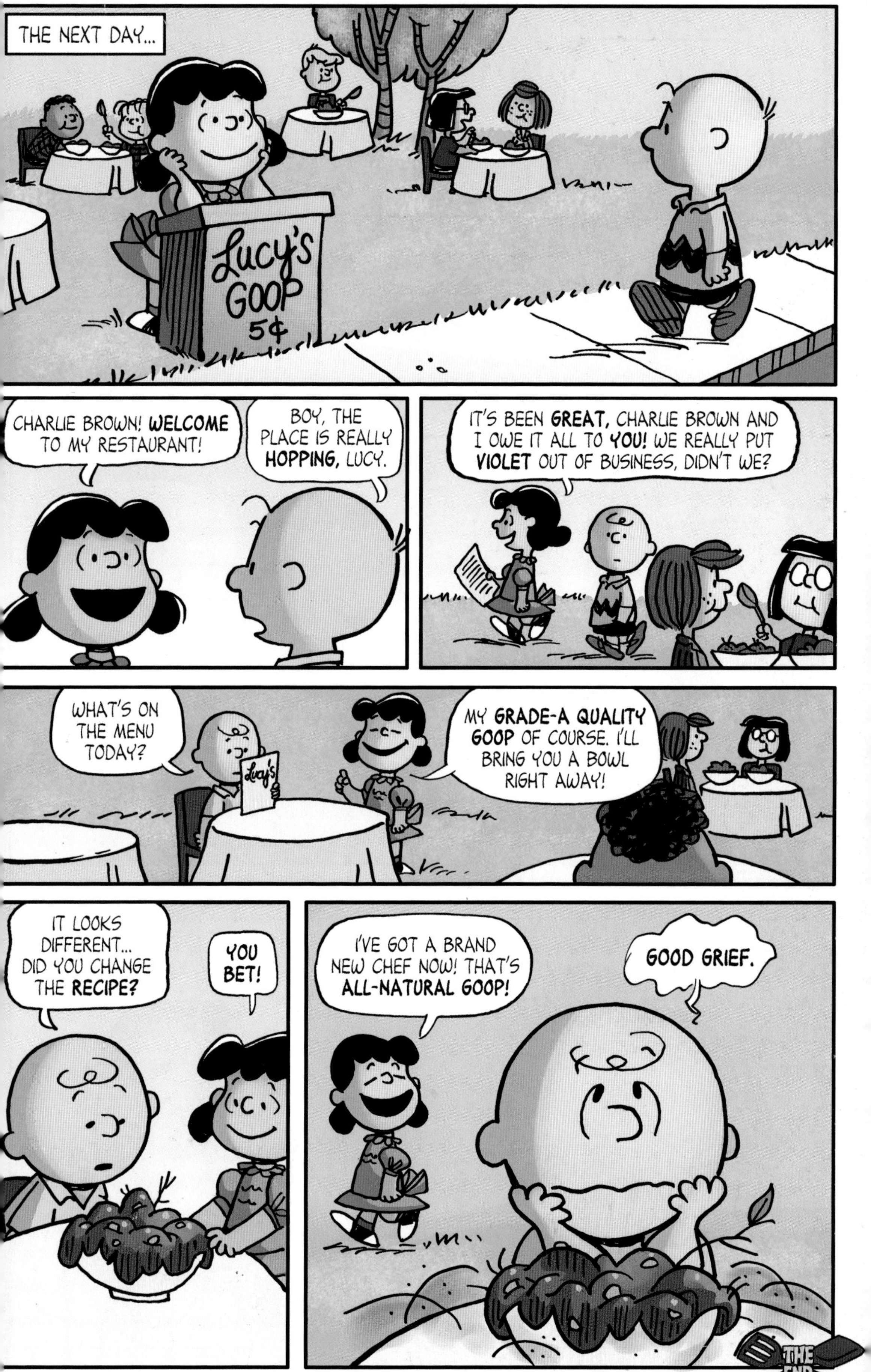
THE NEXT DAY...
Lucy's GOOP 5¢
CHARLIE BROWN! WELCOME TO MY RESTAURANT!
BOY, THE PLACE IS REALLY HOPPING, LUCY.
IT'S BEEN GREAT, CHARLIE BROWN AND I OWE IT ALL TO YOU! WE REALLY PUT VIOLET OUT OF BUSINESS, DIDN'T WE?
WHAT'S ON THE MENU TODAY?
Lucy's
MY GRADE-A QUALITY GOOP OF COURSE. I'LL BRING YOU A BOWL RIGHT AWAY!
IT LOOKS DIFFERENT... DID YOU CHANGE THE RECIPE?
YOU BET!
I'VE GOT A BRAND NEW CHEF NOW! THAT'S ALL-NATURAL GOOP!
GOOD GRIEF.
THE END

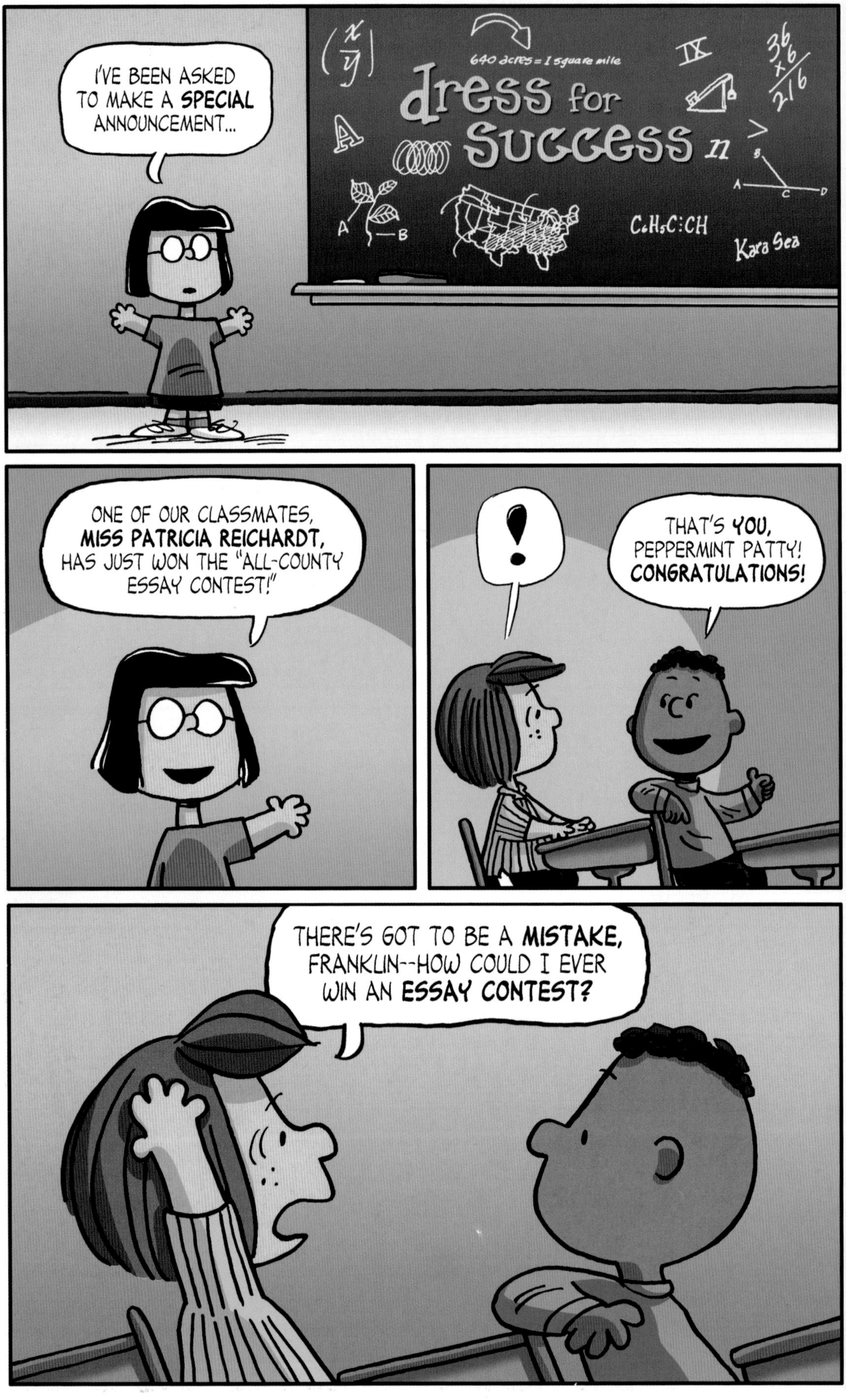
I'VE BEEN ASKED TO MAKE A **SPECIAL** ANNOUNCEMENT...
640 acres = 1 square mile
dress for Success
IX
Kara Sea
ONE OF OUR CLASSMATES, **MISS PATRICIA REICHARDT,** HAS JUST WON THE "ALL-COUNTY ESSAY CONTEST!"
!
THAT'S **YOU,** PEPPERMINT PATTY! **CONGRATULATIONS!**
THERE'S GOT TO BE A **MISTAKE,** FRANKLIN--HOW COULD I EVER WIN AN **ESSAY CONTEST?**

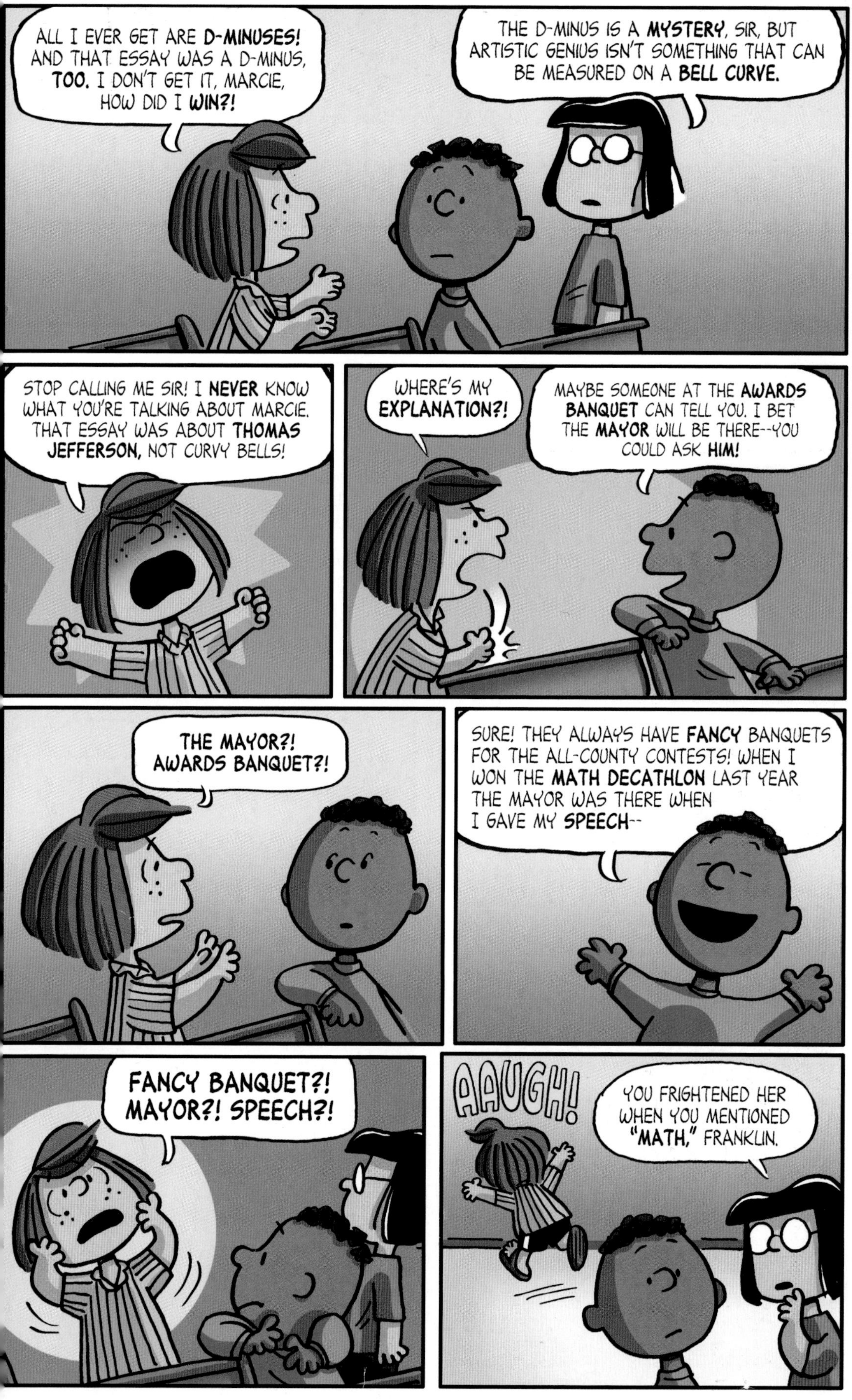

ALL I EVER GET ARE D-MINUSES! AND THAT ESSAY WAS A D-MINUS, TOO. I DON'T GET IT, MARCIE, HOW DID I WIN?!
THE D-MINUS IS A MYSTERY, SIR, BUT ARTISTIC GENIUS ISN'T SOMETHING THAT CAN BE MEASURED ON A BELL CURVE.
STOP CALLING ME SIR! I NEVER KNOW WHAT YOU'RE TALKING ABOUT MARCIE. THAT ESSAY WAS ABOUT THOMAS JEFFERSON, NOT CURVY BELLS!
WHERE'S MY EXPLANATION?!
MAYBE SOMEONE AT THE AWARDS BANQUET CAN TELL YOU. I BET THE MAYOR WILL BE THERE--YOU COULD ASK HIM!
THE MAYOR?! AWARDS BANQUET?!
SURE! THEY ALWAYS HAVE FANCY BANQUETS FOR THE ALL-COUNTY CONTESTS! WHEN I WON THE MATH DECATHLON LAST YEAR THE MAYOR WAS THERE WHEN I GAVE MY SPEECH--
FANCY BANQUET?! MAYOR?! SPEECH?!
AAUGH!
YOU FRIGHTENED HER WHEN YOU MENTIONED "MATH," FRANKLIN.

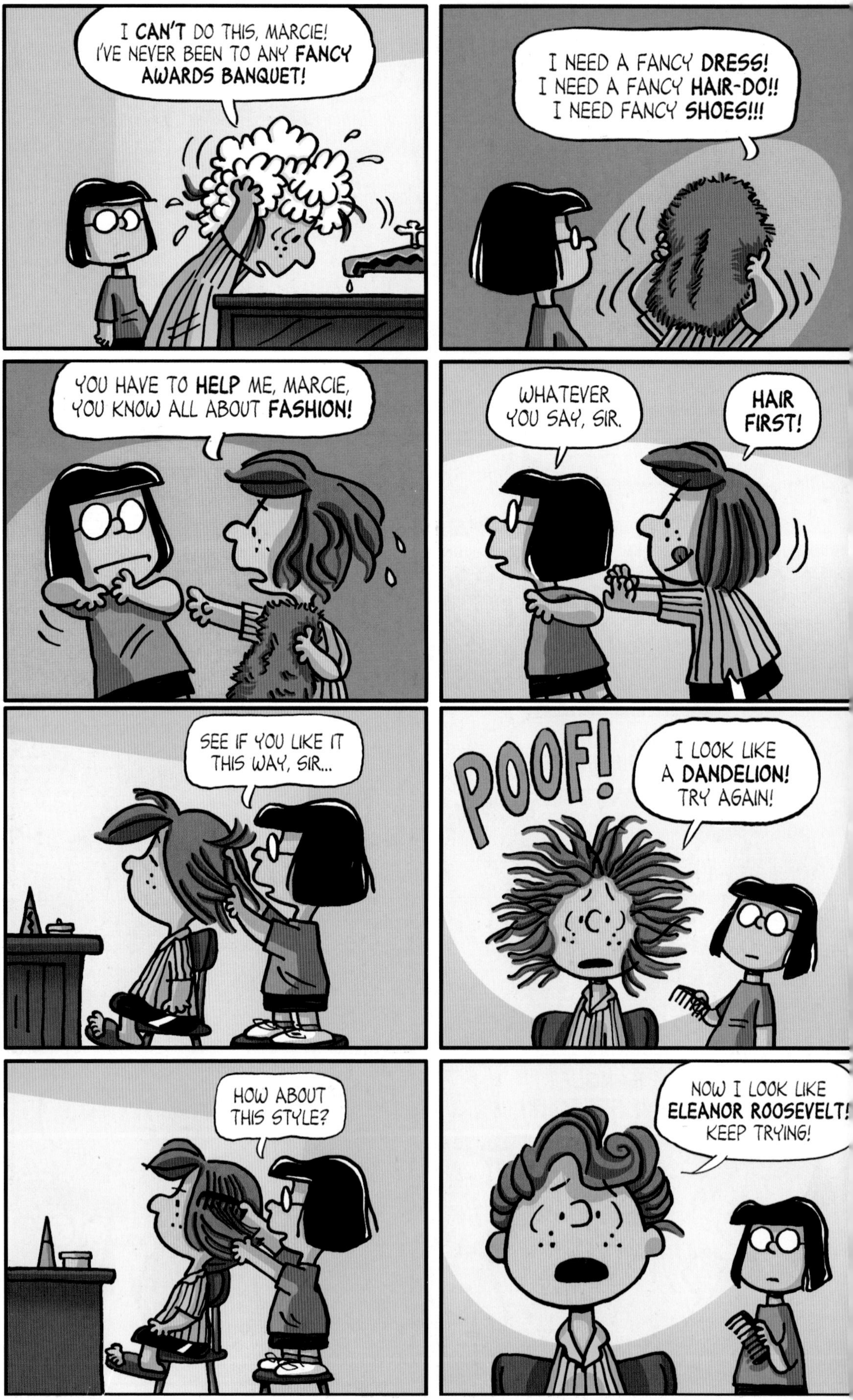
I **CAN'T** DO THIS, MARCIE! I'VE NEVER BEEN TO ANY **FANCY AWARDS BANQUET!**
I NEED A FANCY **DRESS!** I NEED A FANCY **HAIR-DO!!** I NEED FANCY **SHOES!!!**
YOU HAVE TO **HELP** ME, MARCIE, YOU KNOW ALL ABOUT **FASHION!**
WHATEVER YOU SAY, SIR.
HAIR FIRST!
SEE IF YOU LIKE IT THIS WAY, SIR...
POOF!
I LOOK LIKE A **DANDELION!** TRY AGAIN!
HOW ABOUT THIS STYLE?
NOW I LOOK LIKE **ELEANOR ROOSEVELT!** KEEP TRYING!

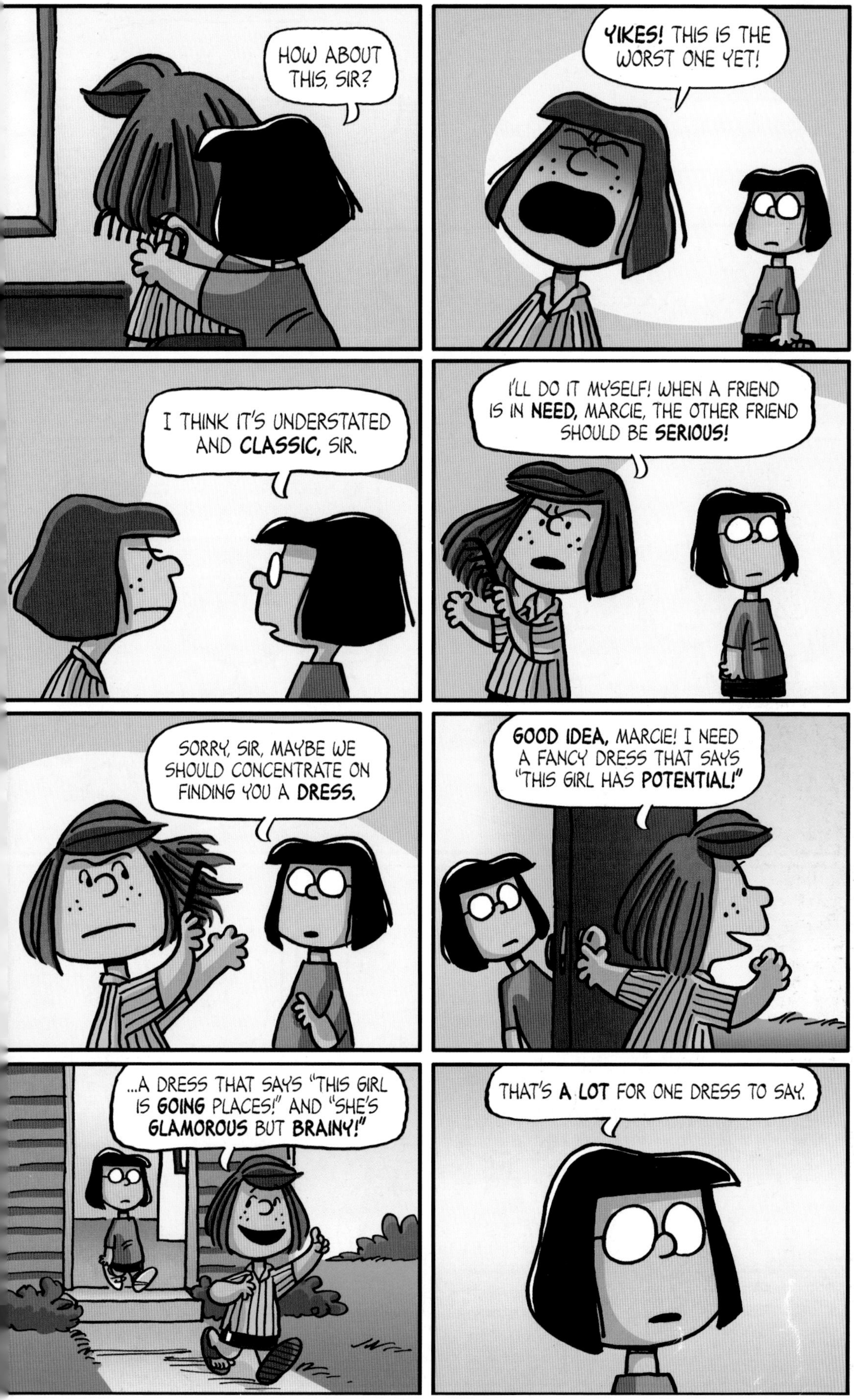
HOW ABOUT THIS, SIR?
YIKES! THIS IS THE WORST ONE YET!
I THINK IT'S UNDERSTATED AND CLASSIC, SIR.
I'LL DO IT MYSELF! WHEN A FRIEND IS IN NEED, MARCIE, THE OTHER FRIEND SHOULD BE SERIOUS!
SORRY, SIR, MAYBE WE SHOULD CONCENTRATE ON FINDING YOU A DRESS.
GOOD IDEA, MARCIE! I NEED A FANCY DRESS THAT SAYS "THIS GIRL HAS POTENTIAL!"
...A DRESS THAT SAYS "THIS GIRL IS GOING PLACES!" AND "SHE'S GLAMOROUS BUT BRAINY!"
THAT'S A LOT FOR ONE DRESS TO SAY.

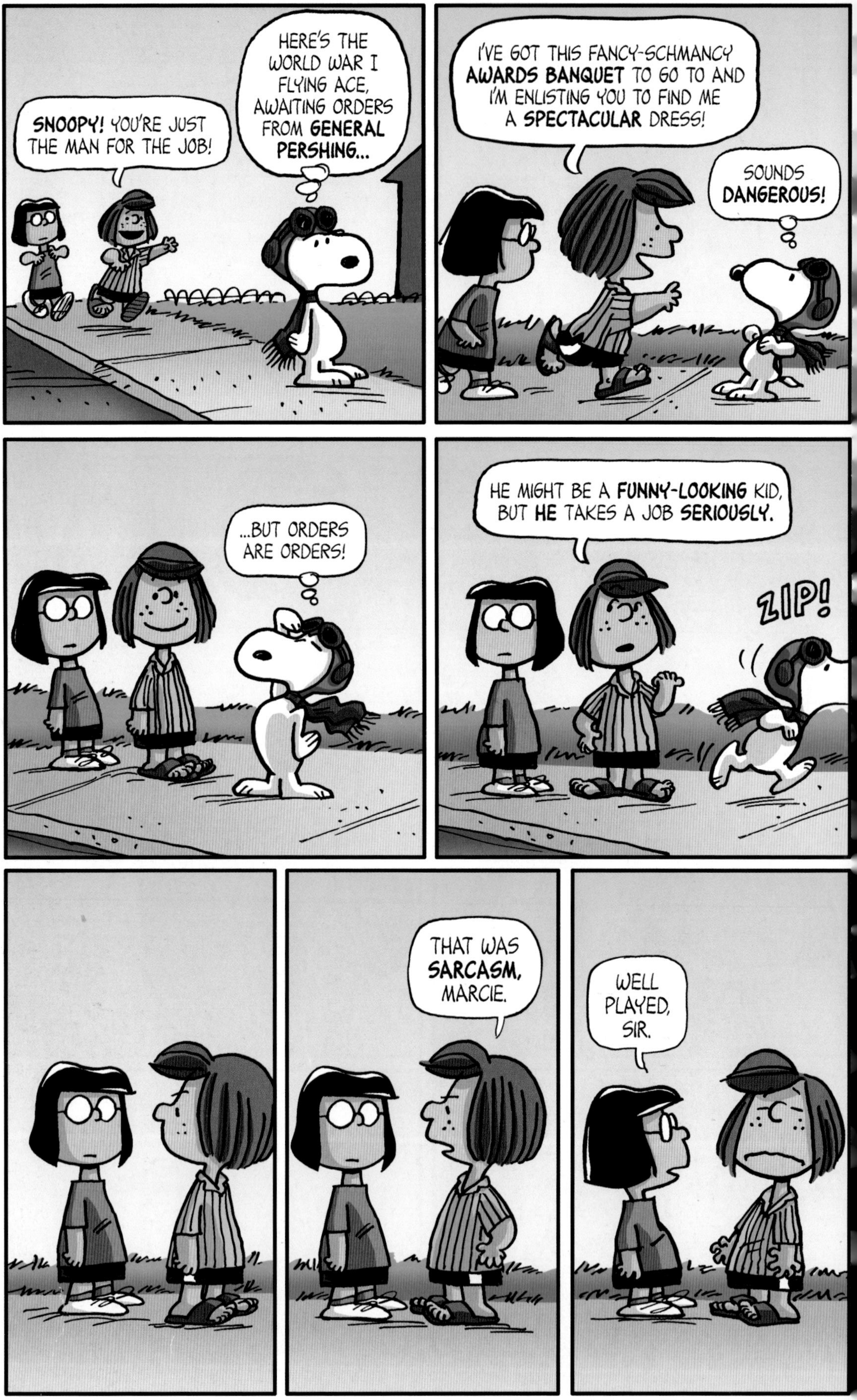

SNOOPY! YOU'RE JUST THE MAN FOR THE JOB!
HERE'S THE WORLD WAR I FLYING ACE, AWAITING ORDERS FROM GENERAL PERSHING...
I'VE GOT THIS FANCY-SCHMANCY AWARDS BANQUET TO GO TO AND I'M ENLISTING YOU TO FIND ME A SPECTACULAR DRESS!
SOUNDS DANGEROUS!
...BUT ORDERS ARE ORDERS!
HE MIGHT BE A FUNNY-LOOKING KID, BUT HE TAKES A JOB SERIOUSLY.
ZIP!
THAT WAS SARCASM, MARCIE.
WELL PLAYED, SIR.

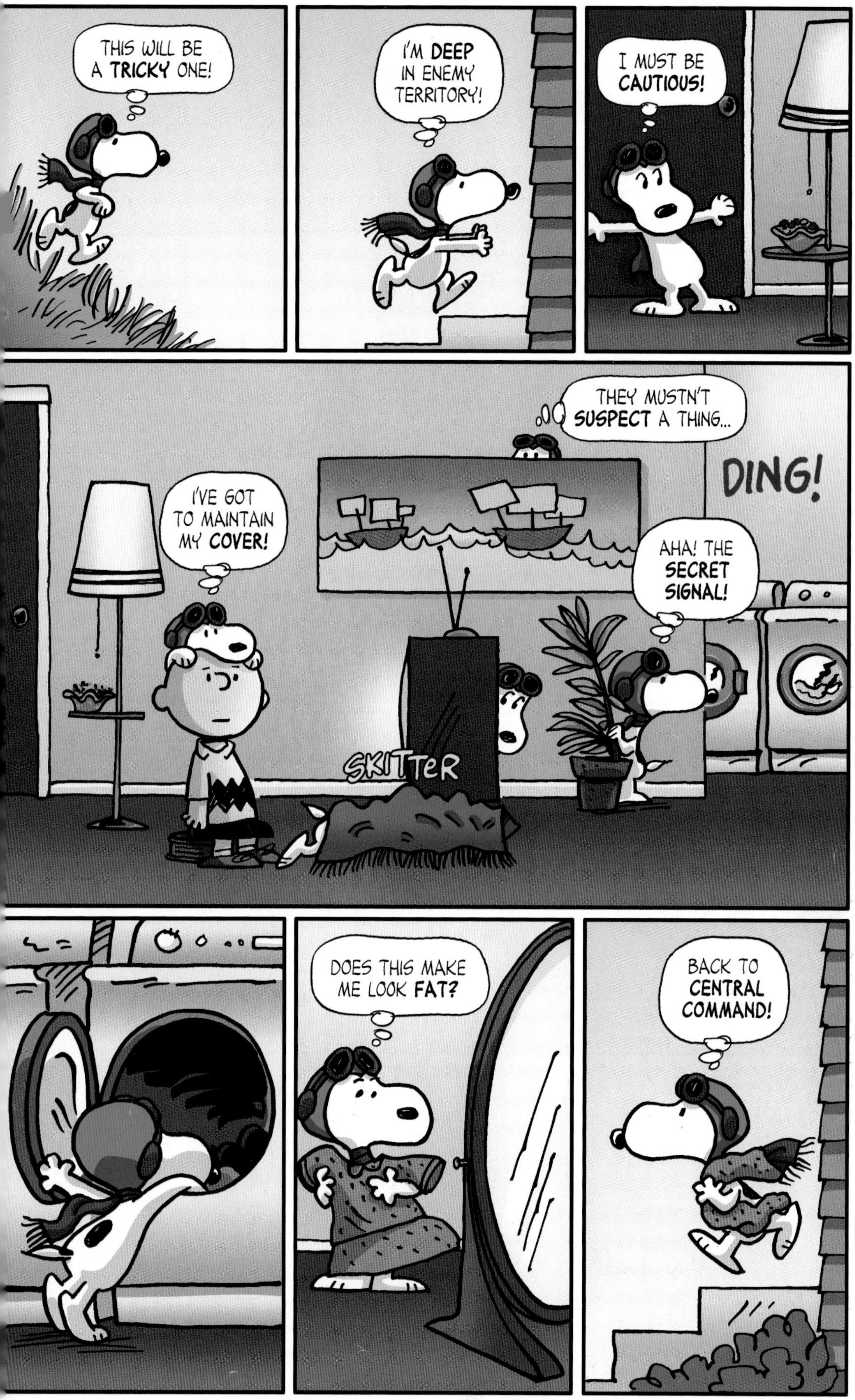

THIS WILL BE A TRICKY ONE!
I'M DEEP IN ENEMY TERRITORY!
I MUST BE CAUTIOUS!
THEY MUSTN'T SUSPECT A THING...
DING!
I'VE GOT TO MAINTAIN MY COVER!
AHA! THE SECRET SIGNAL!
SKITTER
DOES THIS MAKE ME LOOK FAT?
BACK TO CENTRAL COMMAND!

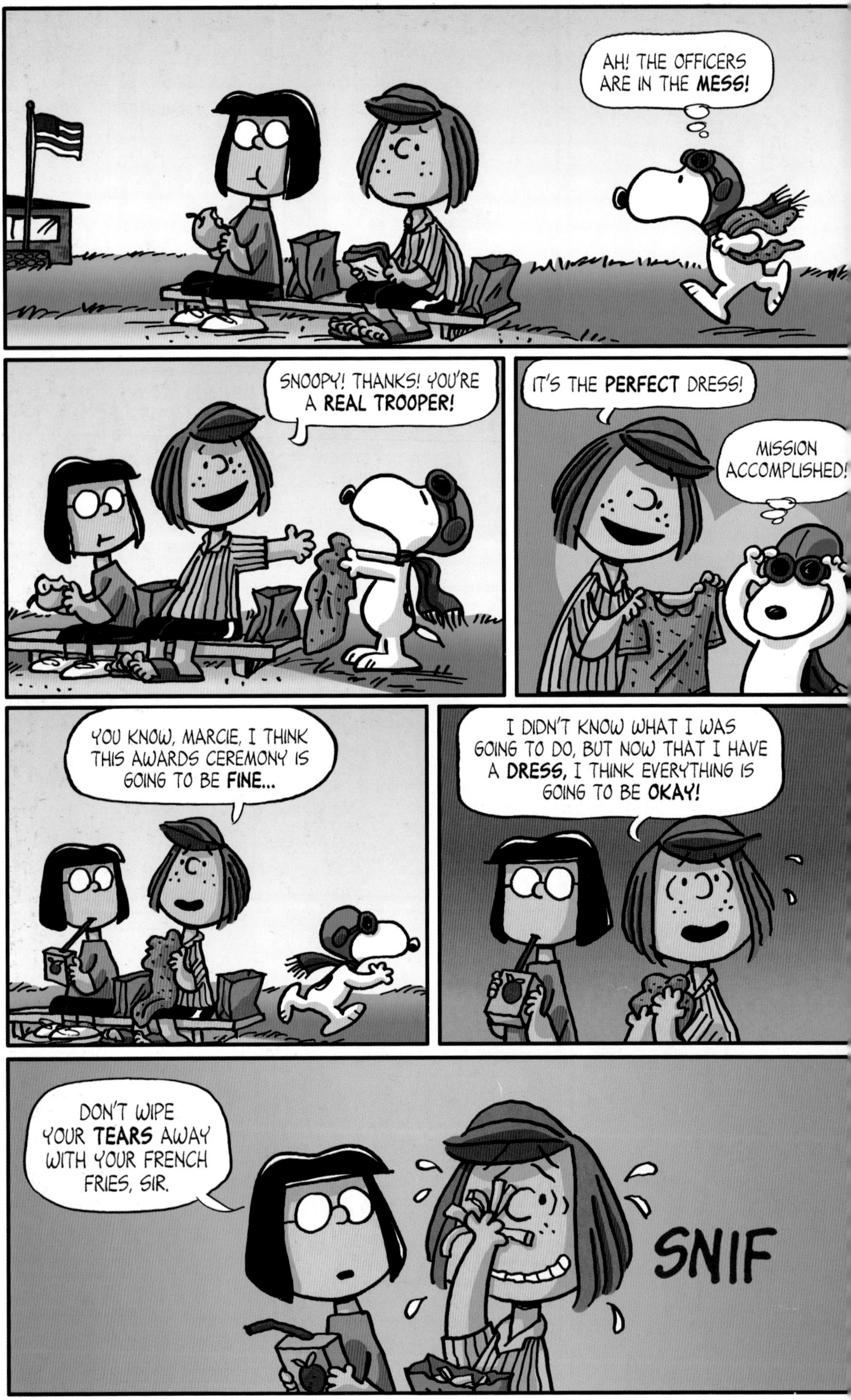
AH! THE OFFICERS ARE IN THE **MESS!**
SNOOPY! THANKS! YOU'RE A **REAL TROOPER!**
IT'S THE **PERFECT** DRESS!
MISSION ACCOMPLISHED!
YOU KNOW, MARCIE, I THINK THIS AWARDS CEREMONY IS GOING TO BE **FINE...**
I DIDN'T KNOW WHAT I WAS GOING TO DO, BUT NOW THAT I HAVE A **DRESS,** I THINK EVERYTHING IS GOING TO BE **OKAY!**
DON'T WIPE YOUR **TEARS** AWAY WITH YOUR FRENCH FRIES, SIR.
SNIF

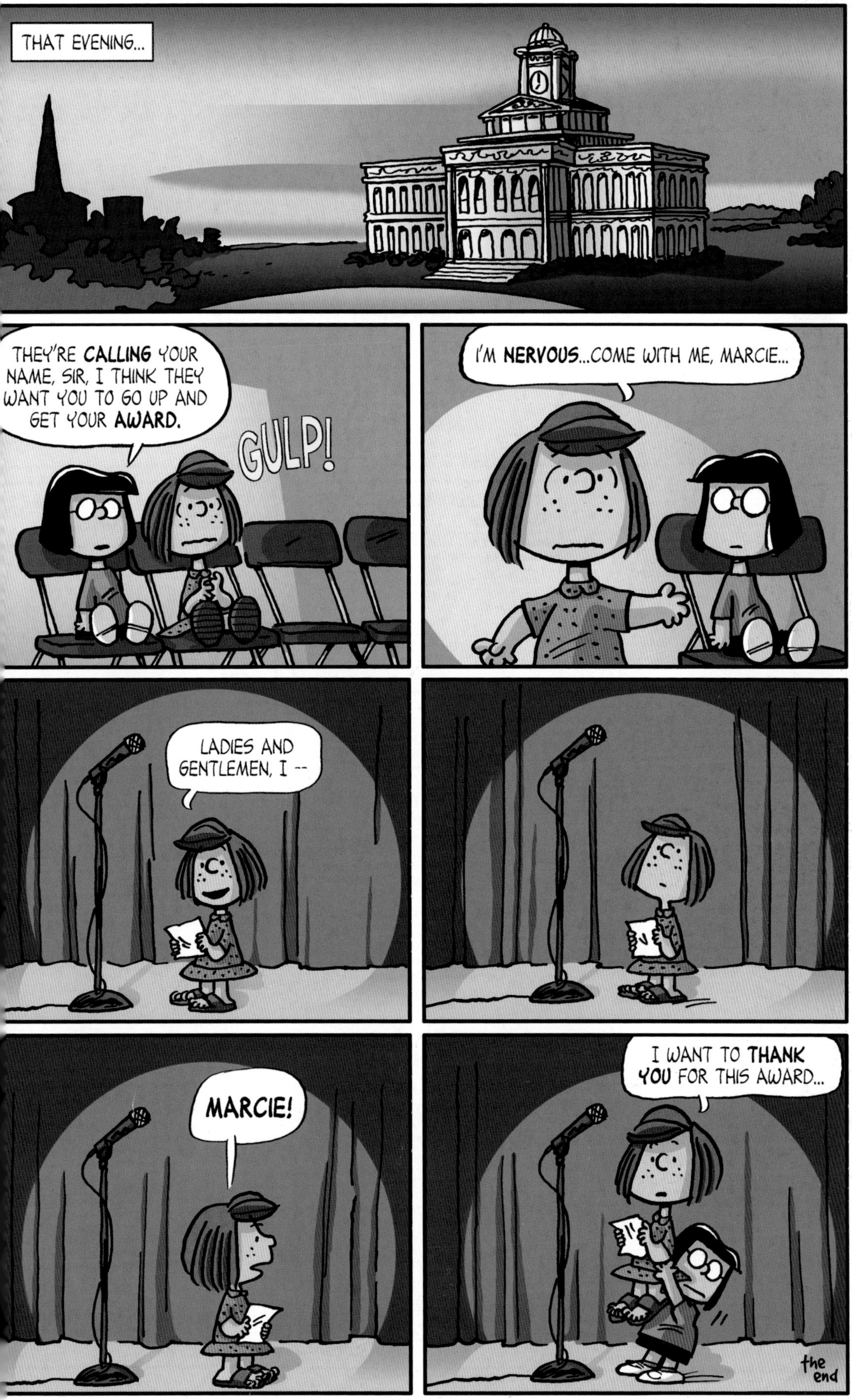
THAT EVENING...
THEY'RE CALLING YOUR NAME, SIR, I THINK THEY WANT YOU TO GO UP AND GET YOUR AWARD.
GULP!
I'M NERVOUS...COME WITH ME, MARCIE...
LADIES AND GENTLEMEN, I --
MARCIE!
I WANT TO THANK YOU FOR THIS AWARD...
the end

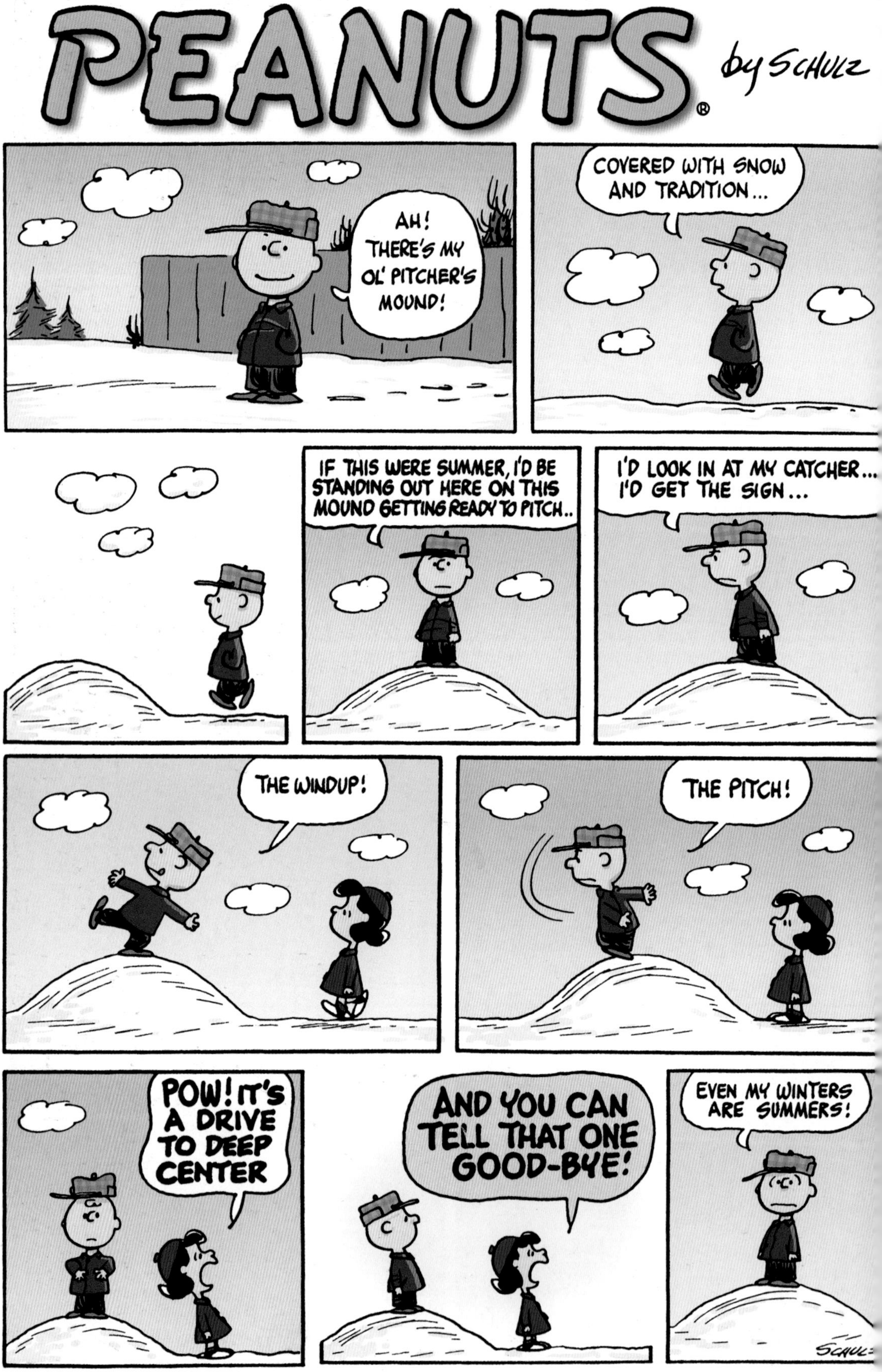
PEANUTS
by SCHULZ
AH! THERE'S MY OL' PITCHER'S MOUND!
COVERED WITH SNOW AND TRADITION...
IF THIS WERE SUMMER, I'D BE STANDING OUT HERE ON THIS MOUND GETTING READY TO PITCH..
I'D LOOK IN AT MY CATCHER... I'D GET THE SIGN...
THE WINDUP!
THE PITCH!
POW! IT'S A DRIVE TO DEEP CENTER
AND YOU CAN TELL THAT ONE GOOD-BYE!
EVEN MY WINTERS ARE SUMMERS!
SCHULZ

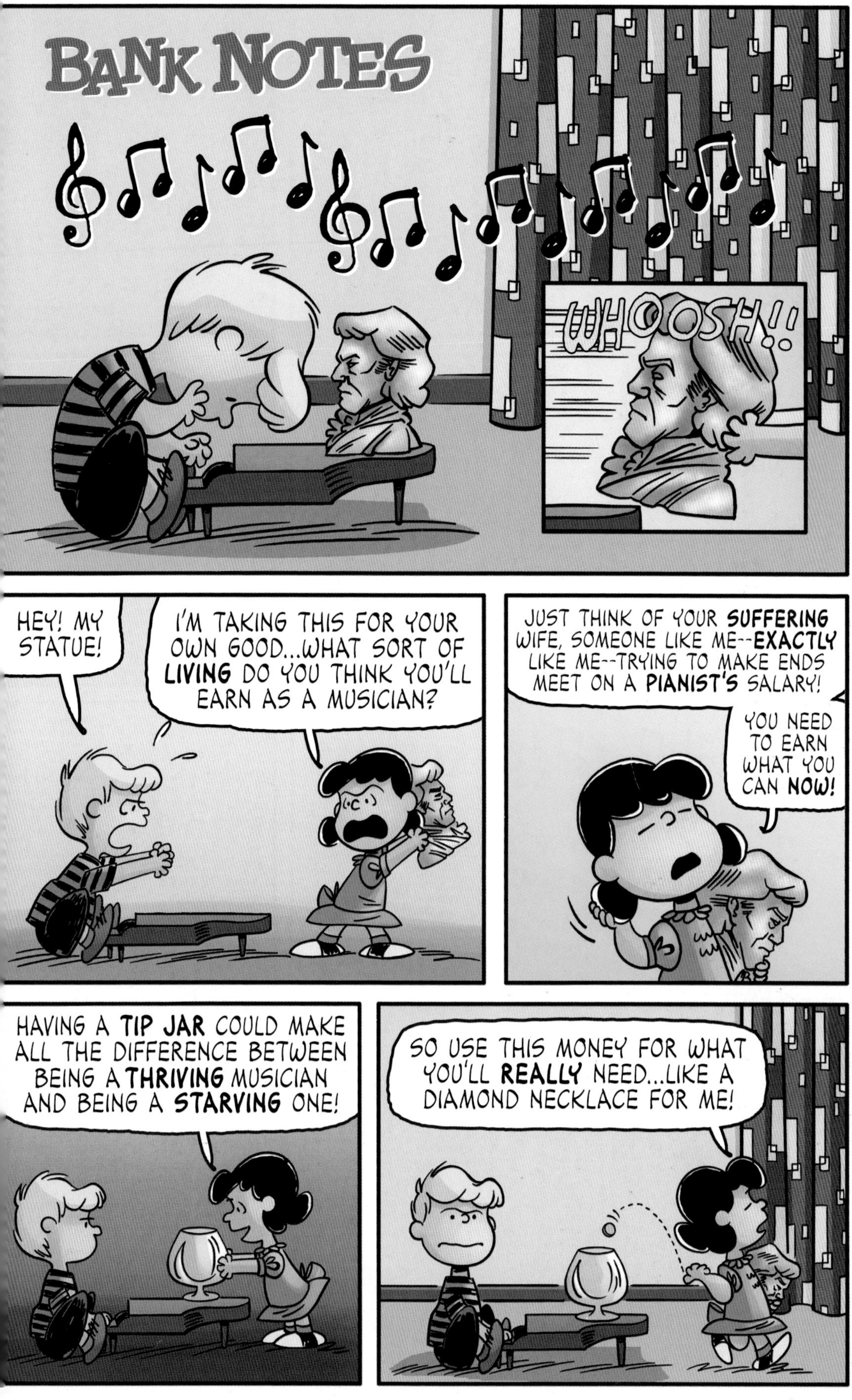
BANK NOTES
WHOOSH!!
HEY! MY STATUE!
I'M TAKING THIS FOR YOUR OWN GOOD...WHAT SORT OF LIVING DO YOU THINK YOU'LL EARN AS A MUSICIAN?
JUST THINK OF YOUR SUFFERING WIFE, SOMEONE LIKE ME--EXACTLY LIKE ME--TRYING TO MAKE ENDS MEET ON A PIANIST'S SALARY!
YOU NEED TO EARN WHAT YOU CAN NOW!
HAVING A TIP JAR COULD MAKE ALL THE DIFFERENCE BETWEEN BEING A THRIVING MUSICIAN AND BEING A STARVING ONE!
SO USE THIS MONEY FOR WHAT YOU'LL REALLY NEED...LIKE A DIAMOND NECKLACE FOR ME!

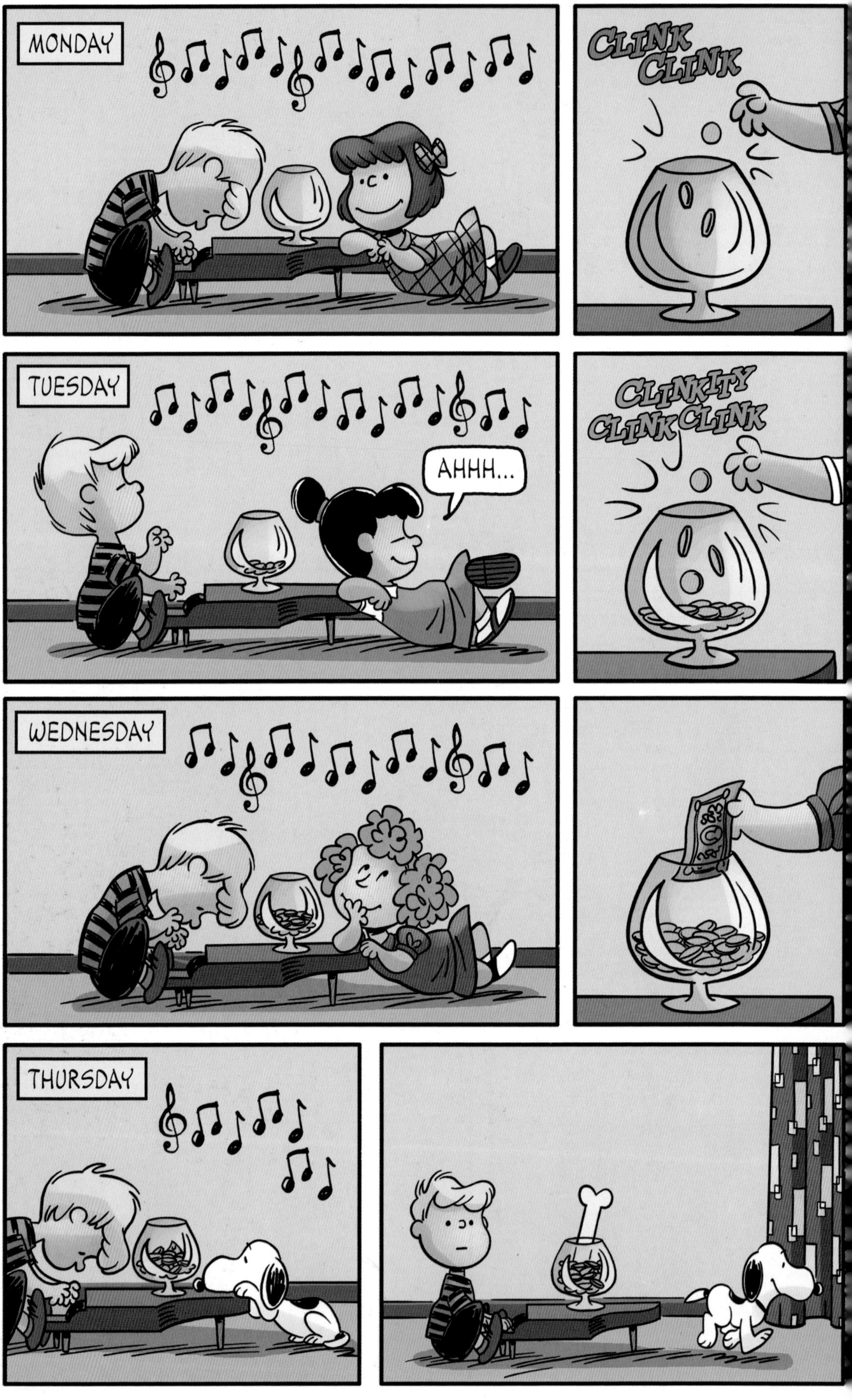
MONDAY
CLINK
CLINK
TUESDAY
AHHH...
CLINKITY
CLINK CLINK
WEDNESDAY
THURSDAY

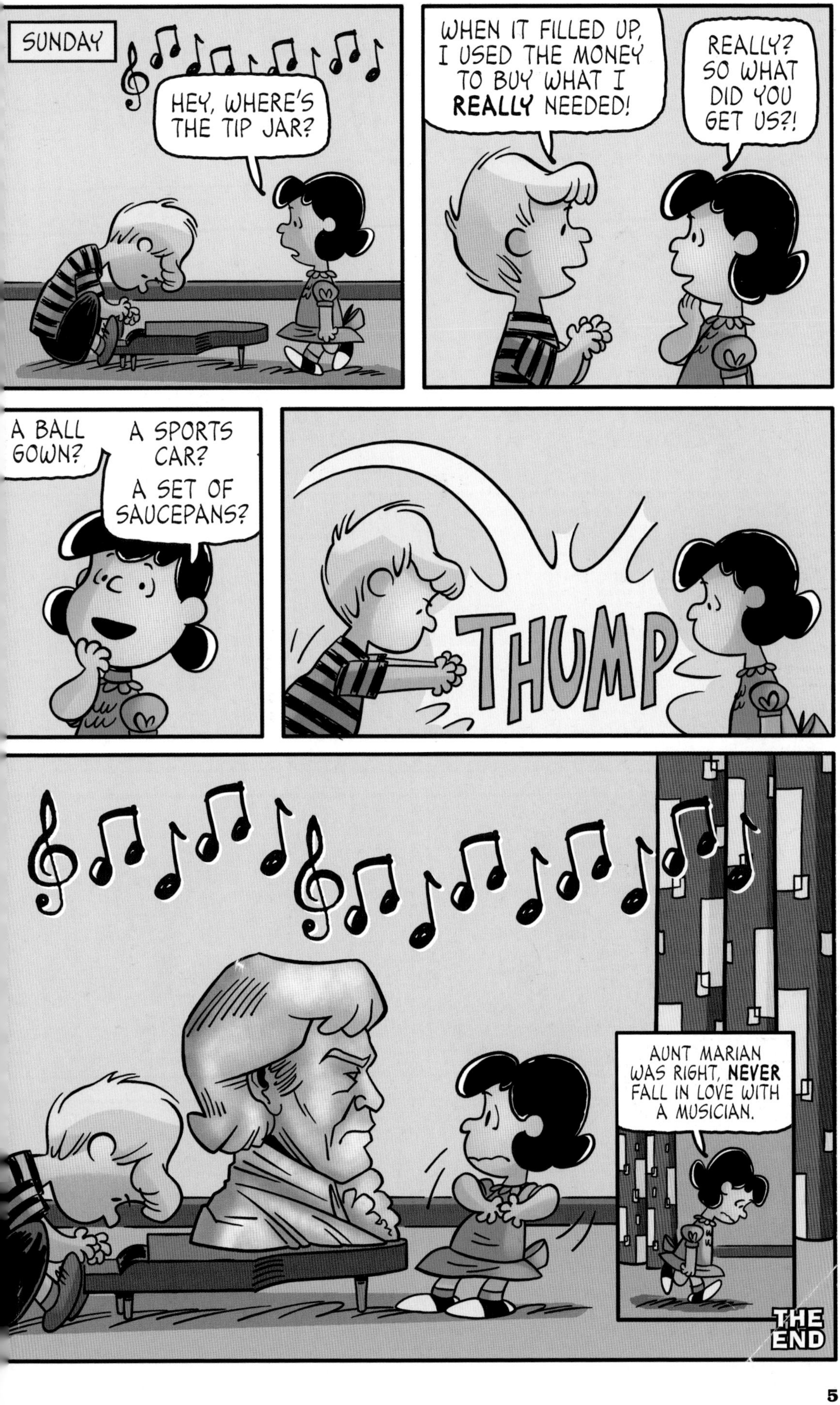
SUNDAY
HEY, WHERE'S THE TIP JAR?
WHEN IT FILLED UP, I USED THE MONEY TO BUY WHAT I **REALLY** NEEDED!
REALLY? SO WHAT DID YOU GET US?!
A BALL GOWN?
A SPORTS CAR?
A SET OF SAUCEPANS?
THUMP
AUNT MARIAN WAS RIGHT, **NEVER** FALL IN LOVE WITH A MUSICIAN.
THE END

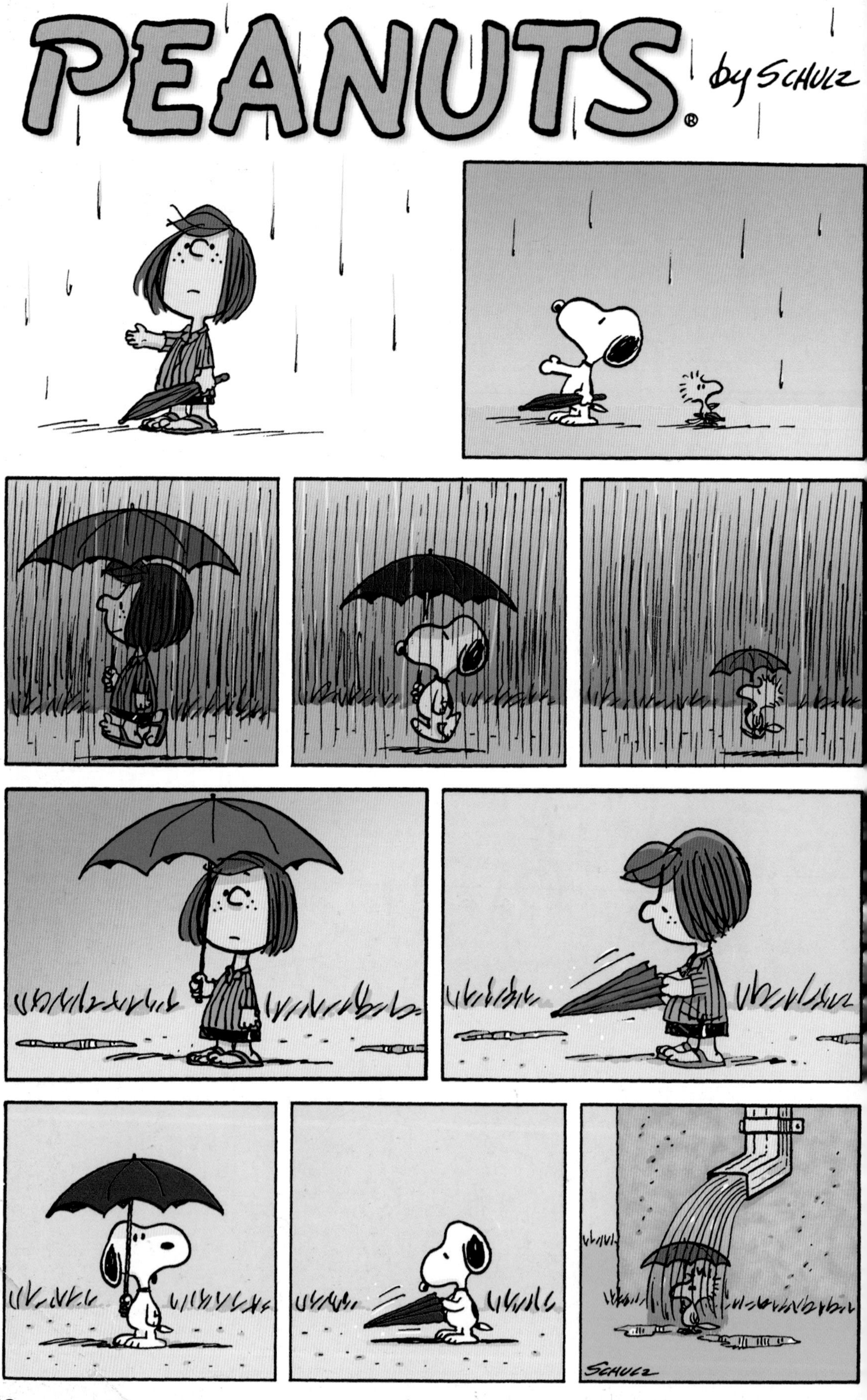
PEANUTS
by SCHULZ
SCHULZ

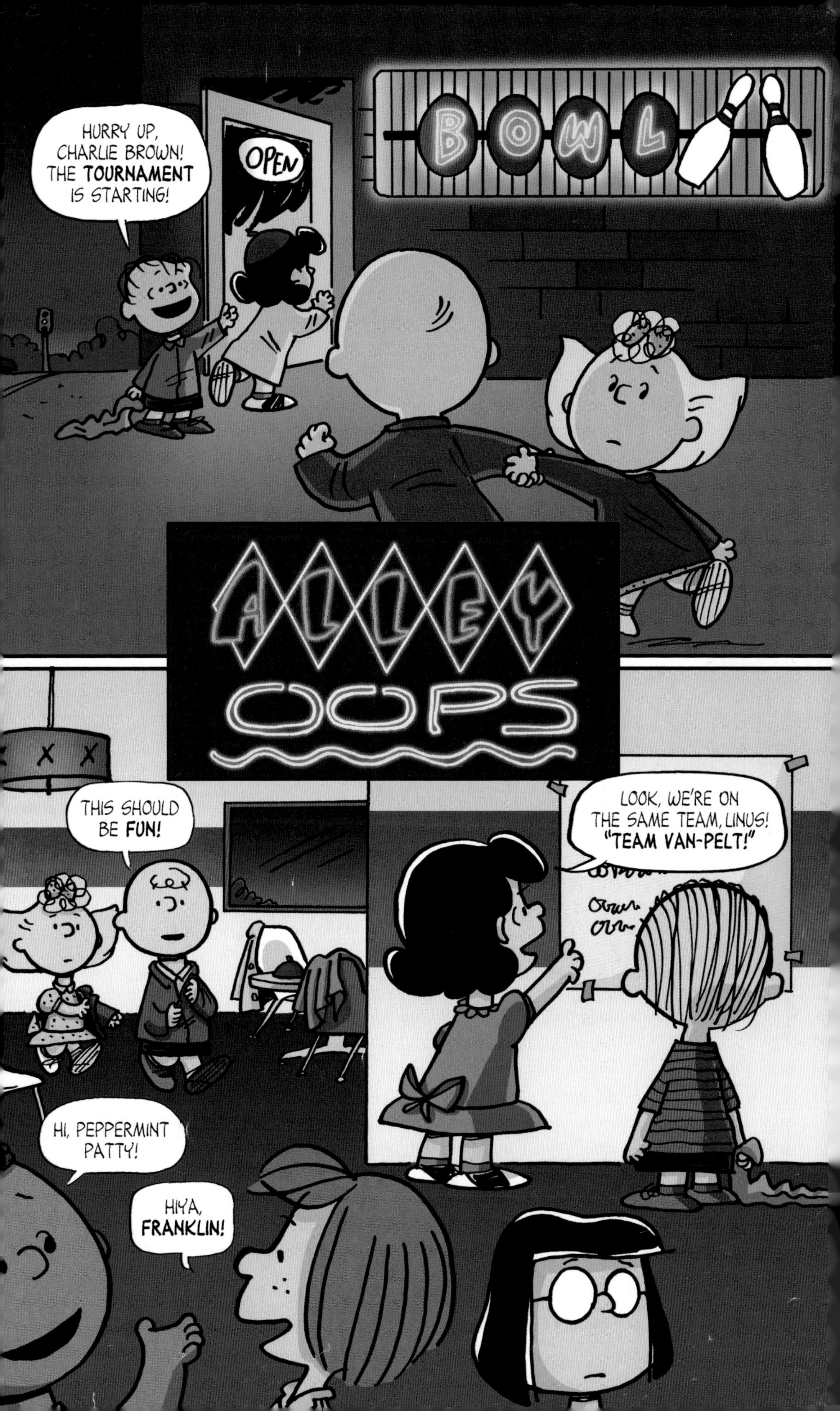

HURRY UP, CHARLIE BROWN! THE TOURNAMENT IS STARTING!
OPEN
BOWL
ALLEY OOPS
THIS SHOULD BE FUN!
LOOK, WE'RE ON THE SAME TEAM, LINUS! "TEAM VAN-PELT!"
HI, PEPPERMINT PATTY!
HIYA, FRANKLIN!

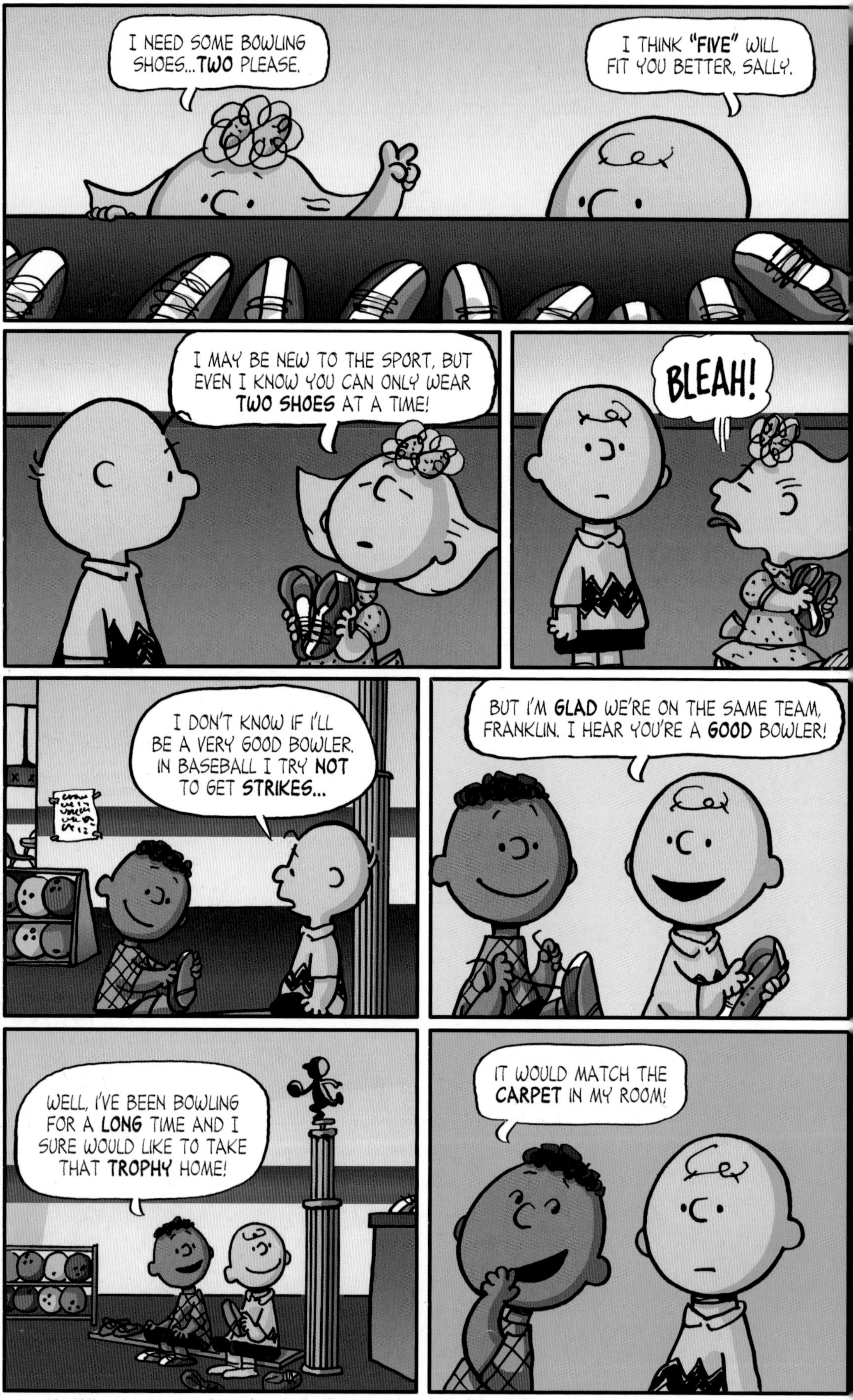
I NEED SOME BOWLING SHOES...**TWO** PLEASE.
I THINK **"FIVE"** WILL FIT YOU BETTER, SALLY.
I MAY BE NEW TO THE SPORT, BUT EVEN I KNOW YOU CAN ONLY WEAR **TWO SHOES** AT A TIME!
BLEAH!
I DON'T KNOW IF I'LL BE A VERY GOOD BOWLER. IN BASEBALL I TRY **NOT** TO GET **STRIKES...**
BUT I'M **GLAD** WE'RE ON THE SAME TEAM, FRANKLIN. I HEAR YOU'RE A **GOOD** BOWLER!
WELL, I'VE BEEN BOWLING FOR A **LONG** TIME AND I SURE WOULD LIKE TO TAKE THAT **TROPHY** HOME!
IT WOULD MATCH THE **CARPET** IN MY ROOM!

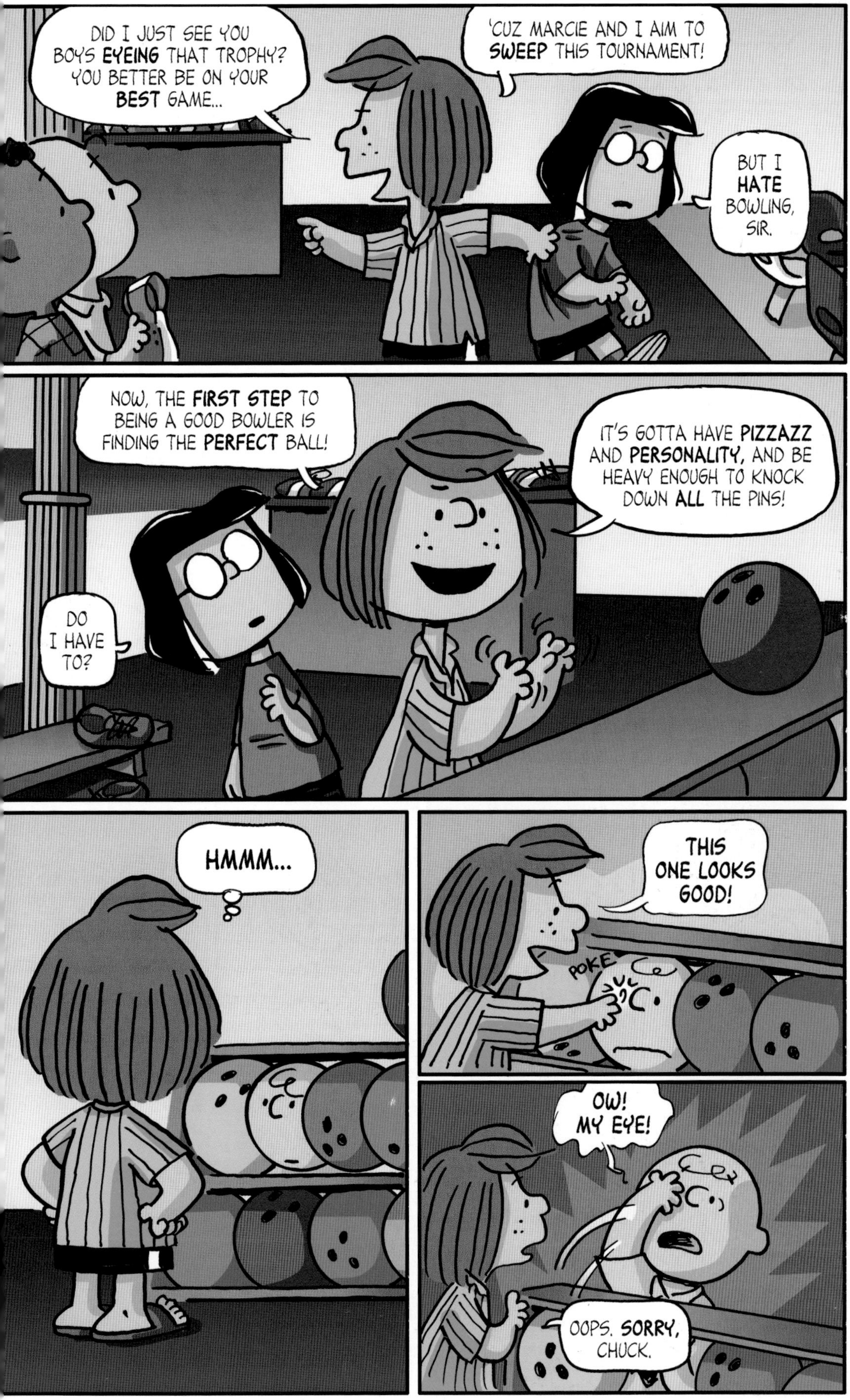
DID I JUST SEE YOU BOYS **EYEING** THAT TROPHY? YOU BETTER BE ON YOUR **BEST** GAME...
'CUZ MARCIE AND I AIM TO **SWEEP** THIS TOURNAMENT!
BUT I **HATE** BOWLING, SIR.
NOW, THE **FIRST STEP** TO BEING A GOOD BOWLER IS FINDING THE **PERFECT** BALL!
IT'S GOTTA HAVE **PIZZAZZ** AND **PERSONALITY,** AND BE HEAVY ENOUGH TO KNOCK DOWN **ALL** THE PINS!
DO I HAVE TO?
HMMM...
THIS ONE LOOKS GOOD!
POKE
OW! MY EYE!
OOPS. **SORRY,** CHUCK.

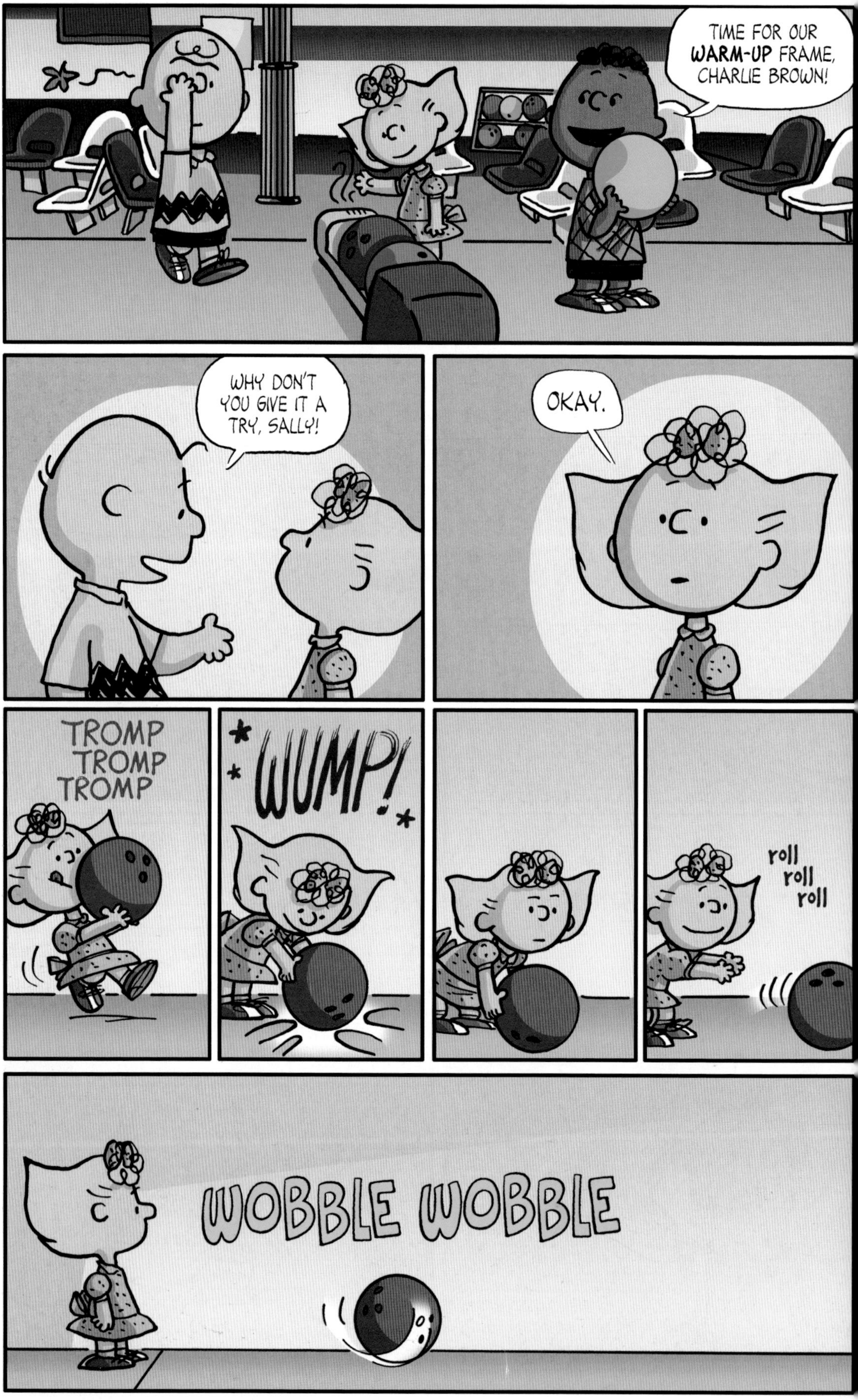
TIME FOR OUR WARM-UP FRAME, CHARLIE BROWN!
WHY DON'T YOU GIVE IT A TRY, SALLY!
OKAY.
TROMP TROMP TROMP
WUMP!
roll roll roll
WOBBLE WOBBLE

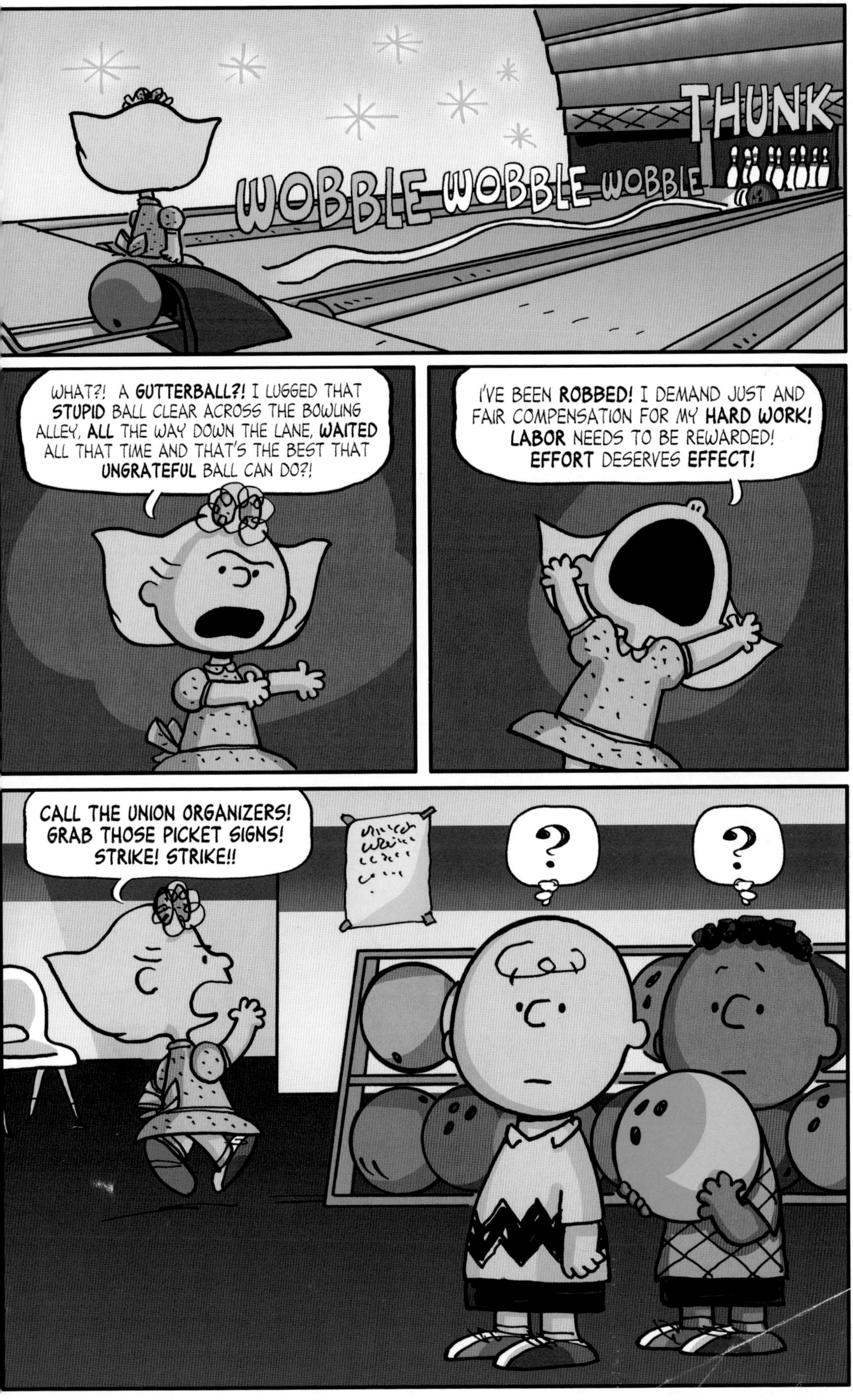
THUNK
WOBBLE WOBBLE WOBBLE
WHAT?! A GUTTERBALL?! I LUGGED THAT STUPID BALL CLEAR ACROSS THE BOWLING ALLEY, ALL THE WAY DOWN THE LANE, WAITED ALL THAT TIME AND THAT'S THE BEST THAT UNGRATEFUL BALL CAN DO?!
I'VE BEEN ROBBED! I DEMAND JUST AND FAIR COMPENSATION FOR MY HARD WORK! LABOR NEEDS TO BE REWARDED! EFFORT DESERVES EFFECT!
CALL THE UNION ORGANIZERS! GRAB THOSE PICKET SIGNS! STRIKE! STRIKE!!
?
?

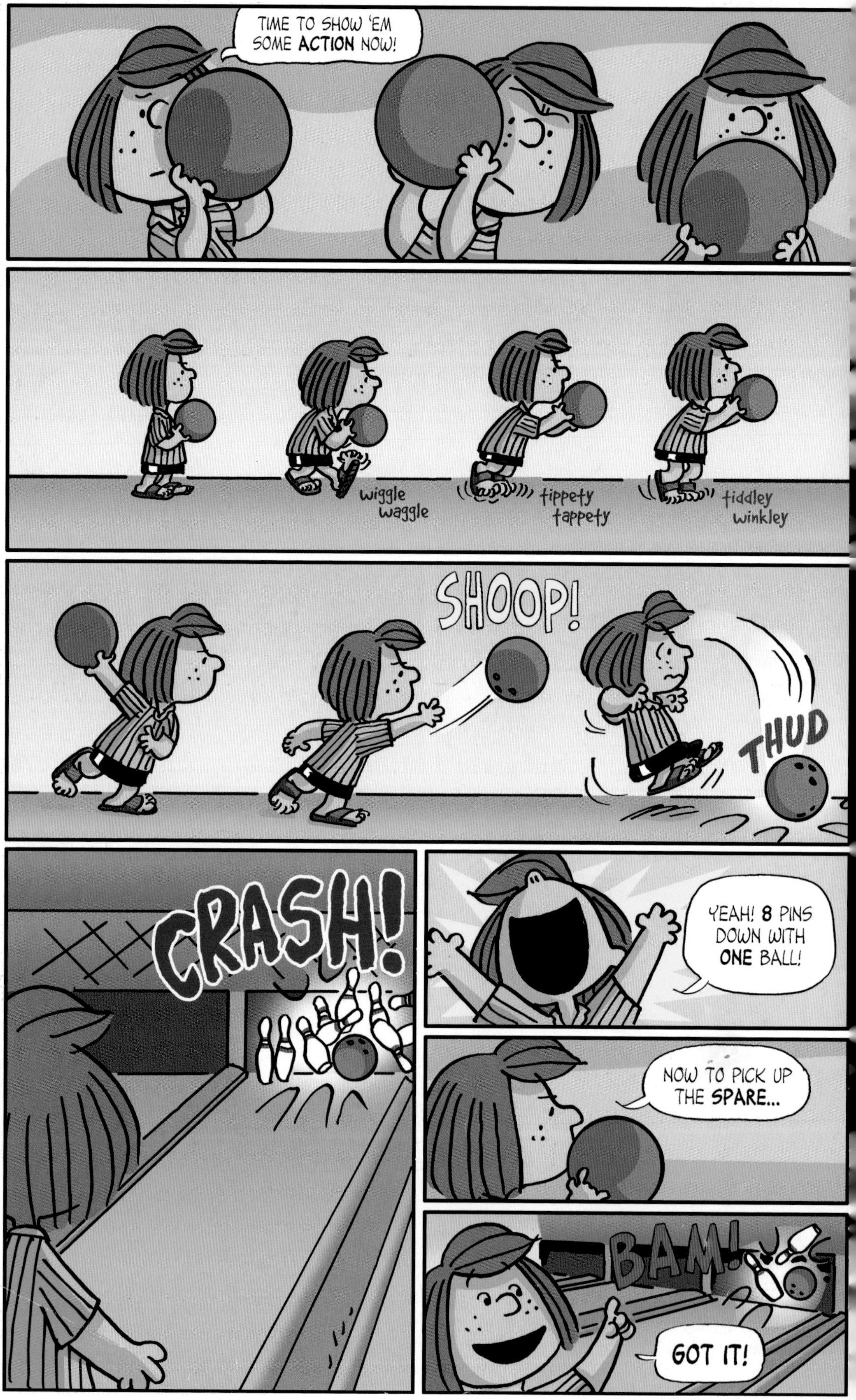
TIME TO SHOW 'EM SOME ACTION NOW!
wiggle waggle
tippety tappety
tiddley winkley
SHOOP!
THUD
CRASH!
YEAH! 8 PINS DOWN WITH ONE BALL!
NOW TO PICK UP THE SPARE...
BAM!
GOT IT!

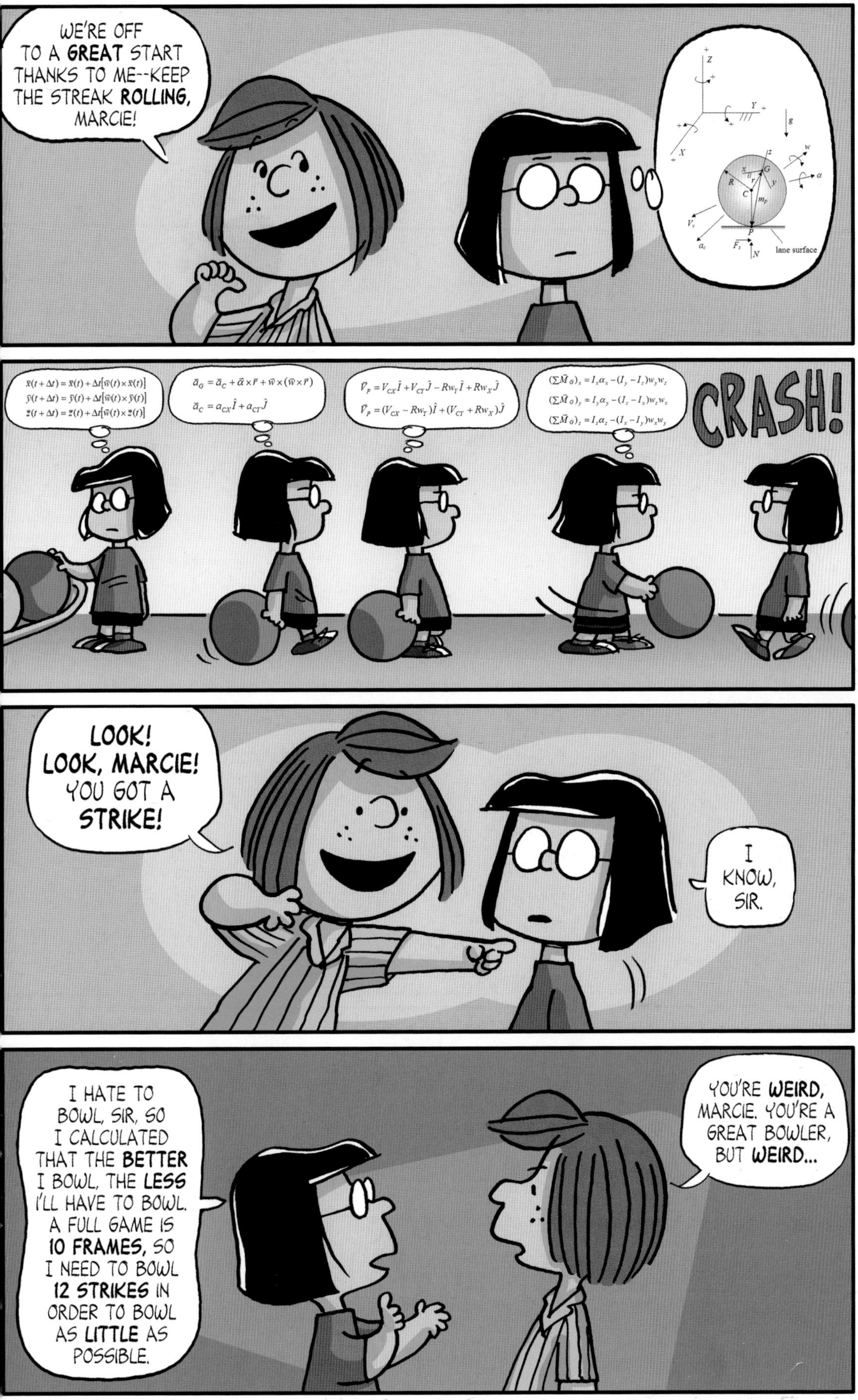
WE'RE OFF TO A **GREAT** START THANKS TO ME--KEEP THE STREAK **ROLLING,** MARCIE!
lane surface
$\bar{x}(t+\Delta t) = \bar{x}(t) + \Delta t[\bar{w}(t) \times \bar{x}(t)]$
$\bar{y}(t+\Delta t) = \bar{y}(t) + \Delta t[\bar{w}(t) \times \bar{y}(t)]$
$\bar{z}(t+\Delta t) = \bar{z}(t) + \Delta t[\bar{w}(t) \times \bar{z}(t)]$
$\vec{a}_G = \vec{a}_C + \vec{\alpha} \times \vec{r} + \vec{w} \times (\vec{w} \times \vec{r})$
$\vec{a}_C = a_{CX}\hat{I} + a_{CT}\hat{J}$
$\vec{V}_P = V_{CX}\hat{I} + V_{CT}\hat{J} - Rw_T\hat{I} + Rw_X\hat{J}$
$\vec{V}_P = (V_{CX} - Rw_T)\hat{I} + (V_{CT} + Rw_X)\hat{J}$
$(\Sigma\vec{M}_G)_x = I_x\alpha_x - (I_y - I_z)w_y w_z$
$(\Sigma\vec{M}_G)_y = I_y\alpha_y - (I_z - I_x)w_z w_x$
$(\Sigma\vec{M}_G)_z = I_z\alpha_z - (I_x - I_y)w_x w_y$
CRASH!
LOOK! LOOK, MARCIE! YOU GOT A **STRIKE!**
I KNOW, SIR.
I HATE TO BOWL, SIR, SO I CALCULATED THAT THE **BETTER** I BOWL, THE **LESS** I'LL HAVE TO BOWL. A FULL GAME IS **10 FRAMES,** SO I NEED TO BOWL **12 STRIKES** IN ORDER TO BOWL AS **LITTLE** AS POSSIBLE.
YOU'RE **WEIRD,** MARCIE. YOU'RE A GREAT BOWLER, BUT **WEIRD...**

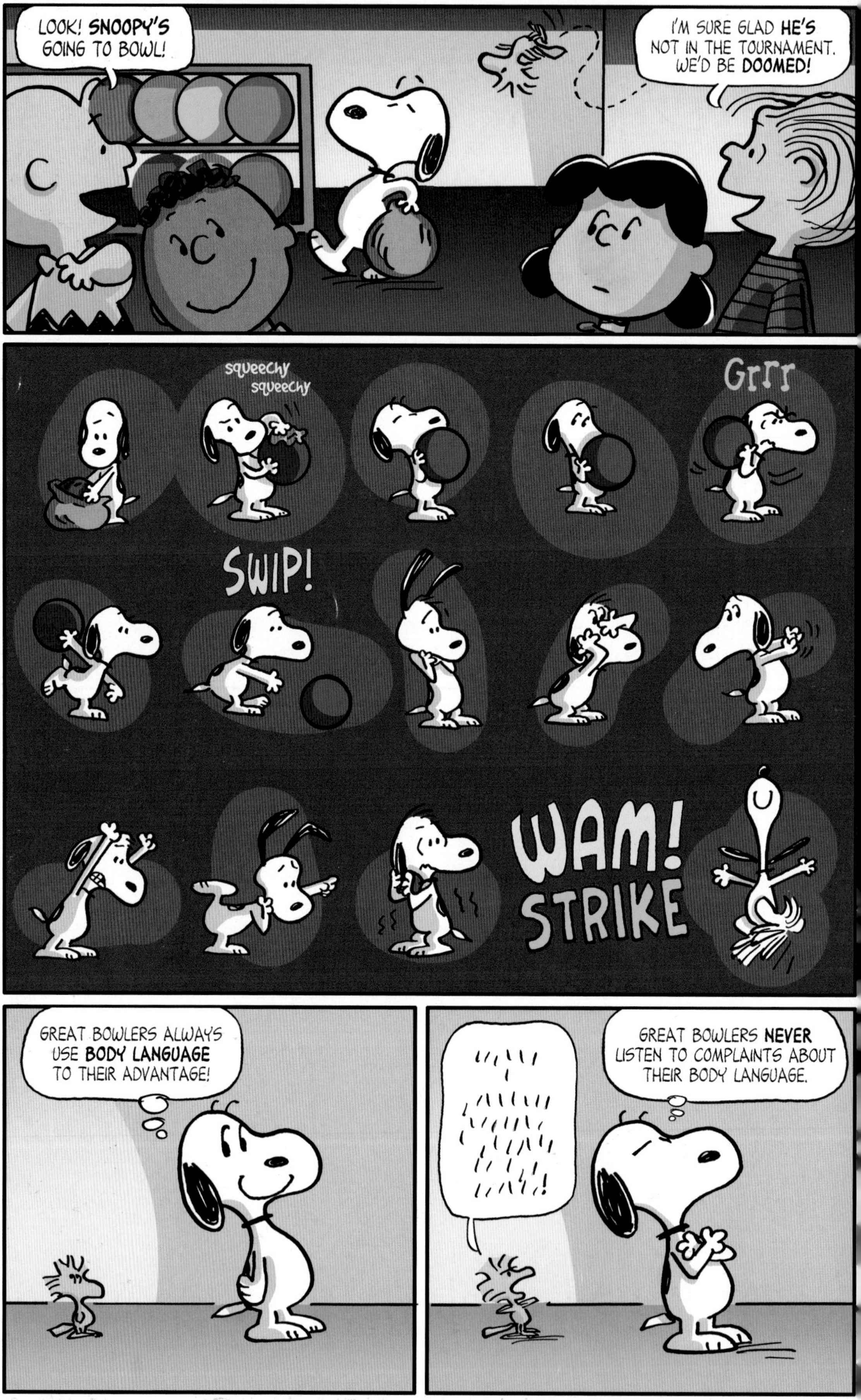
LOOK! SNOOPY'S GOING TO BOWL!
I'M SURE GLAD HE'S NOT IN THE TOURNAMENT. WE'D BE DOOMED!
squeechy squeechy
Grrr
SWIP!
WAM!
STRIKE
GREAT BOWLERS ALWAYS USE BODY LANGUAGE TO THEIR ADVANTAGE!
GREAT BOWLERS NEVER LISTEN TO COMPLAINTS ABOUT THEIR BODY LANGUAGE.

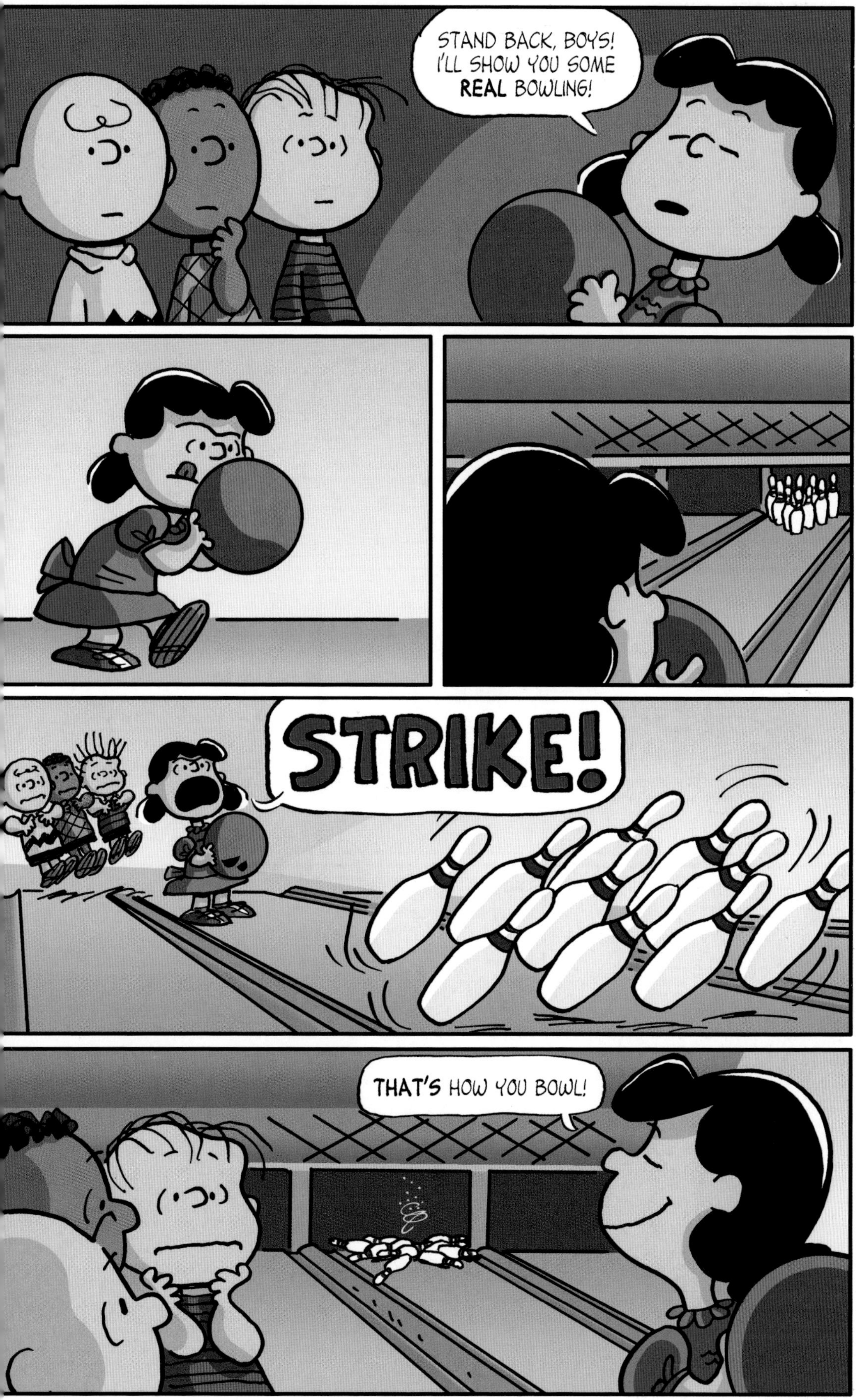
STAND BACK, BOYS! I'LL SHOW YOU SOME REAL BOWLING!
STRIKE!
THAT'S HOW YOU BOWL!

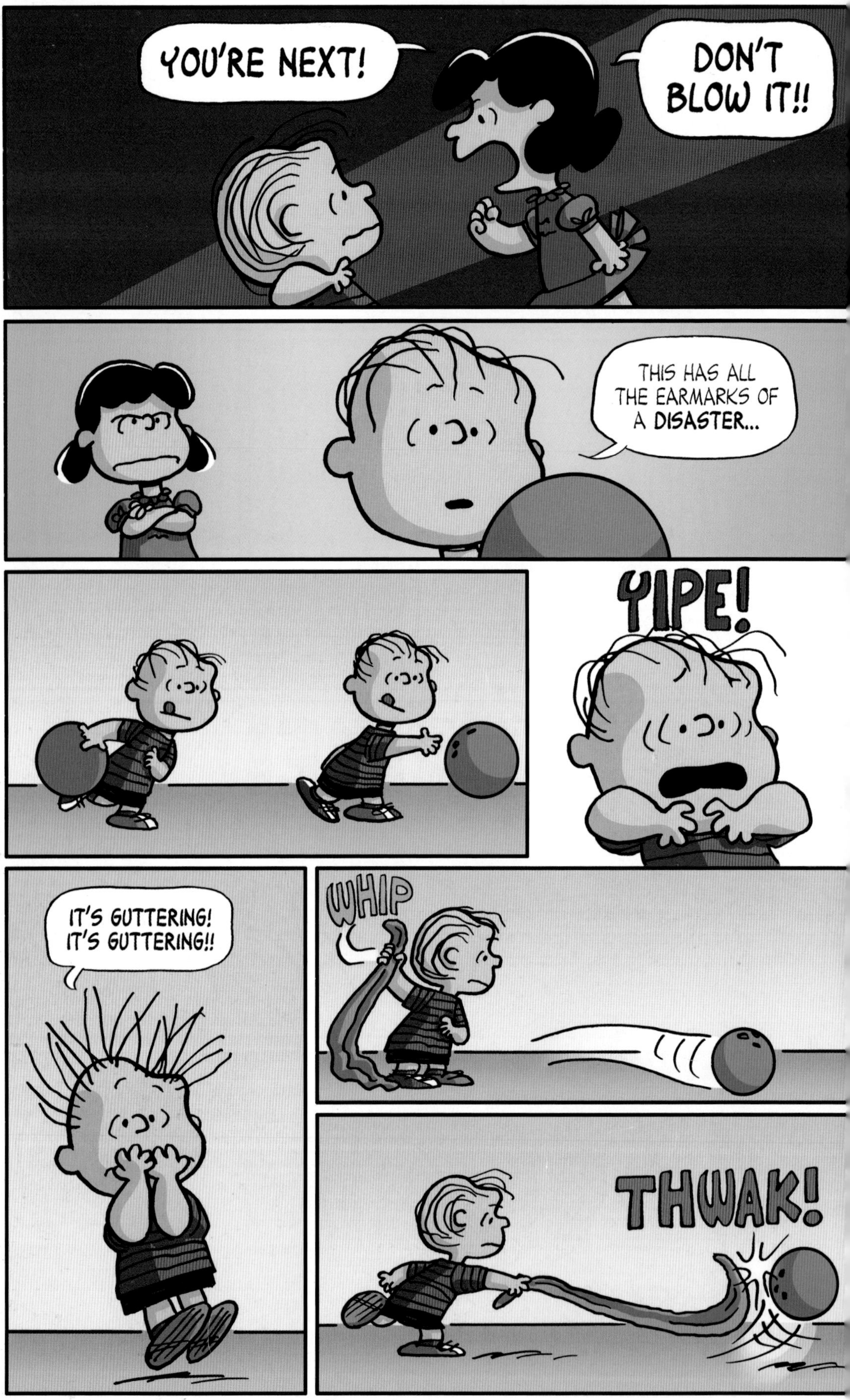
YOU'RE NEXT!
DON'T BLOW IT!!
THIS HAS ALL THE EARMARKS OF A **DISASTER...**
YIPE!
IT'S GUTTERING! IT'S GUTTERING!!
WHIP
THWAK!

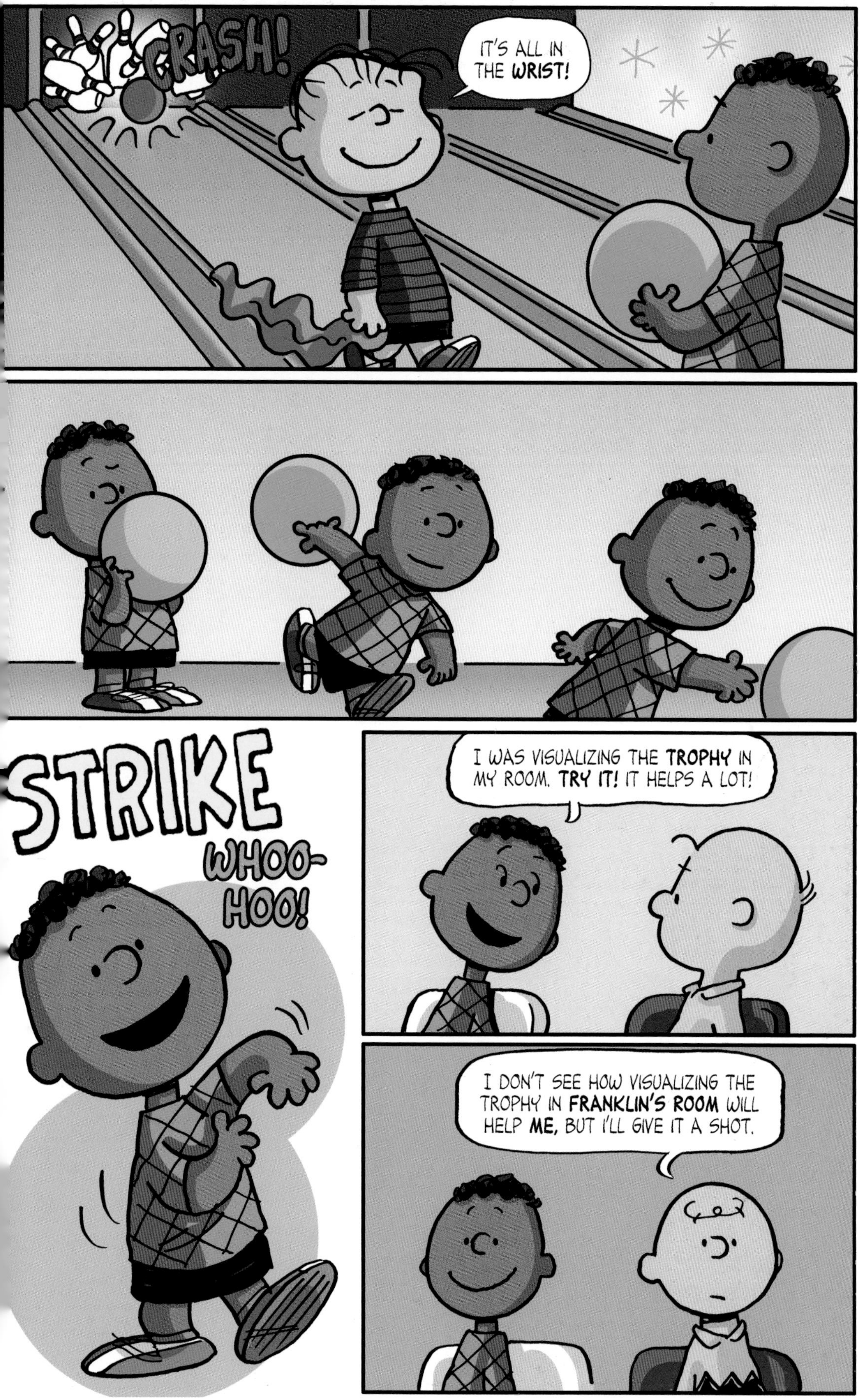
CRASH!
IT'S ALL IN THE WRIST!
STRIKE
WHOO-HOO!
I WAS VISUALIZING THE TROPHY IN MY ROOM. TRY IT! IT HELPS A LOT!
I DON'T SEE HOW VISUALIZING THE TROPHY IN FRANKLIN'S ROOM WILL HELP ME, BUT I'LL GIVE IT A SHOT.

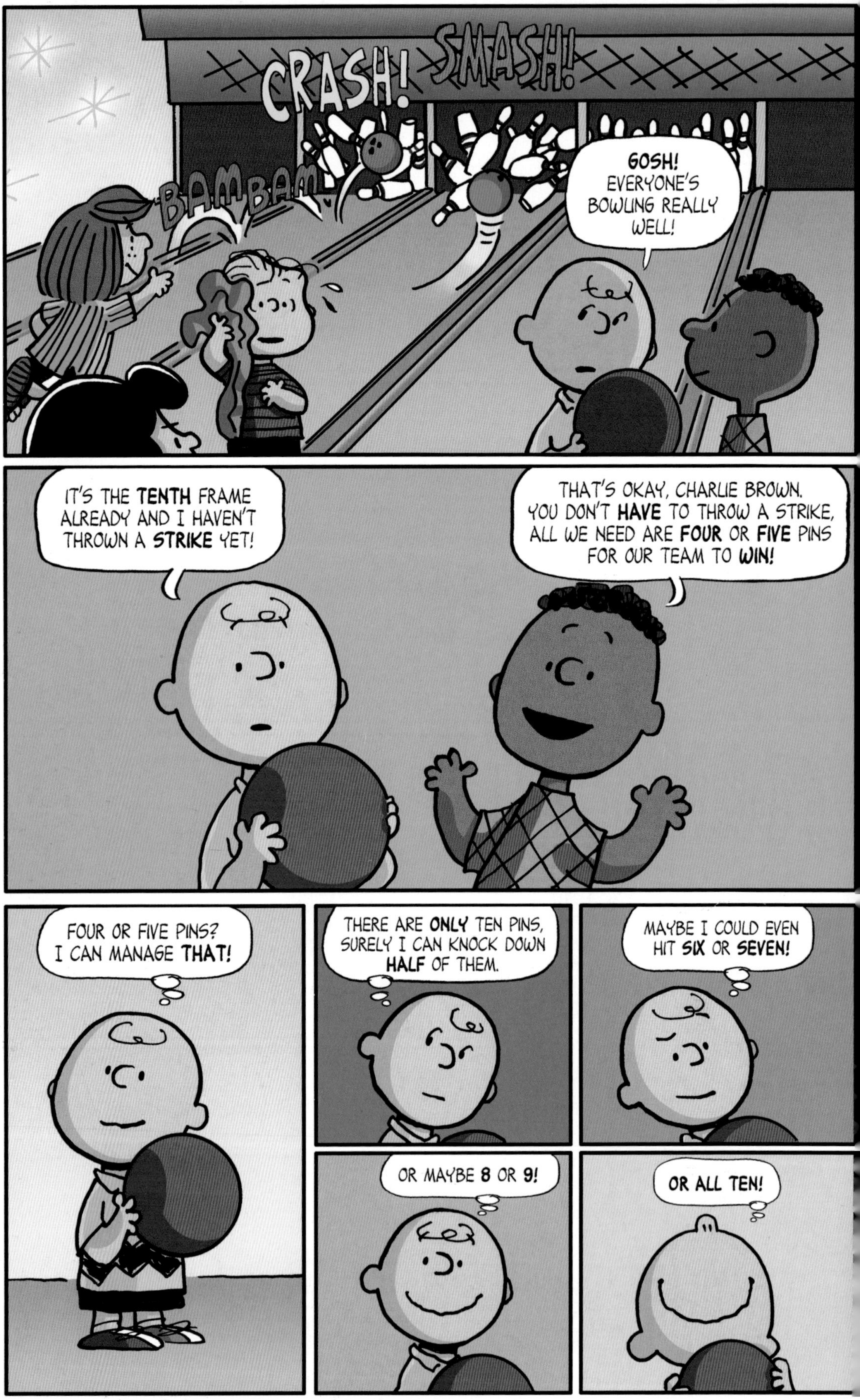
CRASH!
SMASH!
BAMBAM!
GOSH! EVERYONE'S BOWLING REALLY WELL!
IT'S THE TENTH FRAME ALREADY AND I HAVEN'T THROWN A STRIKE YET!
THAT'S OKAY, CHARLIE BROWN. YOU DON'T HAVE TO THROW A STRIKE, ALL WE NEED ARE FOUR OR FIVE PINS FOR OUR TEAM TO WIN!
FOUR OR FIVE PINS? I CAN MANAGE THAT!
THERE ARE ONLY TEN PINS, SURELY I CAN KNOCK DOWN HALF OF THEM.
MAYBE I COULD EVEN HIT SIX OR SEVEN!
OR MAYBE 8 OR 9!
OR ALL TEN!

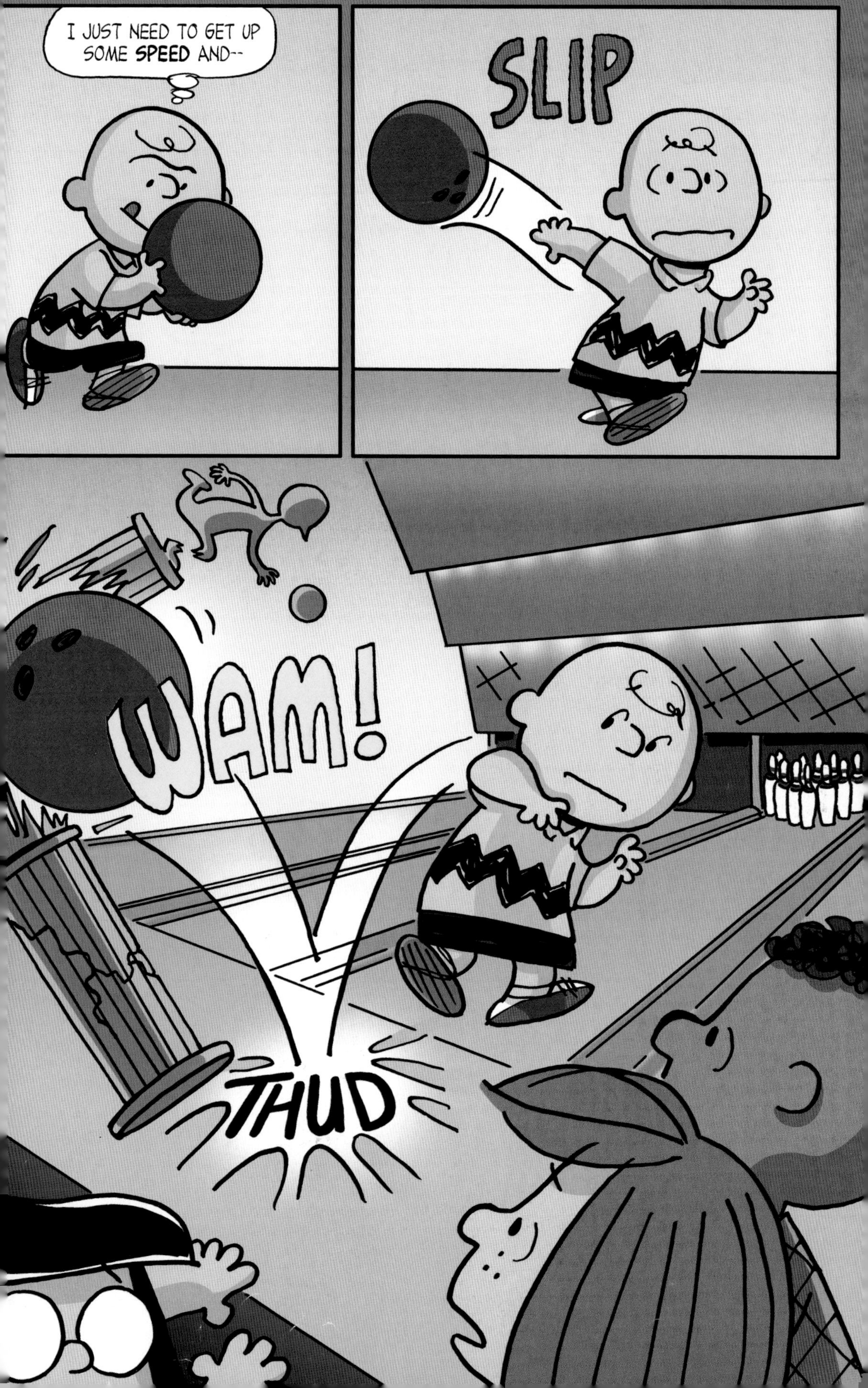
I JUST NEED TO GET UP SOME **SPEED** AND--
SLIP
WAM!
THUD

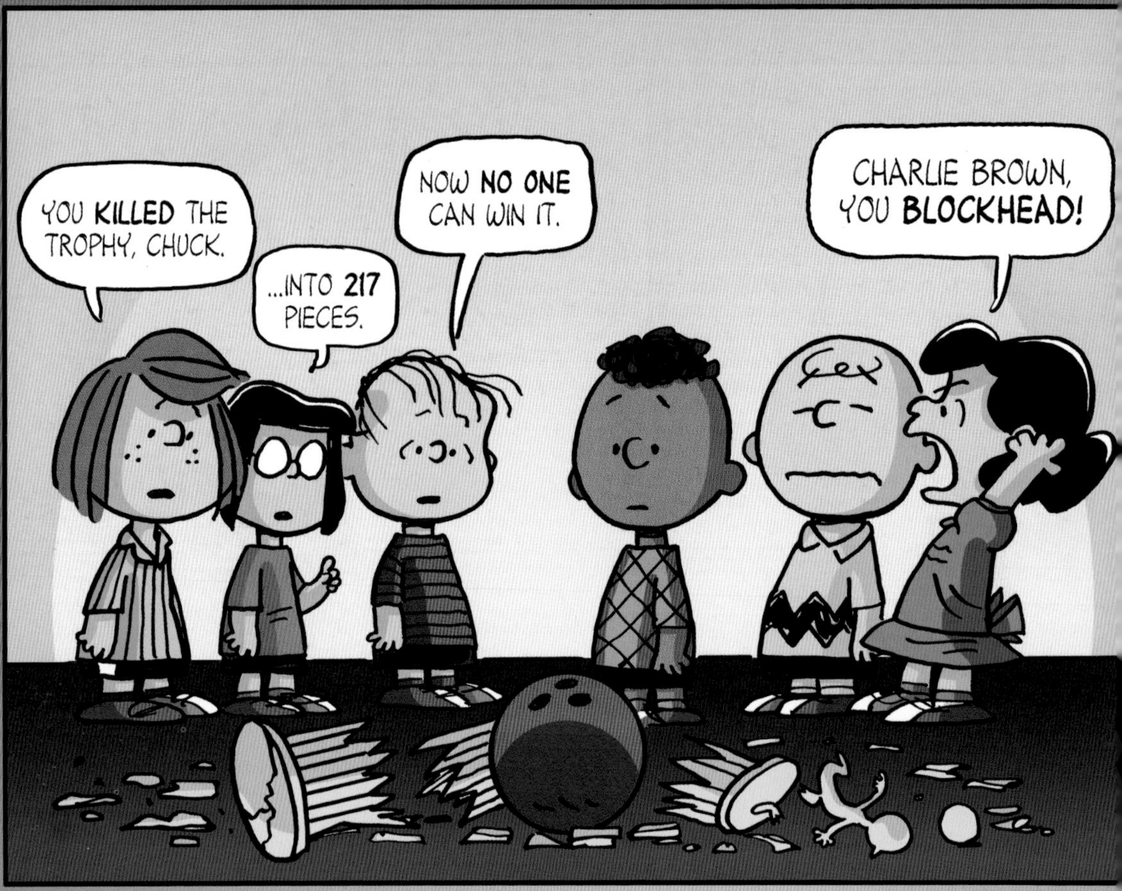
YOU **KILLED** THE TROPHY, CHUCK.
...INTO **217** PIECES.
NOW **NO ONE** CAN WIN IT.
CHARLIE BROWN, YOU **BLOCKHEAD!**

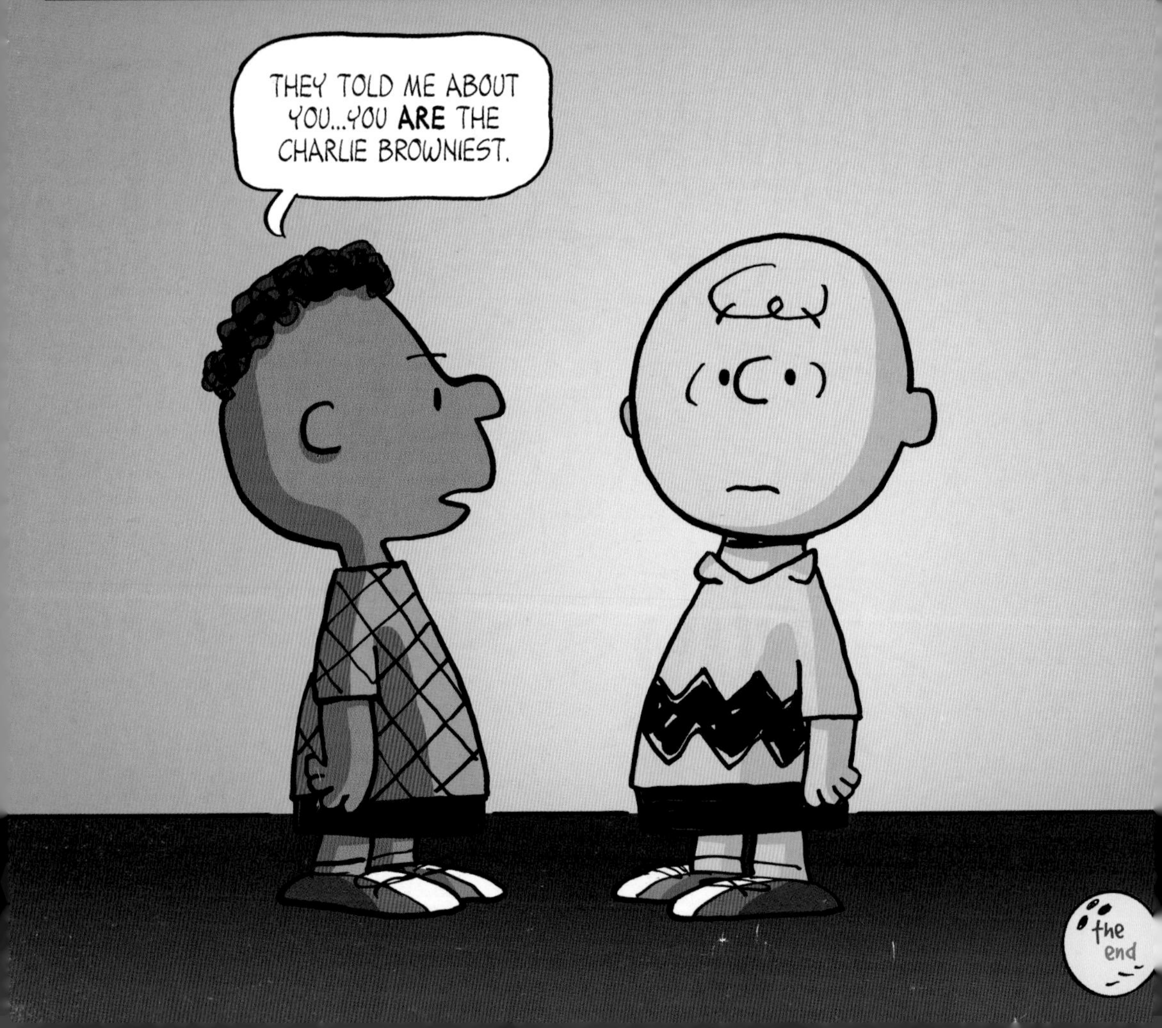
THEY TOLD ME ABOUT YOU...YOU **ARE** THE CHARLIE BROWNIEST.
the end

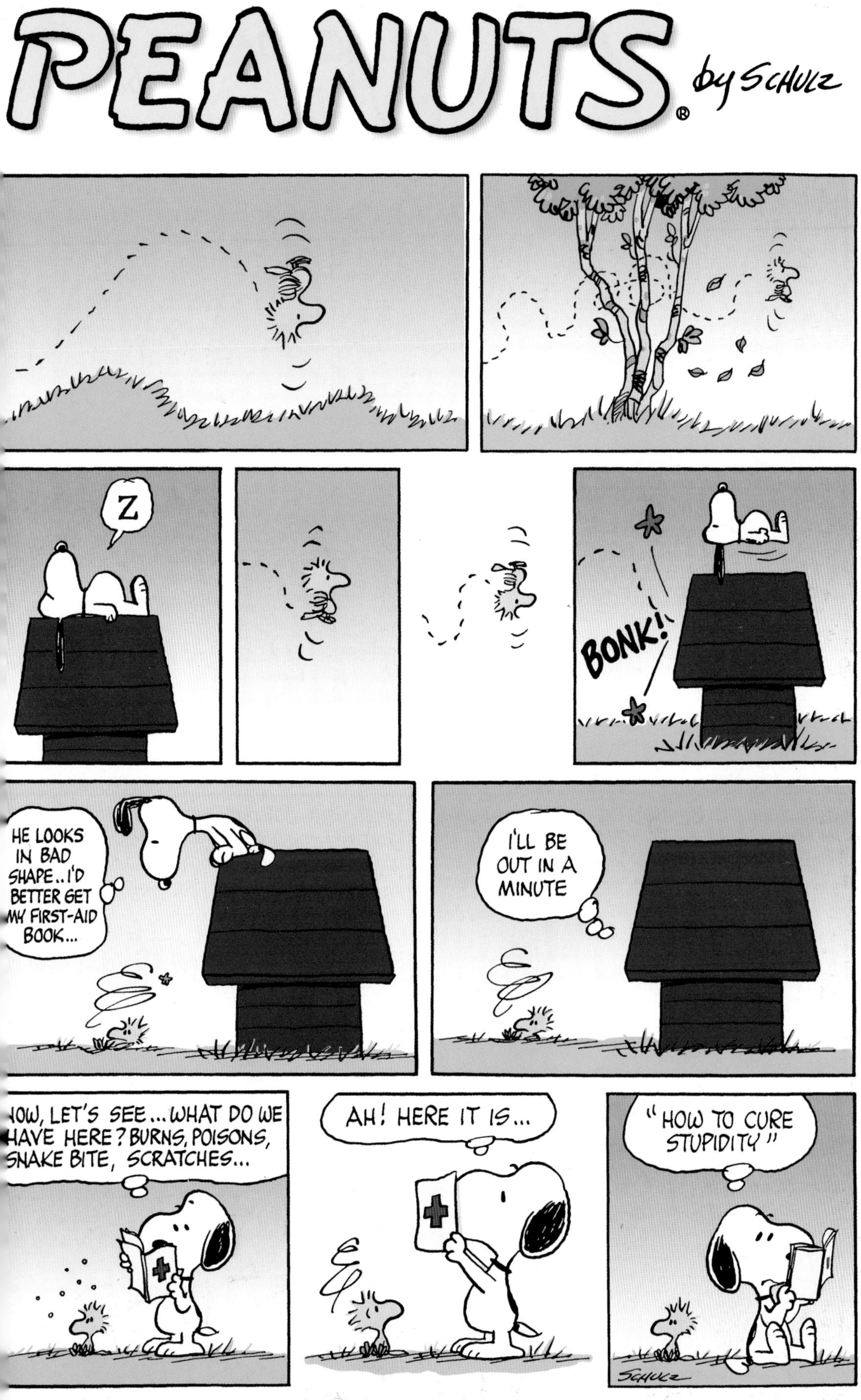
PEANUTS
by SCHULZ
Z
BONK!
HE LOOKS IN BAD SHAPE.. I'D BETTER GET MY FIRST-AID BOOK...
I'LL BE OUT IN A MINUTE
NOW, LET'S SEE... WHAT DO WE HAVE HERE? BURNS, POISONS, SNAKE BITE, SCRATCHES...
AH! HERE IT IS...
"HOW TO CURE STUPIDITY"
SCHULZ

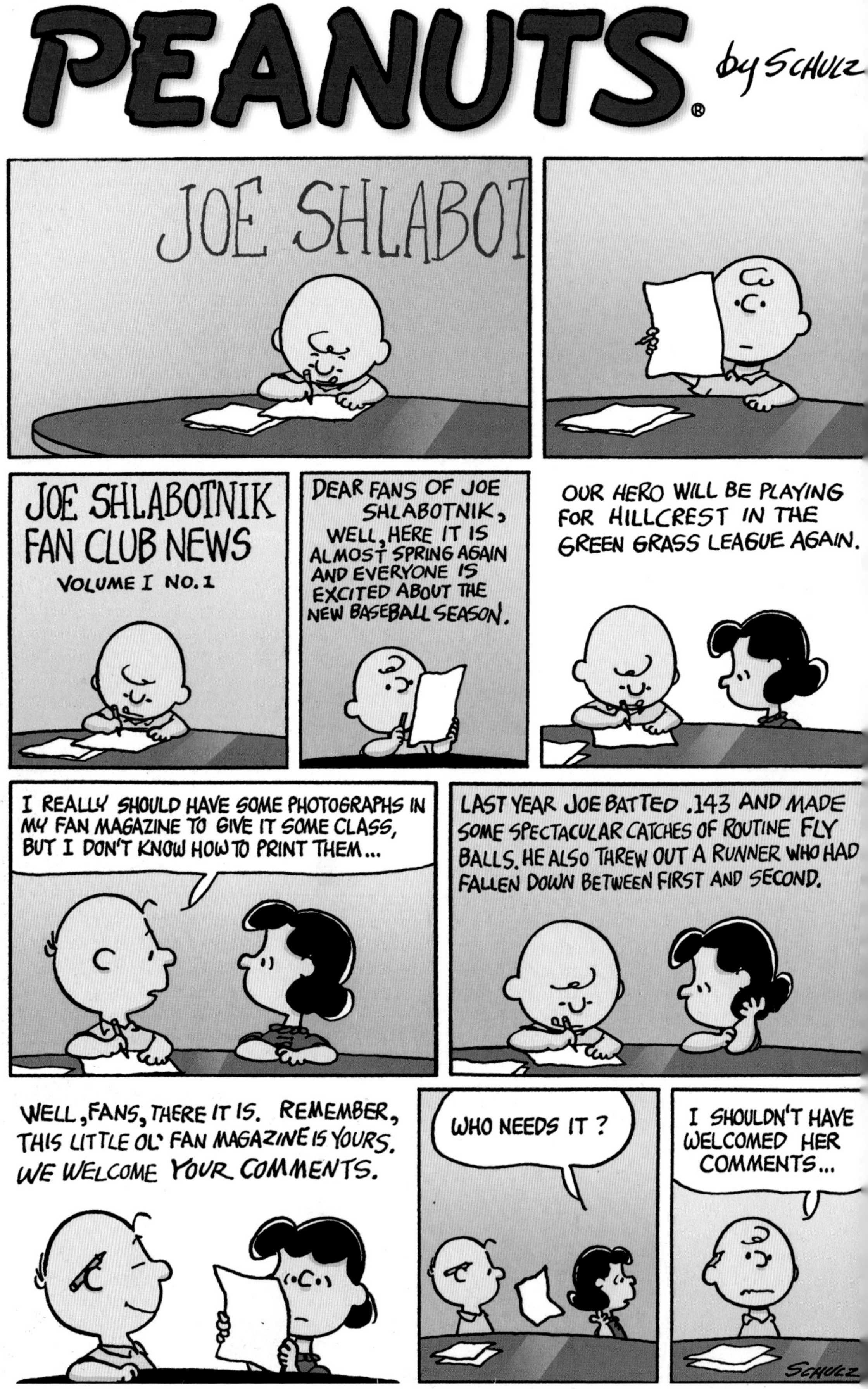
PEANUTS®
by SCHULZ
JOE SHLABOT
JOE SHLABOTNIK FAN CLUB NEWS
VOLUME I NO. 1
DEAR FANS OF JOE SHLABOTNIK, WELL, HERE IT IS ALMOST SPRING AGAIN AND EVERYONE IS EXCITED ABOUT THE NEW BASEBALL SEASON.
OUR HERO WILL BE PLAYING FOR HILLCREST IN THE GREEN GRASS LEAGUE AGAIN.
I REALLY SHOULD HAVE SOME PHOTOGRAPHS IN MY FAN MAGAZINE TO GIVE IT SOME CLASS, BUT I DON'T KNOW HOW TO PRINT THEM...
LAST YEAR JOE BATTED .143 AND MADE SOME SPECTACULAR CATCHES OF ROUTINE FLY BALLS. HE ALSO THREW OUT A RUNNER WHO HAD FALLEN DOWN BETWEEN FIRST AND SECOND.
WELL, FANS, THERE IT IS. REMEMBER, THIS LITTLE OL' FAN MAGAZINE IS YOURS. WE WELCOME YOUR COMMENTS.
WHO NEEDS IT ?
I SHOULDN'T HAVE WELCOMED HER COMMENTS...
SCHULZ

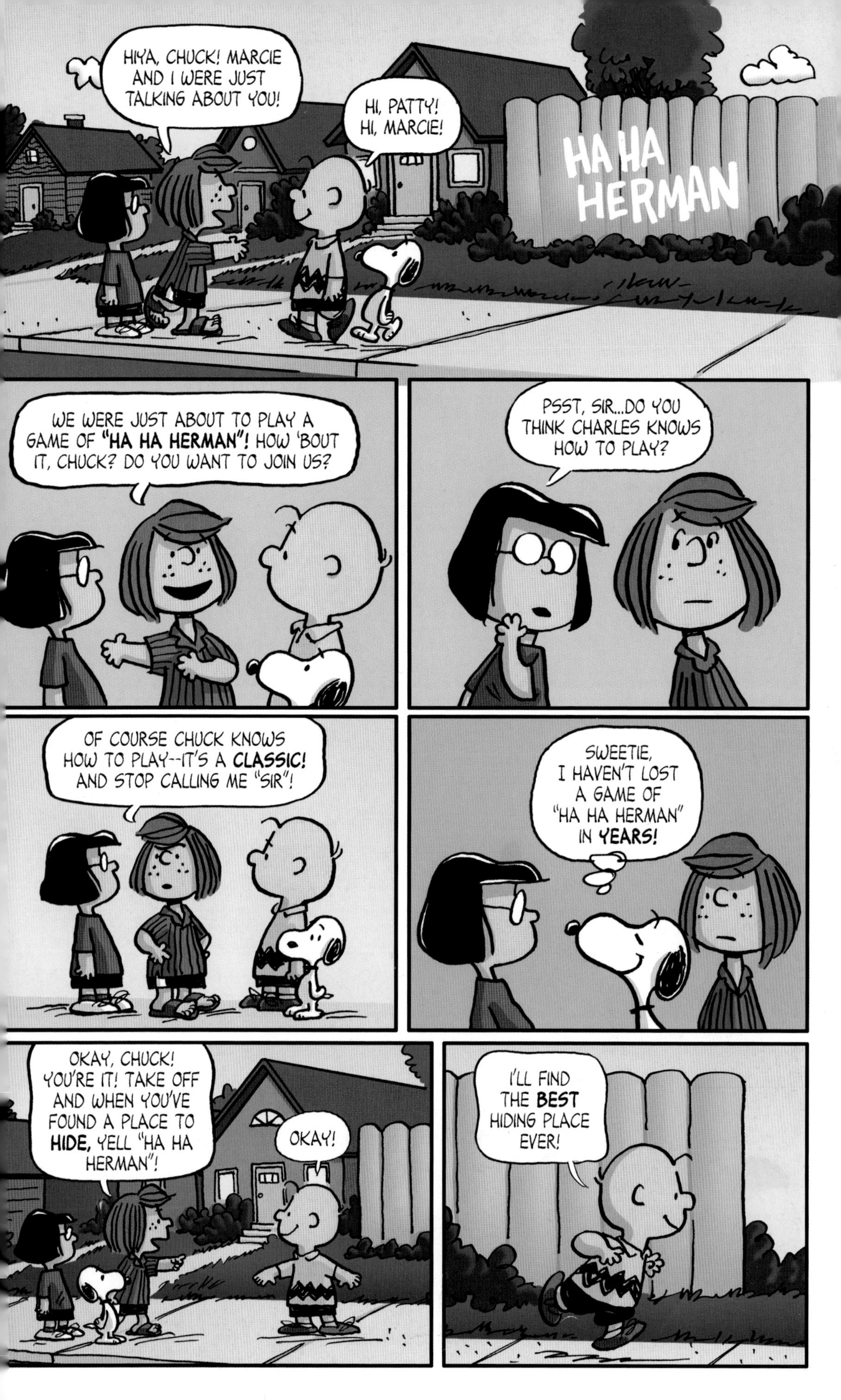
HIYA, CHUCK! MARCIE AND I WERE JUST TALKING ABOUT YOU!
HI, PATTY! HI, MARCIE!
HA HA HERMAN
WE WERE JUST ABOUT TO PLAY A GAME OF "HA HA HERMAN"! HOW 'BOUT IT, CHUCK? DO YOU WANT TO JOIN US?
PSST, SIR...DO YOU THINK CHARLES KNOWS HOW TO PLAY?
OF COURSE CHUCK KNOWS HOW TO PLAY--IT'S A CLASSIC! AND STOP CALLING ME "SIR"!
SWEETIE, I HAVEN'T LOST A GAME OF "HA HA HERMAN" IN YEARS!
OKAY, CHUCK! YOU'RE IT! TAKE OFF AND WHEN YOU'VE FOUND A PLACE TO HIDE, YELL "HA HA HERMAN"!
OKAY!
I'LL FIND THE BEST HIDING PLACE EVER!

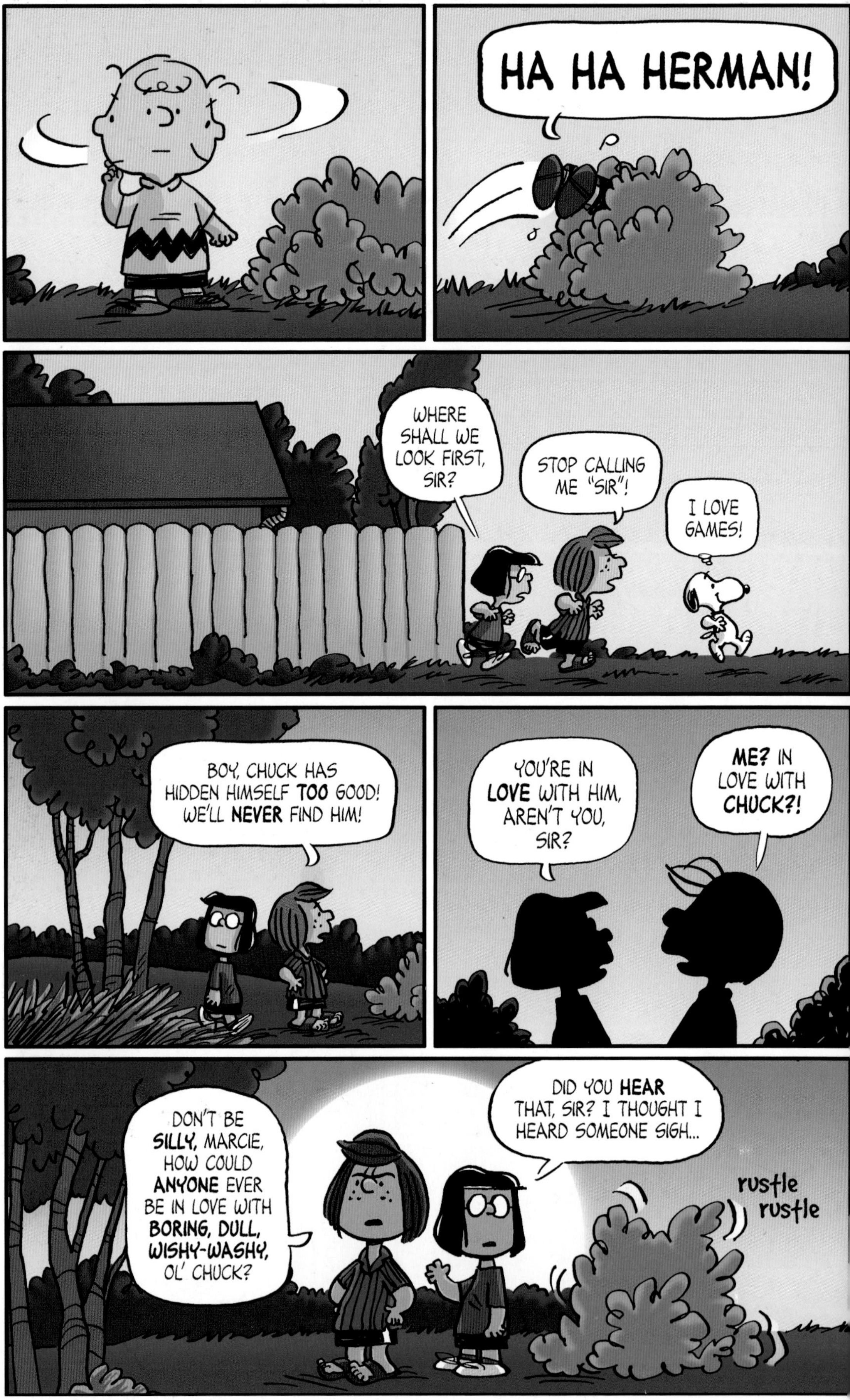
HA HA HERMAN!
WHERE SHALL WE LOOK FIRST, SIR?
STOP CALLING ME "SIR"!
I LOVE GAMES!
BOY, CHUCK HAS HIDDEN HIMSELF TOO GOOD! WE'LL NEVER FIND HIM!
YOU'RE IN LOVE WITH HIM, AREN'T YOU, SIR?
ME? IN LOVE WITH CHUCK?!
DID YOU HEAR THAT, SIR? I THOUGHT I HEARD SOMEONE SIGH...
DON'T BE SILLY, MARCIE, HOW COULD ANYONE EVER BE IN LOVE WITH BORING, DULL, WISHY-WASHY, OL' CHUCK?
rustle rustle

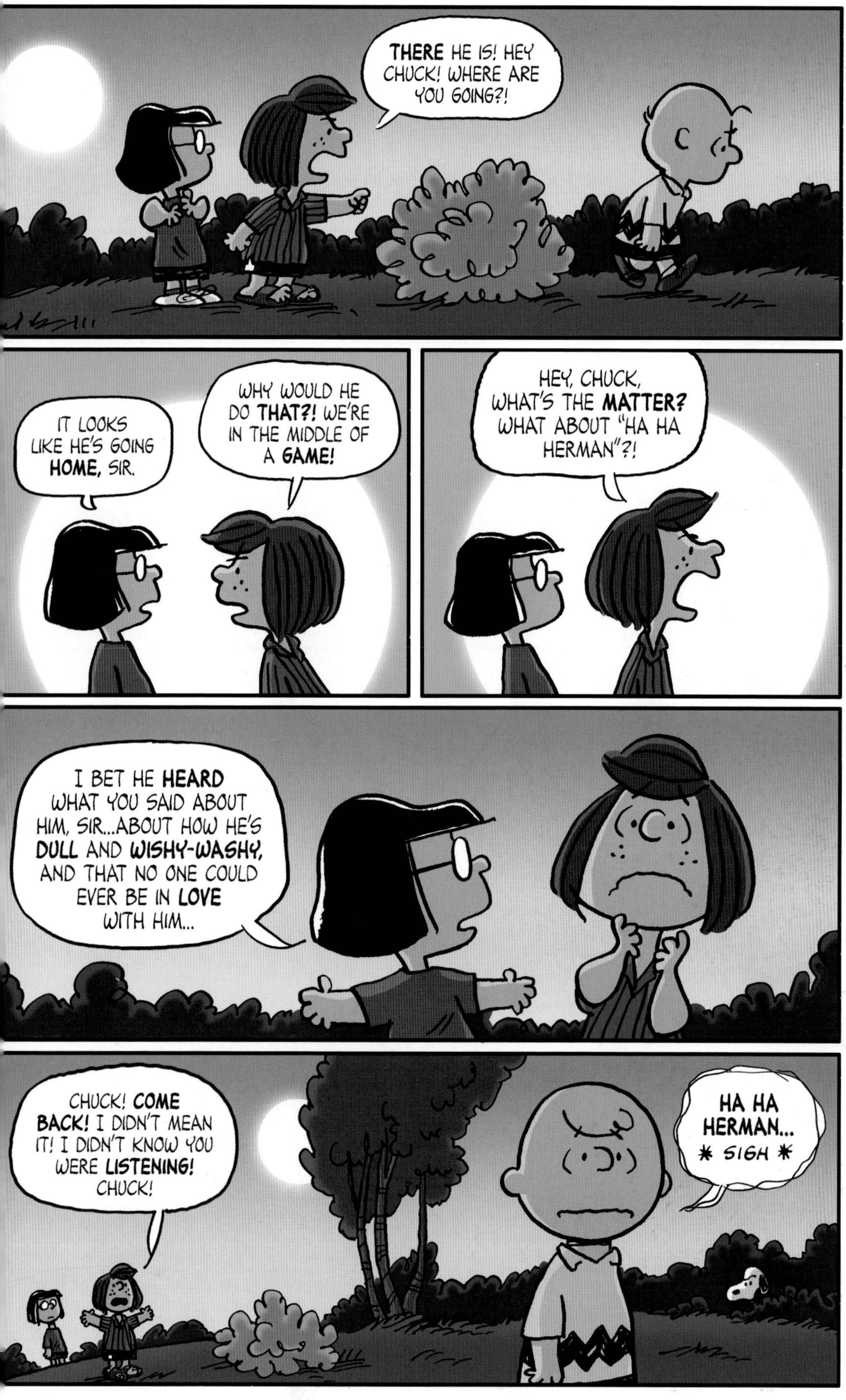
THERE HE IS! HEY CHUCK! WHERE ARE YOU GOING?!
IT LOOKS LIKE HE'S GOING HOME, SIR.
WHY WOULD HE DO THAT?! WE'RE IN THE MIDDLE OF A GAME!
HEY, CHUCK, WHAT'S THE MATTER? WHAT ABOUT "HA HA HERMAN"?!
I BET HE HEARD WHAT YOU SAID ABOUT HIM, SIR...ABOUT HOW HE'S DULL AND WISHY-WASHY, AND THAT NO ONE COULD EVER BE IN LOVE WITH HIM...
CHUCK! COME BACK! I DIDN'T MEAN IT! I DIDN'T KNOW YOU WERE LISTENING! CHUCK!
HA HA HERMAN... * SIGH *

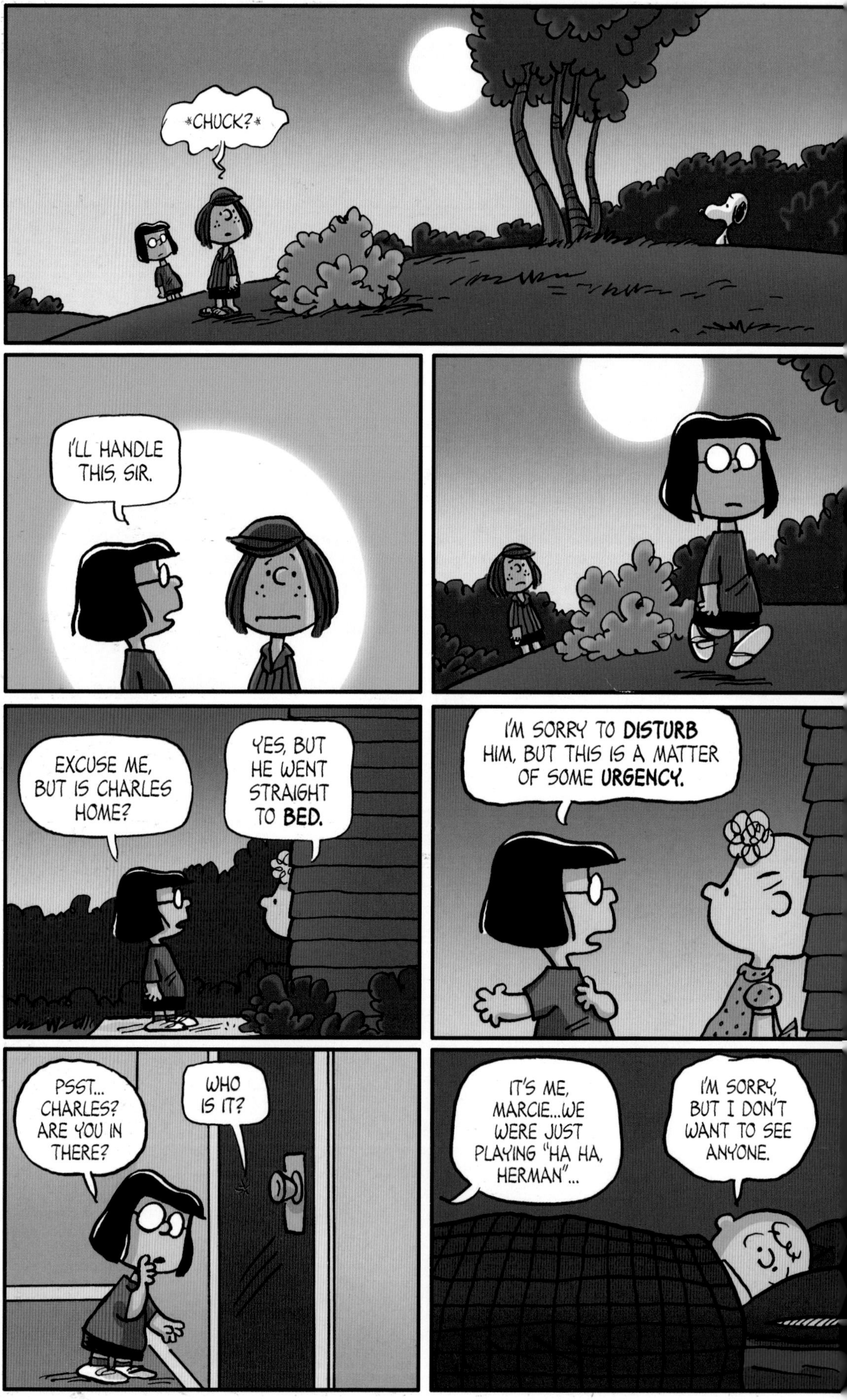
CHUCK?
I'LL HANDLE THIS, SIR.
EXCUSE ME, BUT IS CHARLES HOME?
YES, BUT HE WENT STRAIGHT TO **BED.**
I'M SORRY TO **DISTURB** HIM, BUT THIS IS A MATTER OF SOME **URGENCY.**
PSST... CHARLES? ARE YOU IN THERE?
WHO IS IT?
IT'S ME, MARCIE...WE WERE JUST PLAYING "HA HA, HERMAN"...
I'M SORRY, BUT I DON'T WANT TO SEE ANYONE.

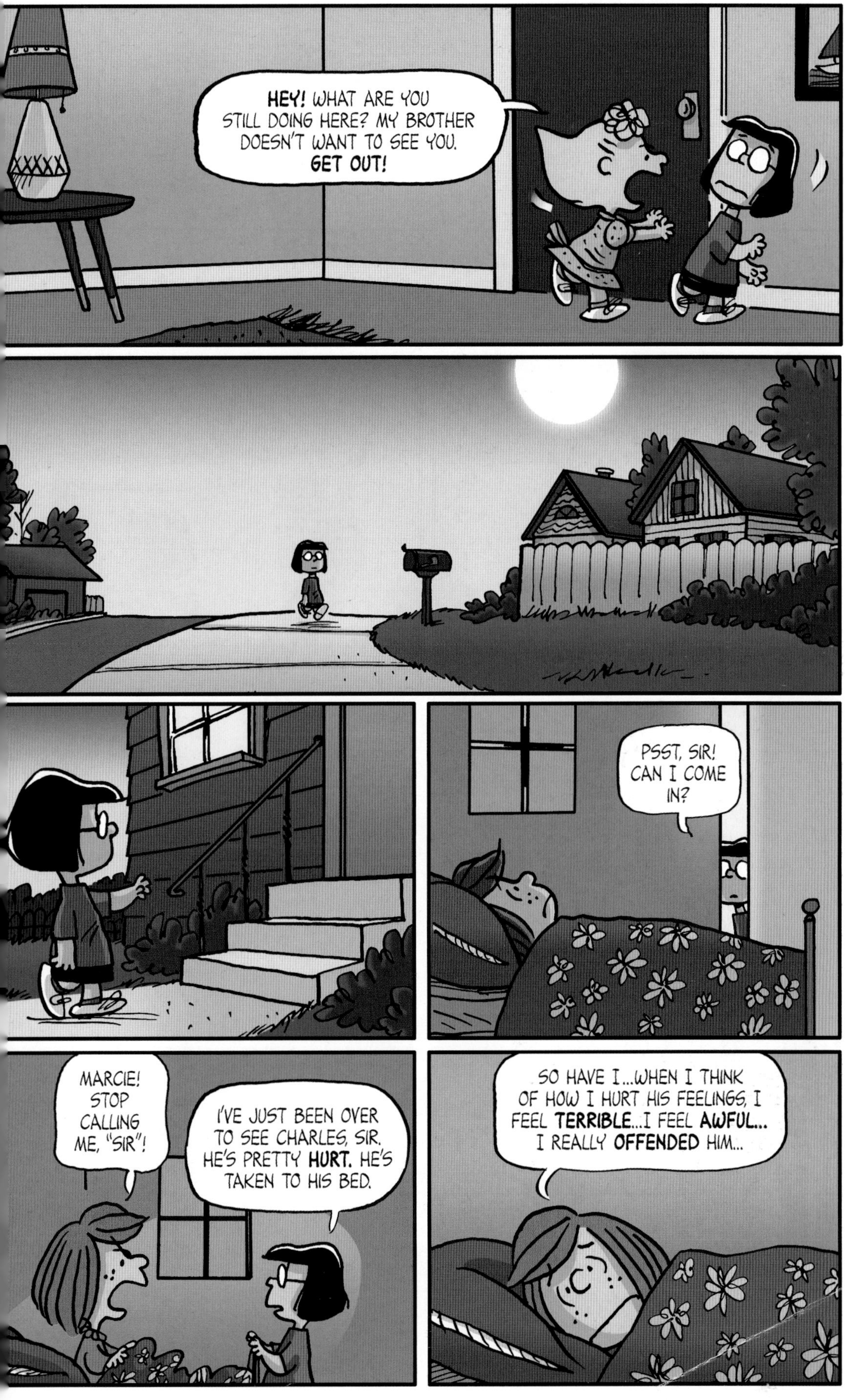
HEY! WHAT ARE YOU STILL DOING HERE? MY BROTHER DOESN'T WANT TO SEE YOU. GET OUT!
PSST, SIR! CAN I COME IN?
MARCIE! STOP CALLING ME, "SIR"!
I'VE JUST BEEN OVER TO SEE CHARLES, SIR. HE'S PRETTY HURT. HE'S TAKEN TO HIS BED.
SO HAVE I...WHEN I THINK OF HOW I HURT HIS FEELINGS, I FEEL TERRIBLE...I FEEL AWFUL... I REALLY OFFENDED HIM...

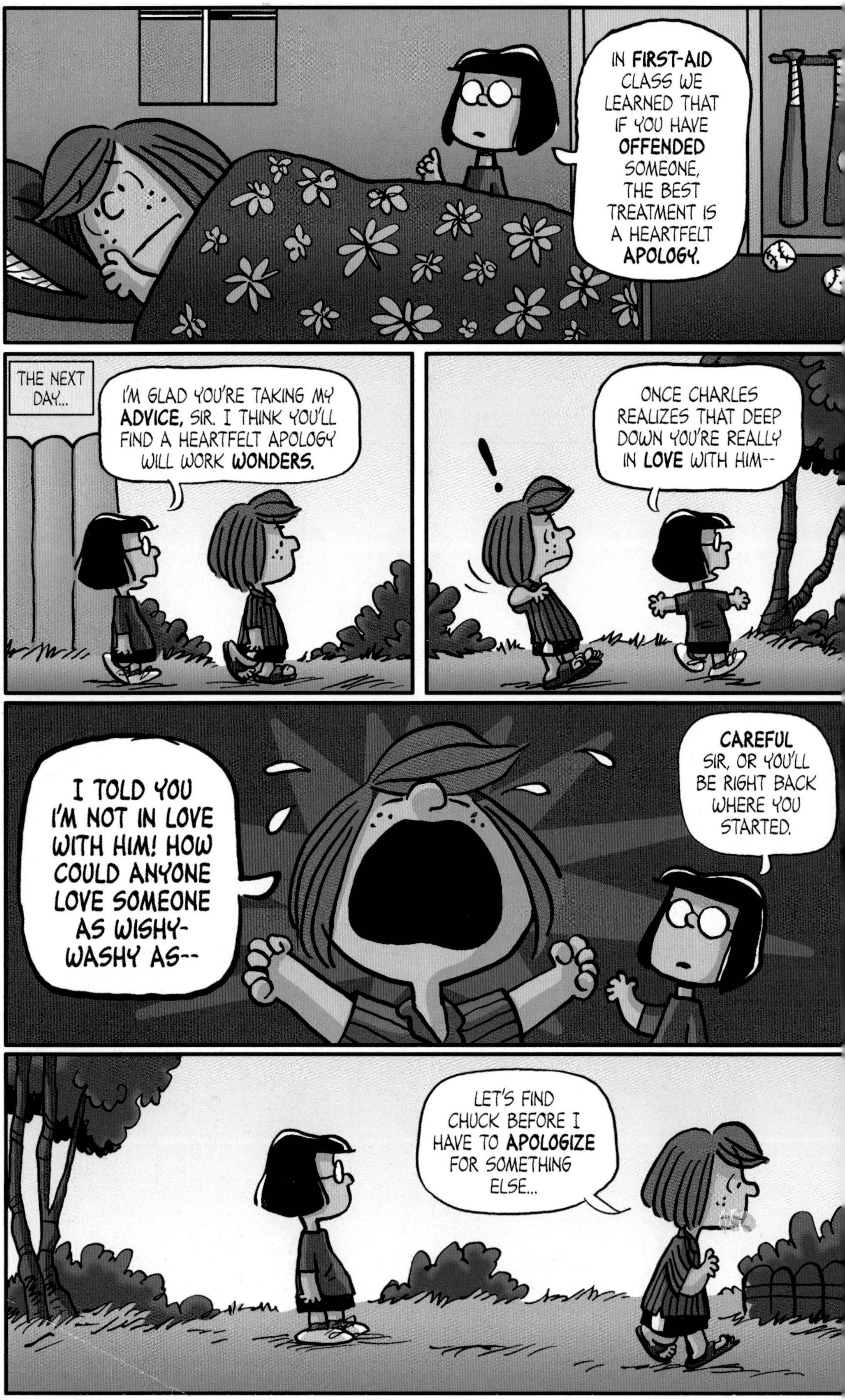
IN **FIRST-AID** CLASS WE LEARNED THAT IF YOU HAVE **OFFENDED** SOMEONE, THE BEST TREATMENT IS A HEARTFELT **APOLOGY.**
THE NEXT DAY...
I'M GLAD YOU'RE TAKING MY **ADVICE,** SIR. I THINK YOU'LL FIND A HEARTFELT APOLOGY WILL WORK **WONDERS.**
!
ONCE CHARLES REALIZES THAT DEEP DOWN YOU'RE REALLY IN **LOVE** WITH HIM--
I TOLD YOU I'M NOT IN LOVE WITH HIM! HOW COULD ANYONE LOVE SOMEONE AS WISHY-WASHY AS--
CAREFUL SIR, OR YOU'LL BE RIGHT BACK WHERE YOU STARTED.
LET'S FIND CHUCK BEFORE I HAVE TO **APOLOGIZE** FOR SOMETHING ELSE...

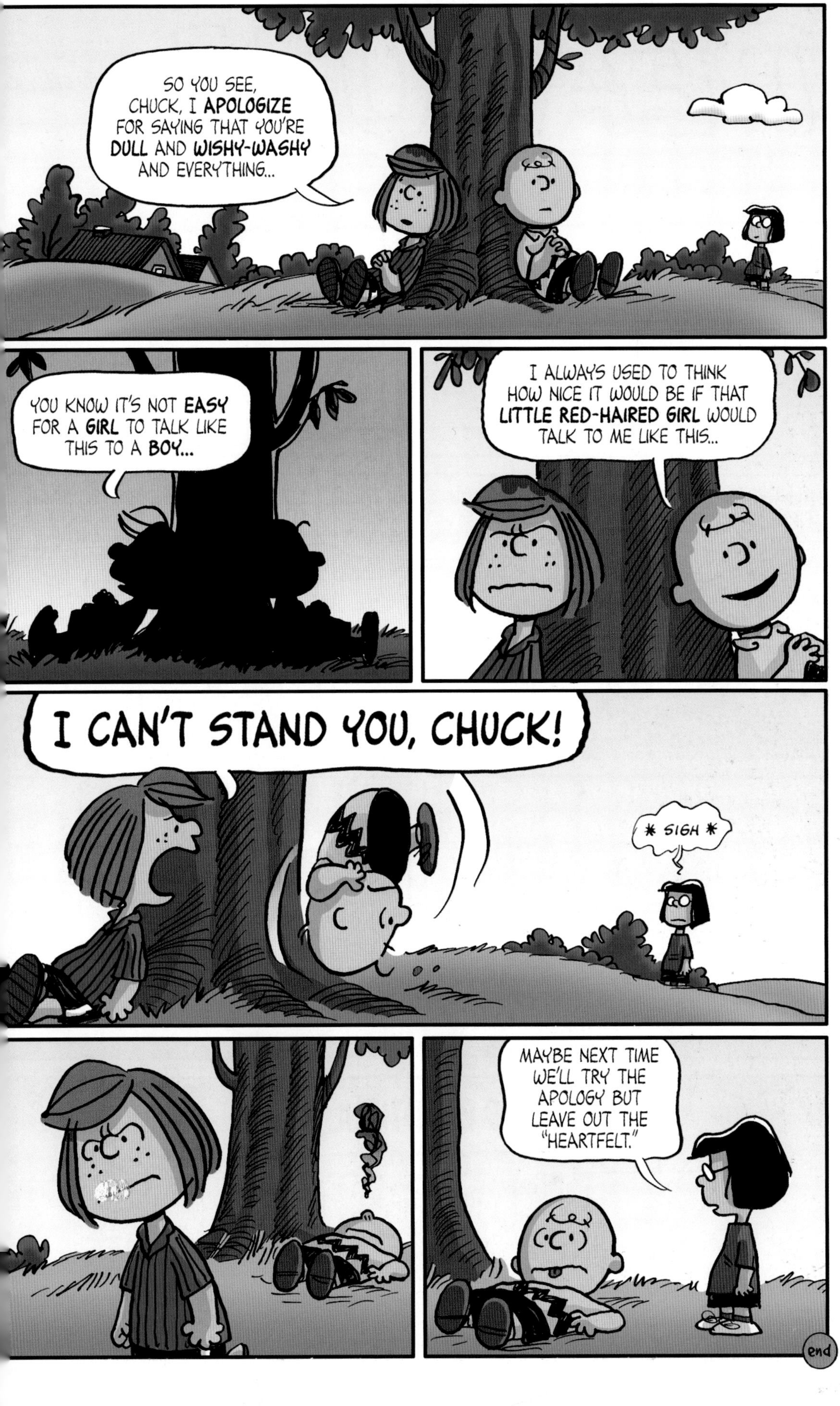
SO YOU SEE, CHUCK, I APOLOGIZE FOR SAYING THAT YOU'RE DULL AND WISHY-WASHY AND EVERYTHING...
YOU KNOW IT'S NOT EASY FOR A GIRL TO TALK LIKE THIS TO A BOY...
I ALWAYS USED TO THINK HOW NICE IT WOULD BE IF THAT LITTLE RED-HAIRED GIRL WOULD TALK TO ME LIKE THIS...
I CAN'T STAND YOU, CHUCK!
* SIGH *
MAYBE NEXT TIME WE'LL TRY THE APOLOGY BUT LEAVE OUT THE "HEARTFELT."
end

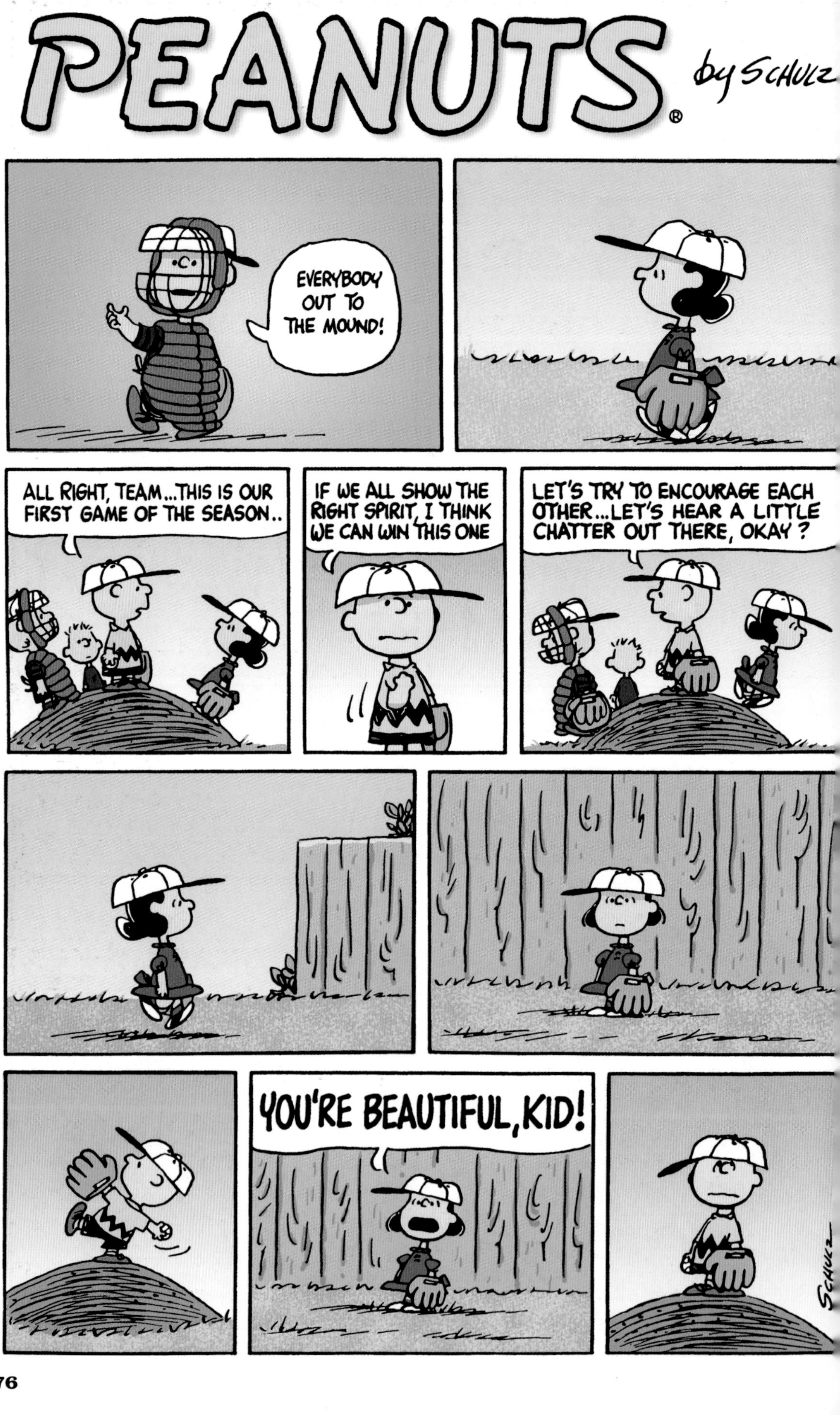
PEANUTS
by SCHULZ
EVERYBODY OUT TO THE MOUND!
ALL RIGHT, TEAM...THIS IS OUR FIRST GAME OF THE SEASON..
IF WE ALL SHOW THE RIGHT SPIRIT, I THINK WE CAN WIN THIS ONE
LET'S TRY TO ENCOURAGE EACH OTHER...LET'S HEAR A LITTLE CHATTER OUT THERE, OKAY?
YOU'RE BEAUTIFUL, KID!
SCHULZ

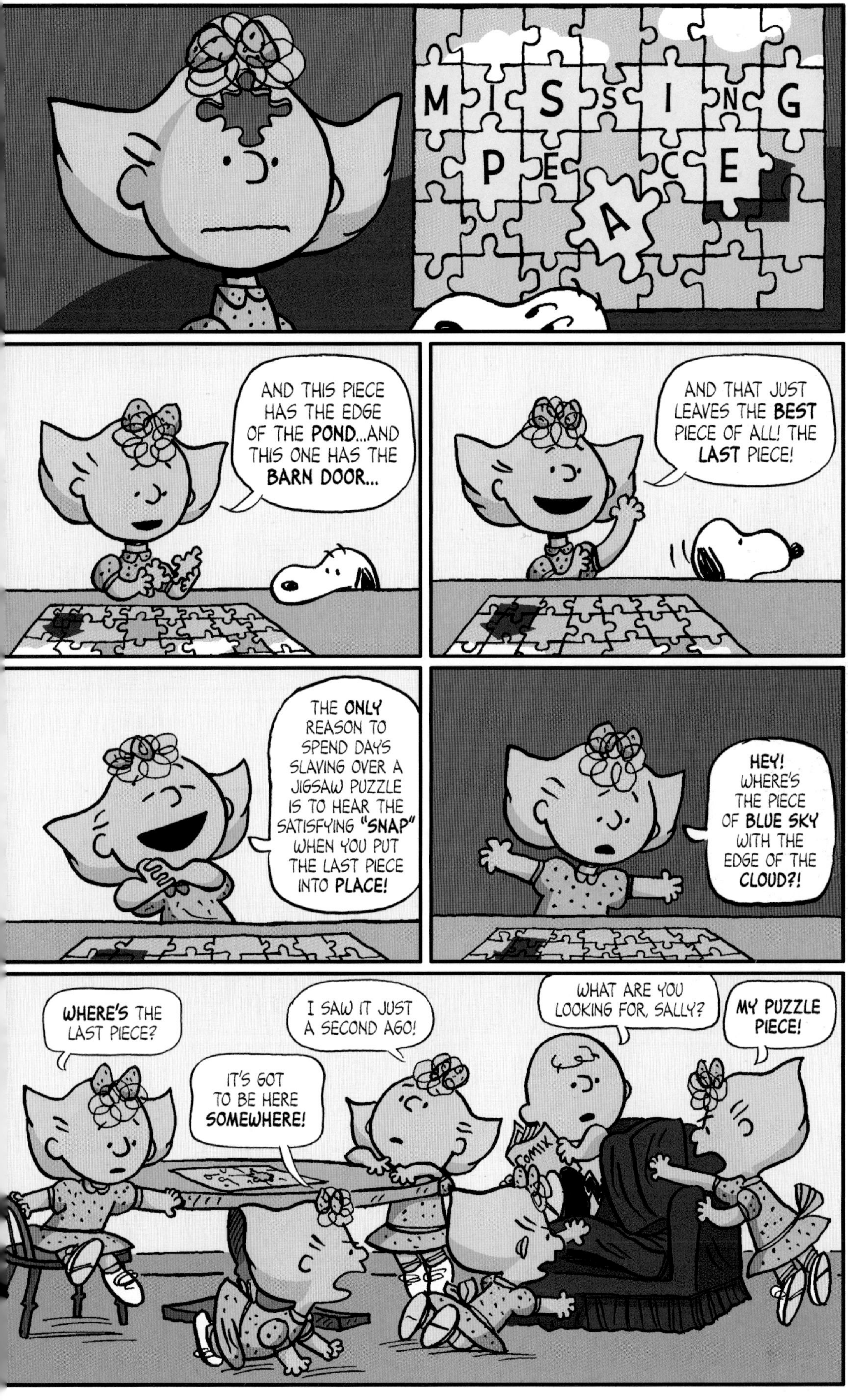

MISSING PIECE
AND THIS PIECE HAS THE EDGE OF THE POND...AND THIS ONE HAS THE BARN DOOR...
AND THAT JUST LEAVES THE BEST PIECE OF ALL! THE LAST PIECE!
THE ONLY REASON TO SPEND DAYS SLAVING OVER A JIGSAW PUZZLE IS TO HEAR THE SATISFYING "SNAP" WHEN YOU PUT THE LAST PIECE INTO PLACE!
HEY! WHERE'S THE PIECE OF BLUE SKY WITH THE EDGE OF THE CLOUD?!
WHERE'S THE LAST PIECE?
IT'S GOT TO BE HERE SOMEWHERE!
I SAW IT JUST A SECOND AGO!
WHAT ARE YOU LOOKING FOR, SALLY?
MY PUZZLE PIECE!
COMIX

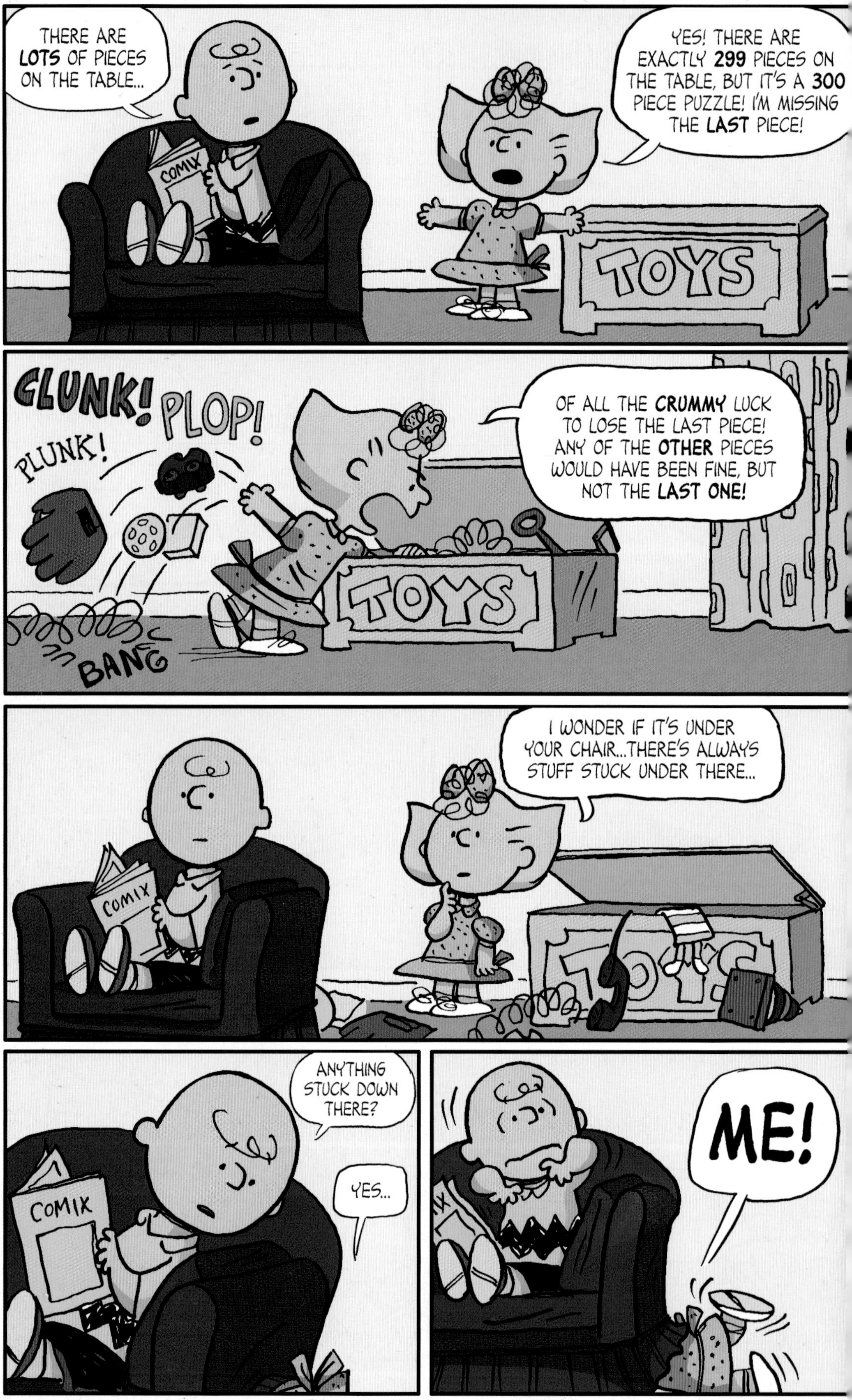
THERE ARE LOTS OF PIECES ON THE TABLE...
YES! THERE ARE EXACTLY 299 PIECES ON THE TABLE, BUT IT'S A 300 PIECE PUZZLE! I'M MISSING THE LAST PIECE!
TOYS
COMIX
CLUNK!
PLOP!
PLUNK!
BANG
OF ALL THE CRUMMY LUCK TO LOSE THE LAST PIECE! ANY OF THE OTHER PIECES WOULD HAVE BEEN FINE, BUT NOT THE LAST ONE!
TOYS
I WONDER IF IT'S UNDER YOUR CHAIR...THERE'S ALWAYS STUFF STUCK UNDER THERE...
COMIX
ANYTHING STUCK DOWN THERE?
YES...
COMIX
ME!

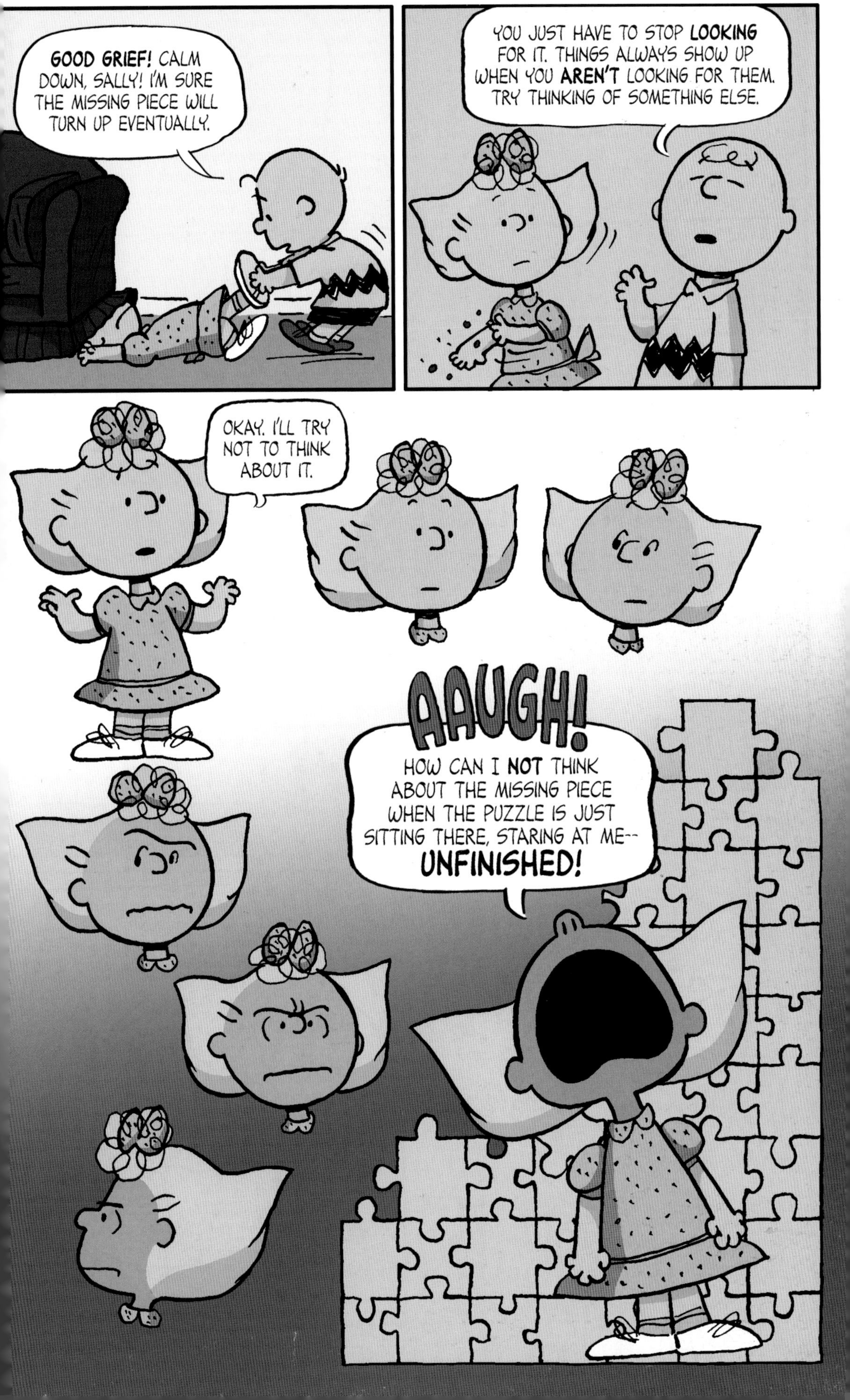

GOOD GRIEF! CALM DOWN, SALLY! I'M SURE THE MISSING PIECE WILL TURN UP EVENTUALLY.
YOU JUST HAVE TO STOP LOOKING FOR IT. THINGS ALWAYS SHOW UP WHEN YOU AREN'T LOOKING FOR THEM. TRY THINKING OF SOMETHING ELSE.
OKAY. I'LL TRY NOT TO THINK ABOUT IT.
AAUGH!
HOW CAN I NOT THINK ABOUT THE MISSING PIECE WHEN THE PUZZLE IS JUST SITTING THERE, STARING AT ME-- UNFINISHED!

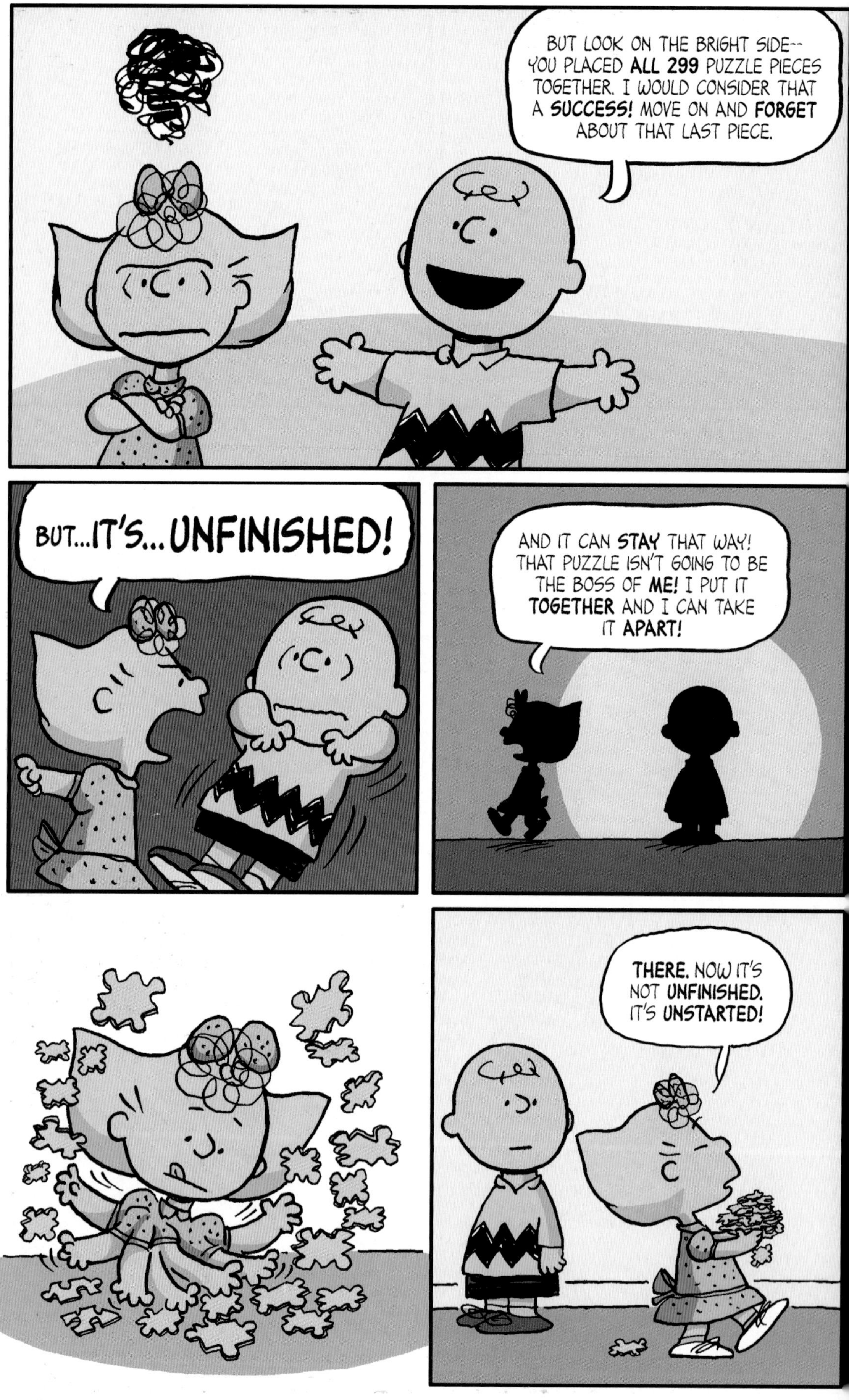
BUT LOOK ON THE BRIGHT SIDE-- YOU PLACED ALL 299 PUZZLE PIECES TOGETHER. I WOULD CONSIDER THAT A SUCCESS! MOVE ON AND FORGET ABOUT THAT LAST PIECE.
BUT...IT'S...UNFINISHED!
AND IT CAN STAY THAT WAY! THAT PUZZLE ISN'T GOING TO BE THE BOSS OF ME! I PUT IT TOGETHER AND I CAN TAKE IT APART!
THERE. NOW IT'S NOT UNFINISHED. IT'S UNSTARTED!

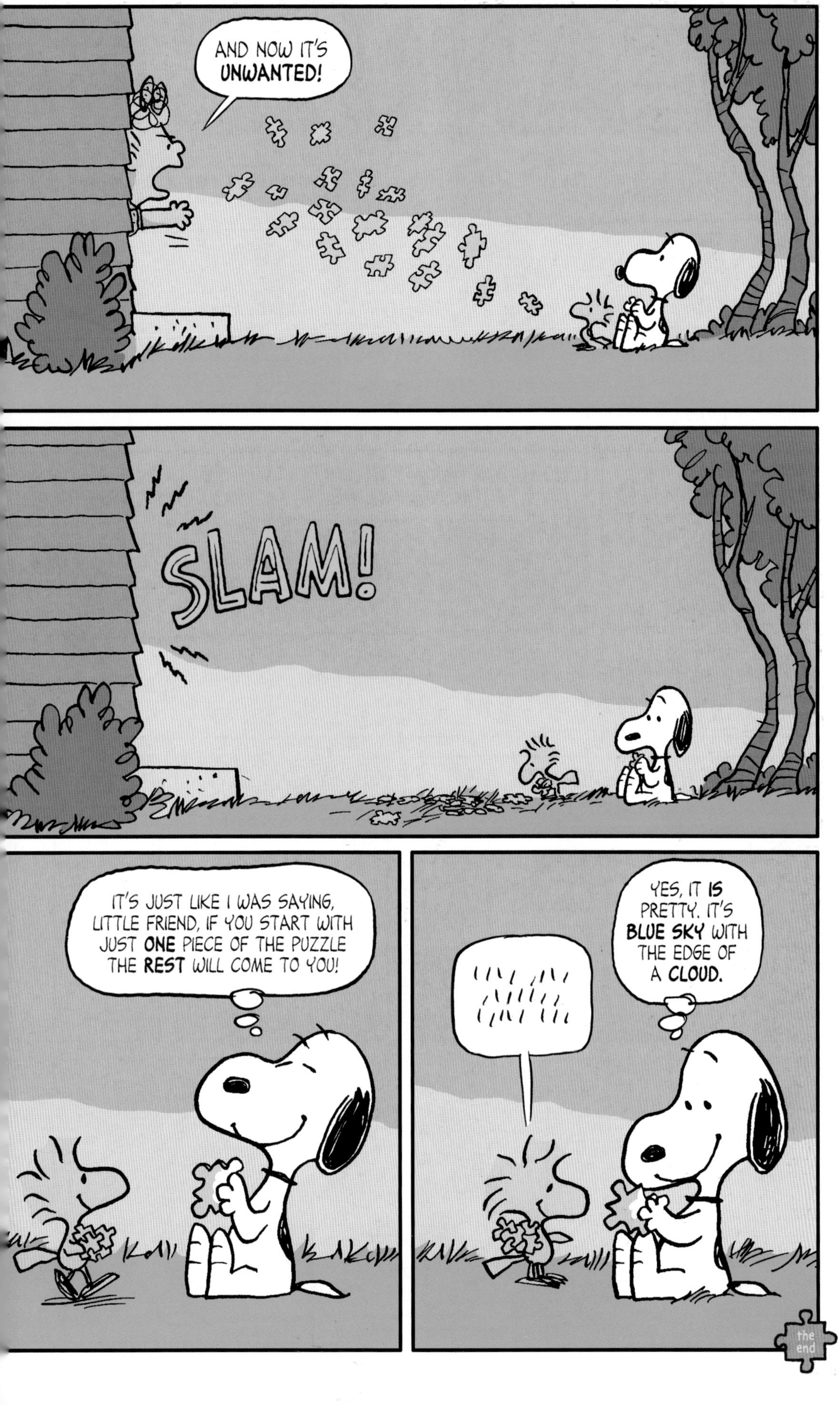
AND NOW IT'S UNWANTED!
SLAM!
IT'S JUST LIKE I WAS SAYING, LITTLE FRIEND, IF YOU START WITH JUST ONE PIECE OF THE PUZZLE THE REST WILL COME TO YOU!
YES, IT IS PRETTY. IT'S BLUE SKY WITH THE EDGE OF A CLOUD.
the end

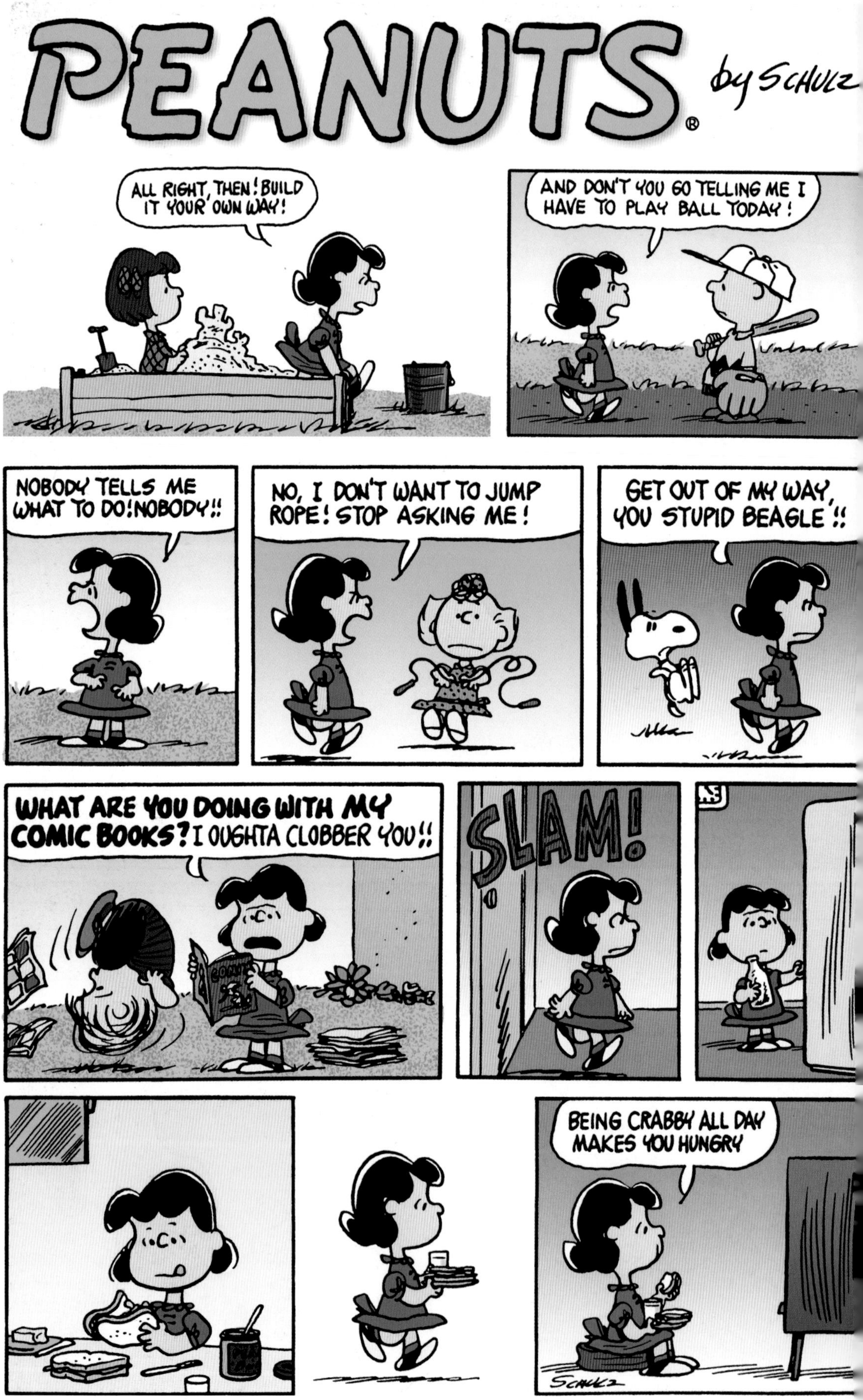
PEANUTS
by SCHULZ
ALL RIGHT, THEN! BUILD IT YOUR OWN WAY!
AND DON'T YOU GO TELLING ME I HAVE TO PLAY BALL TODAY!
NOBODY TELLS ME WHAT TO DO! NOBODY!!
NO, I DON'T WANT TO JUMP ROPE! STOP ASKING ME!
GET OUT OF MY WAY, YOU STUPID BEAGLE!!
WHAT ARE YOU DOING WITH MY COMIC BOOKS? I OUGHTA CLOBBER YOU!!
SLAM!
BEING CRABBY ALL DAY MAKES YOU HUNGRY
SCHULZ

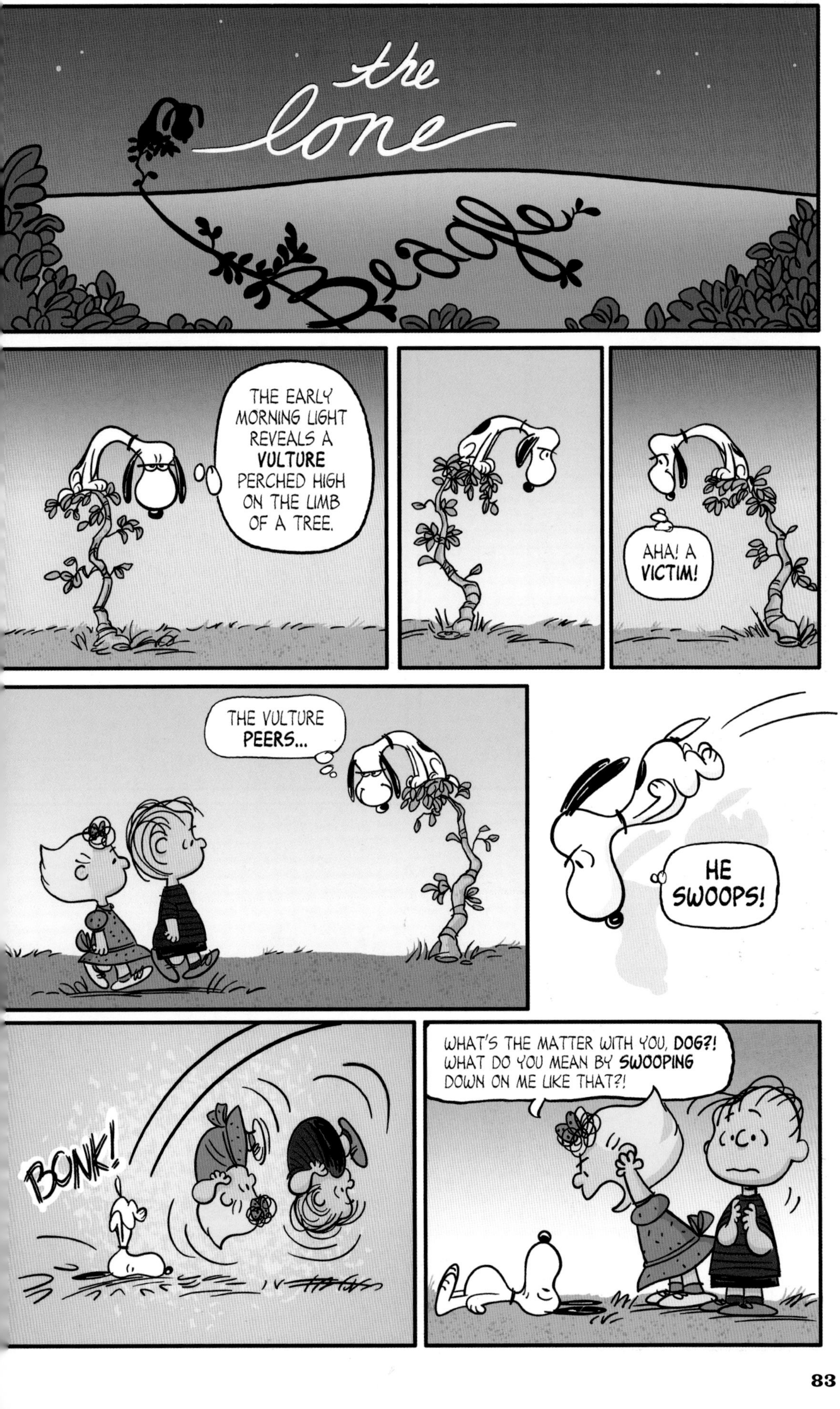
the lone beagle
THE EARLY MORNING LIGHT REVEALS A **VULTURE** PERCHED HIGH ON THE LIMB OF A TREE.
AHA! A **VICTIM!**
THE VULTURE **PEERS...**
HE SWOOPS!
BONK!
WHAT'S THE MATTER WITH YOU, **DOG?!** WHAT DO YOU MEAN BY **SWOOPING** DOWN ON ME LIKE THAT?!

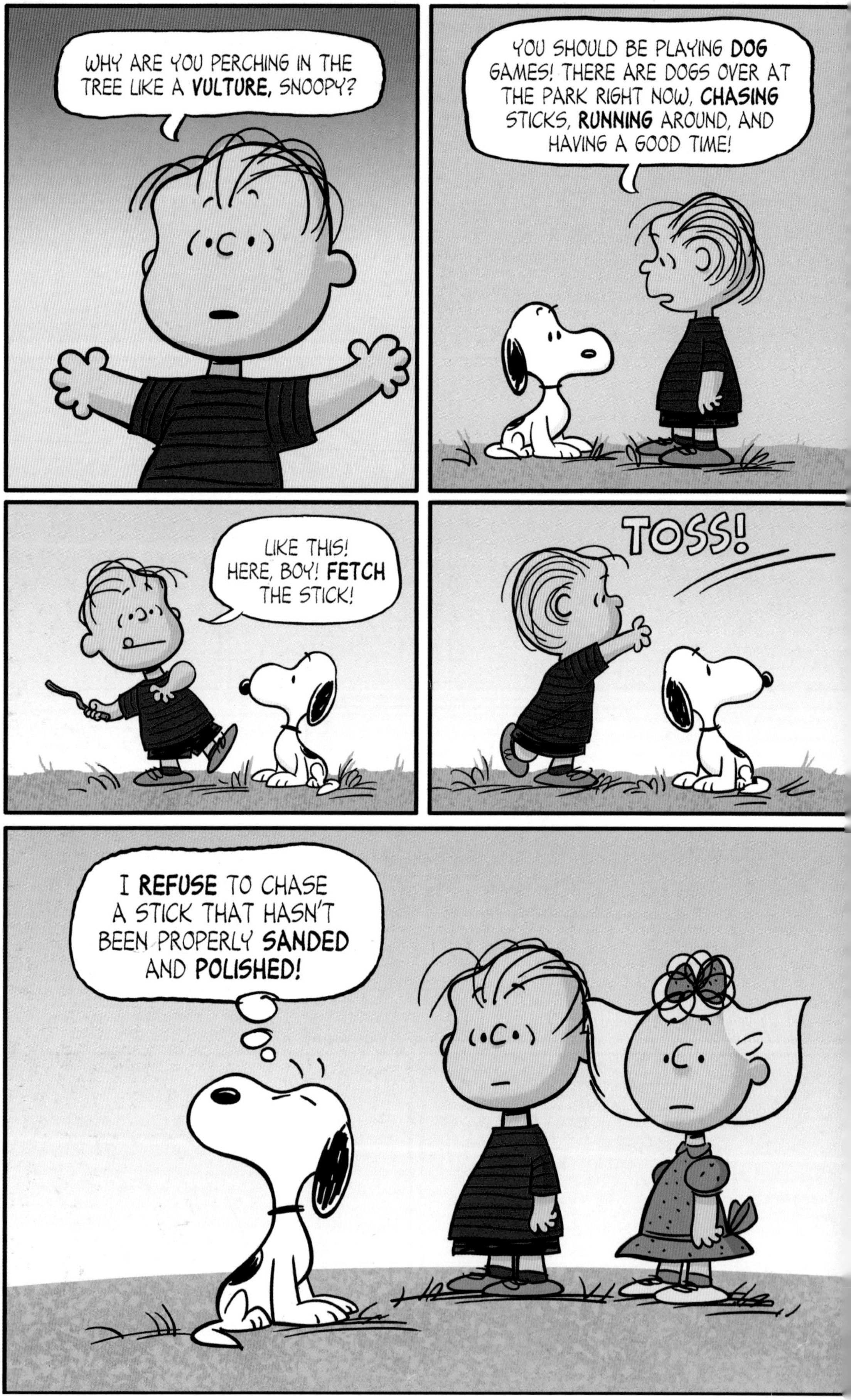
WHY ARE YOU PERCHING IN THE TREE LIKE A **VULTURE,** SNOOPY?
YOU SHOULD BE PLAYING **DOG** GAMES! THERE ARE DOGS OVER AT THE PARK RIGHT NOW, **CHASING** STICKS, **RUNNING** AROUND, AND HAVING A GOOD TIME!
LIKE THIS! HERE, BOY! **FETCH** THE STICK!
TOSS!
I **REFUSE** TO CHASE A STICK THAT HASN'T BEEN PROPERLY **SANDED** AND **POLISHED!**

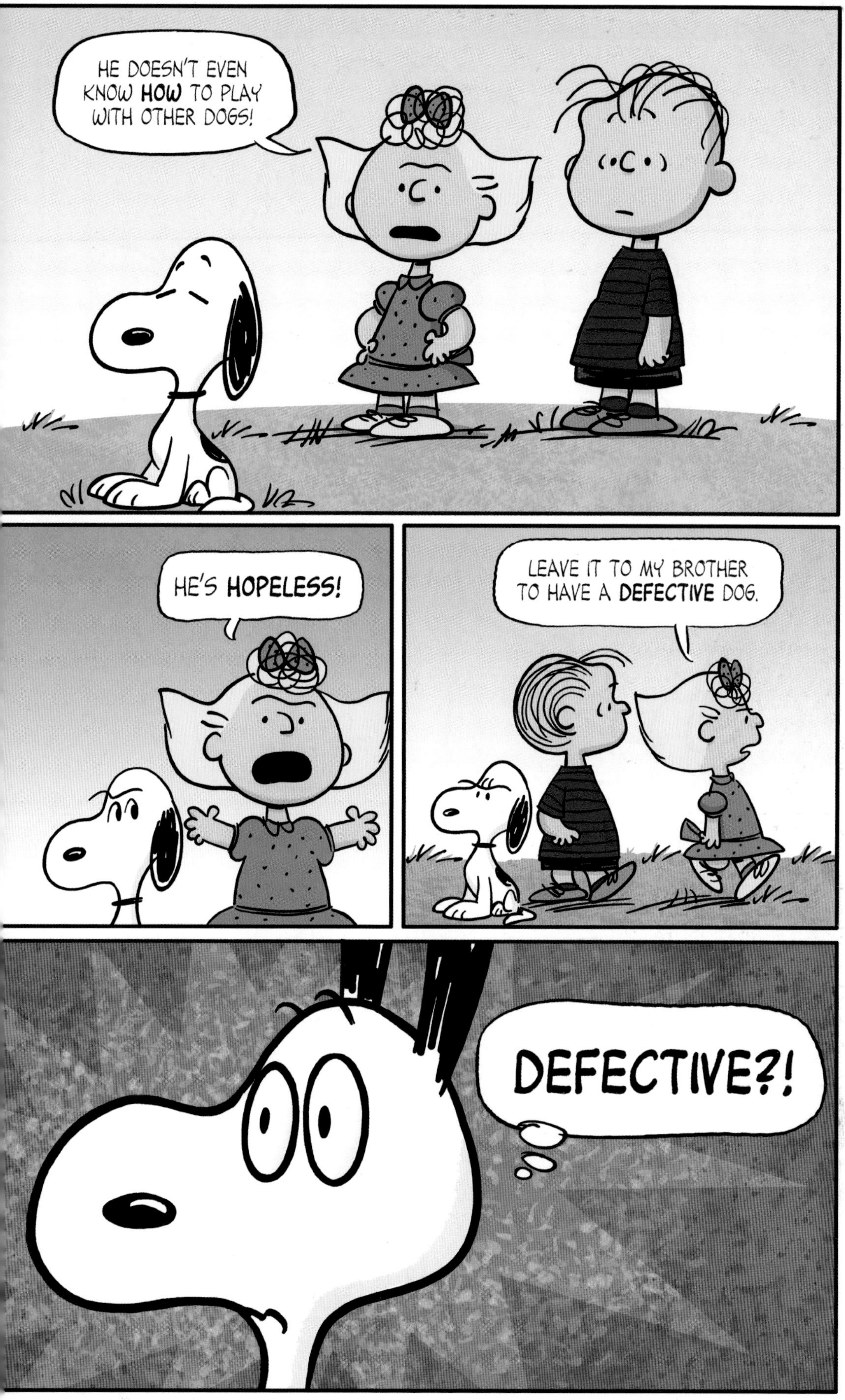
HE DOESN'T EVEN KNOW **HOW** TO PLAY WITH OTHER DOGS!
HE'S **HOPELESS!**
LEAVE IT TO MY BROTHER TO HAVE A **DEFECTIVE** DOG.
DEFECTIVE?!

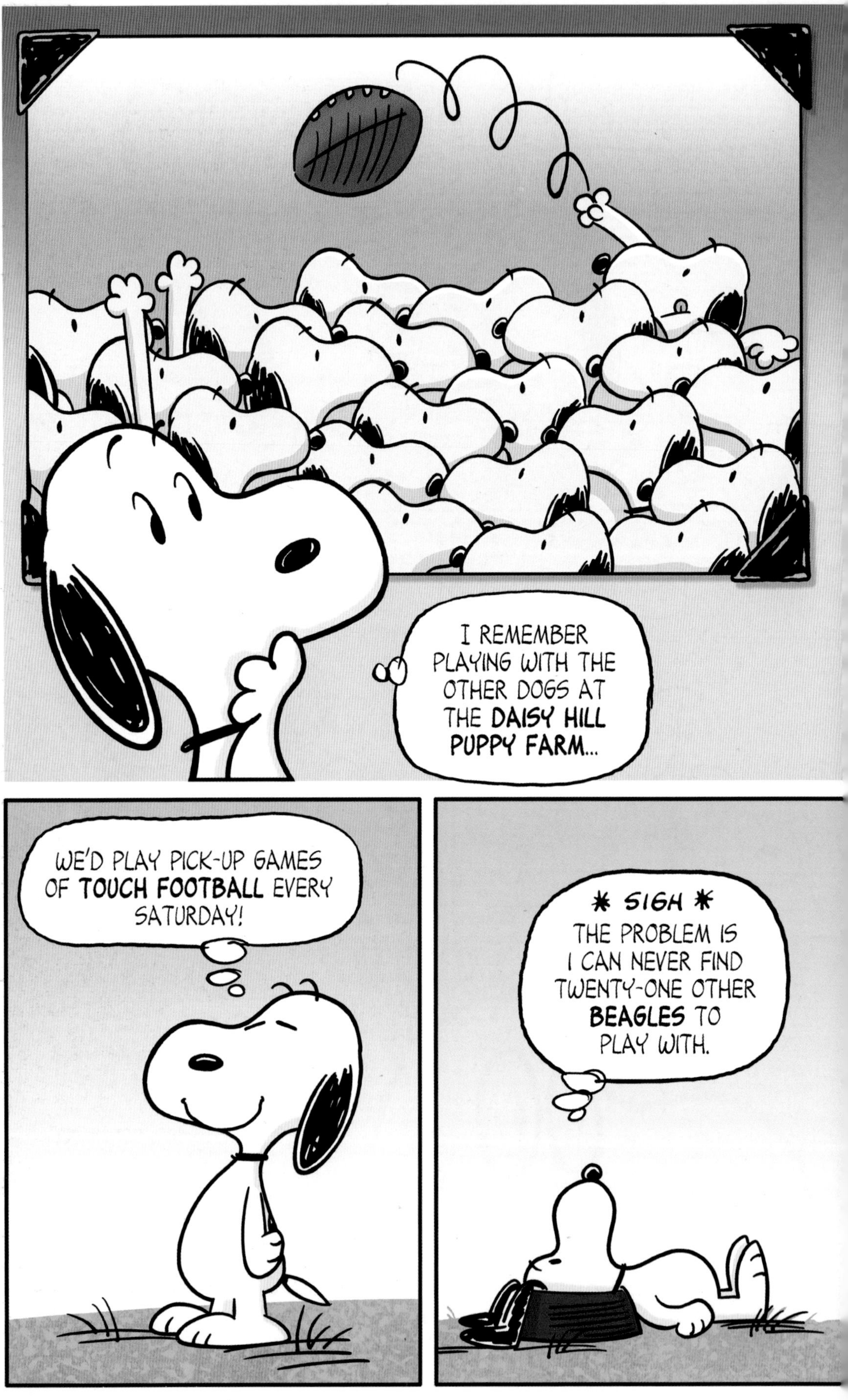
I REMEMBER PLAYING WITH THE OTHER DOGS AT THE DAISY HILL PUPPY FARM...
WE'D PLAY PICK-UP GAMES OF TOUCH FOOTBALL EVERY SATURDAY!
* SIGH * THE PROBLEM IS I CAN NEVER FIND TWENTY-ONE OTHER BEAGLES TO PLAY WITH.

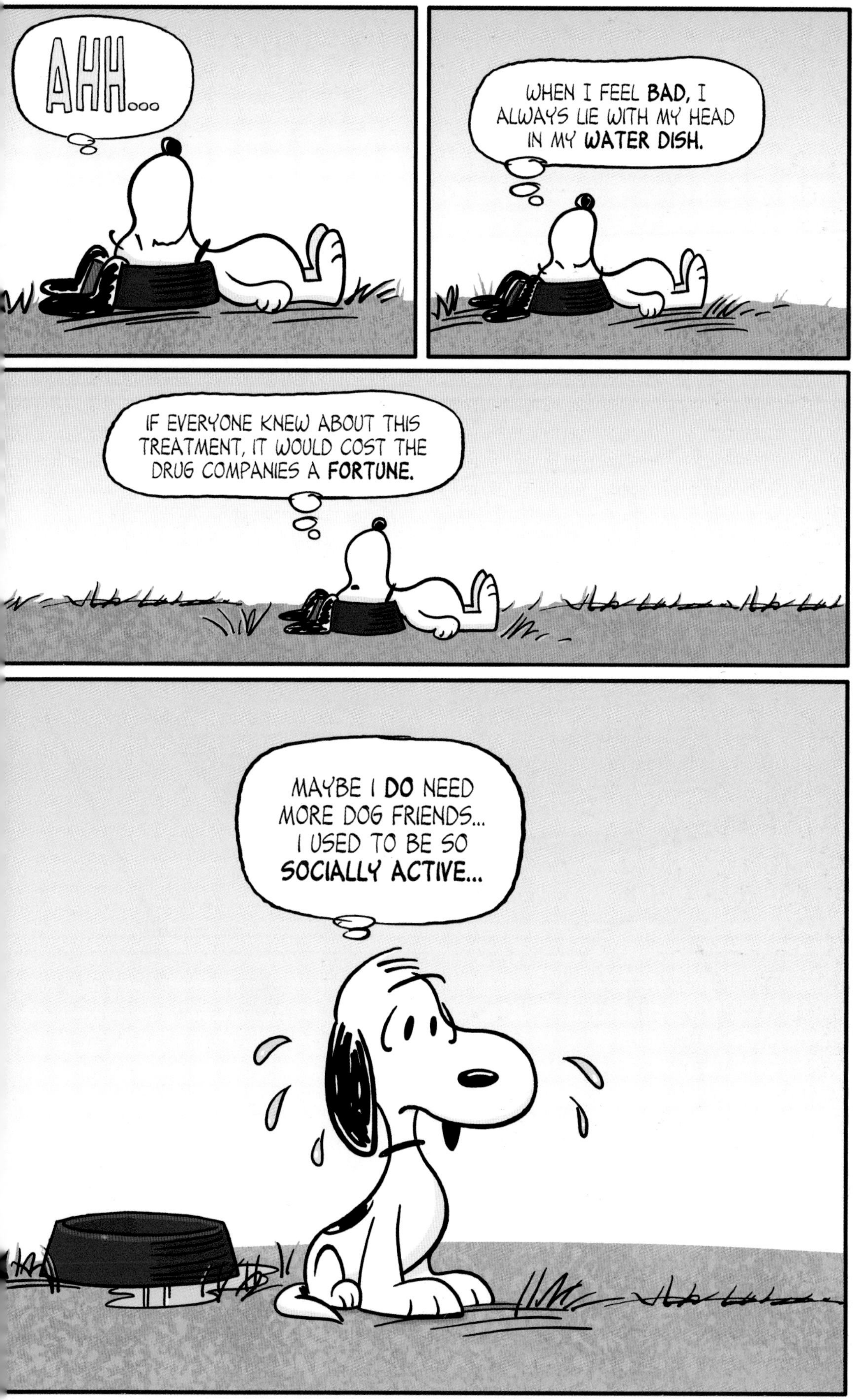
AHH...
WHEN I FEEL BAD, I ALWAYS LIE WITH MY HEAD IN MY WATER DISH.
IF EVERYONE KNEW ABOUT THIS TREATMENT, IT WOULD COST THE DRUG COMPANIES A FORTUNE.
MAYBE I DO NEED MORE DOG FRIENDS... I USED TO BE SO SOCIALLY ACTIVE...

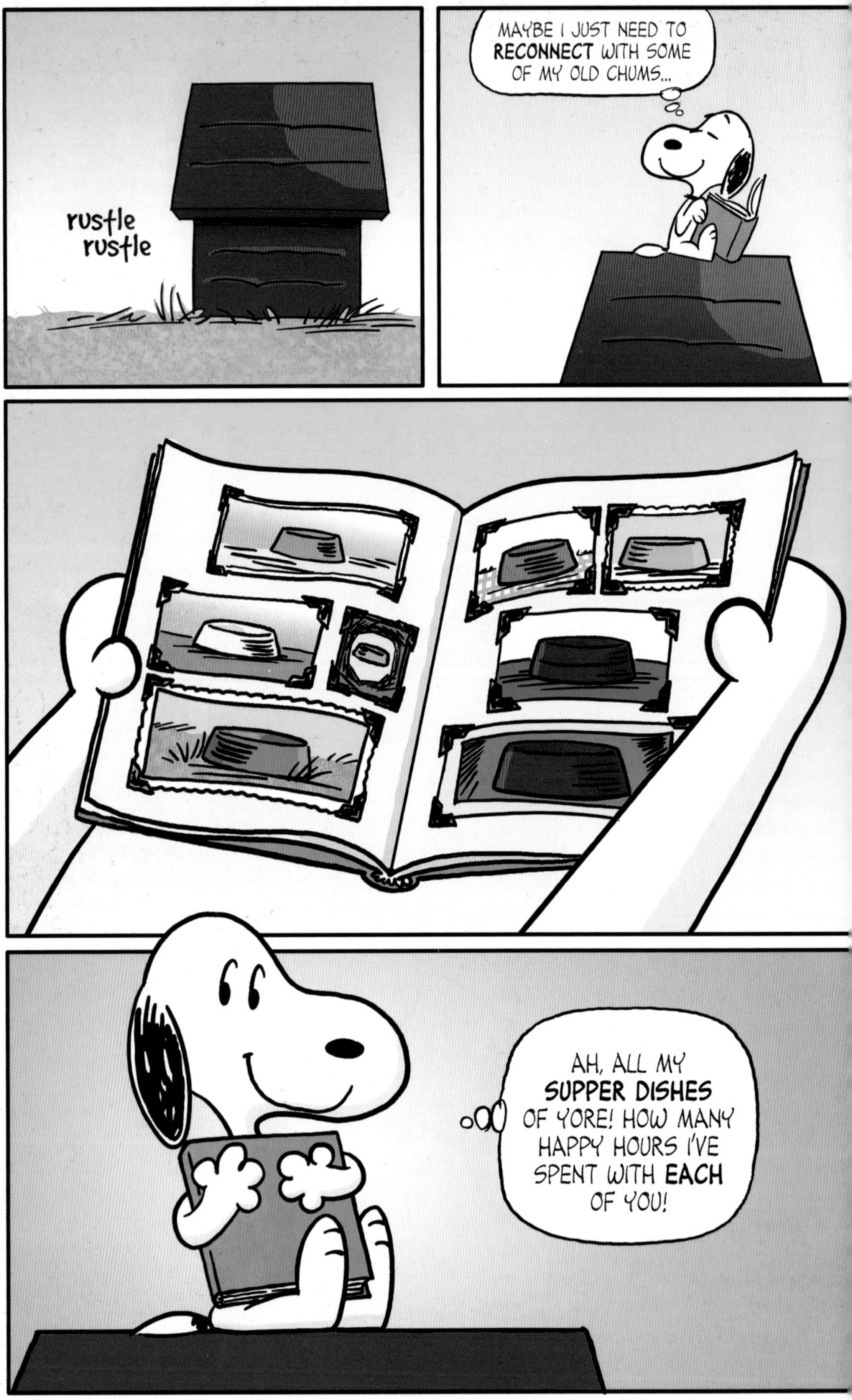
rustle rustle
MAYBE I JUST NEED TO RECONNECT WITH SOME OF MY OLD CHUMS...
AH, ALL MY SUPPER DISHES OF YORE! HOW MANY HAPPY HOURS I'VE SPENT WITH EACH OF YOU!

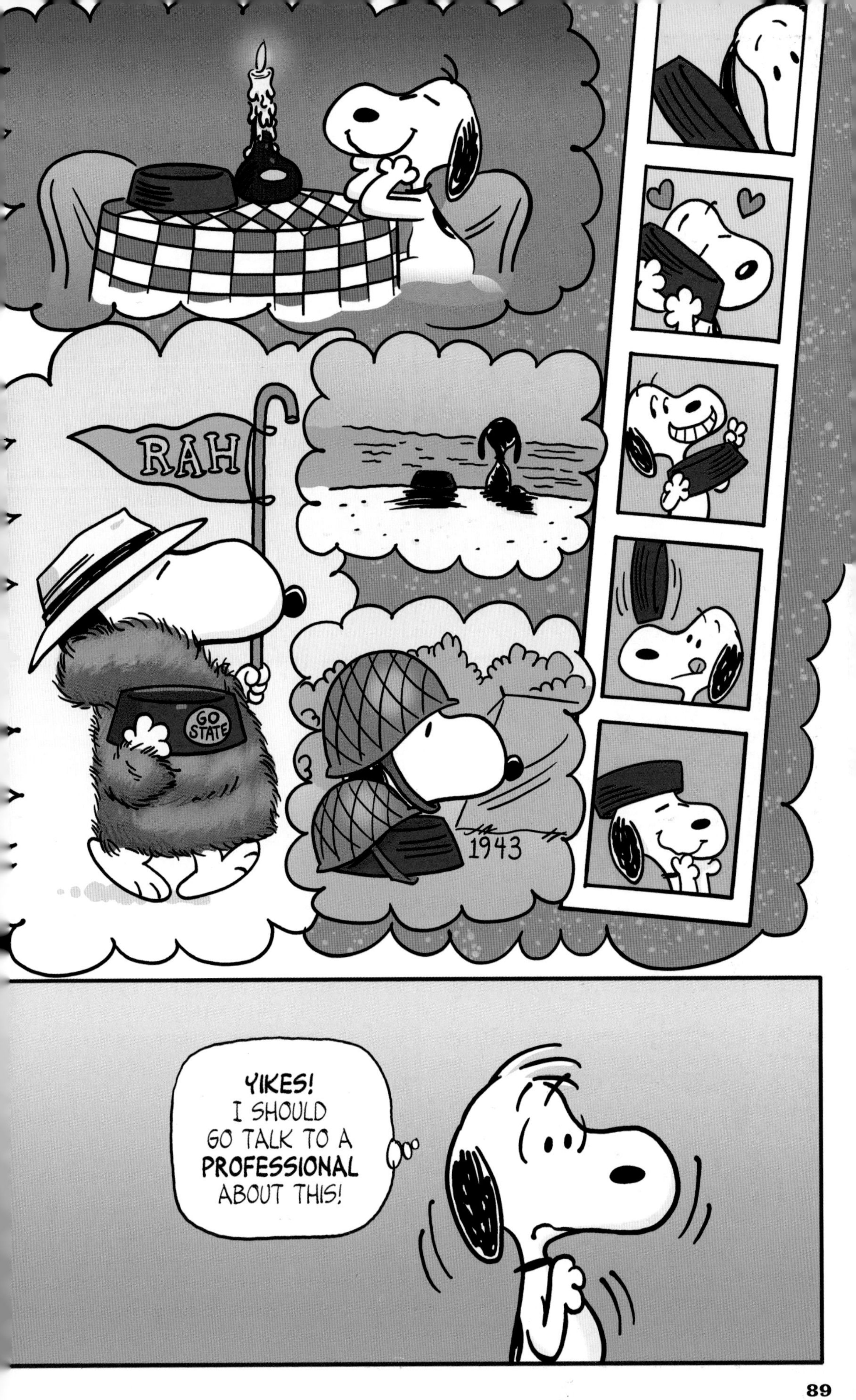
RAH
GO STATE
1943
YIKES! I SHOULD GO TALK TO A PROFESSIONAL ABOUT THIS!

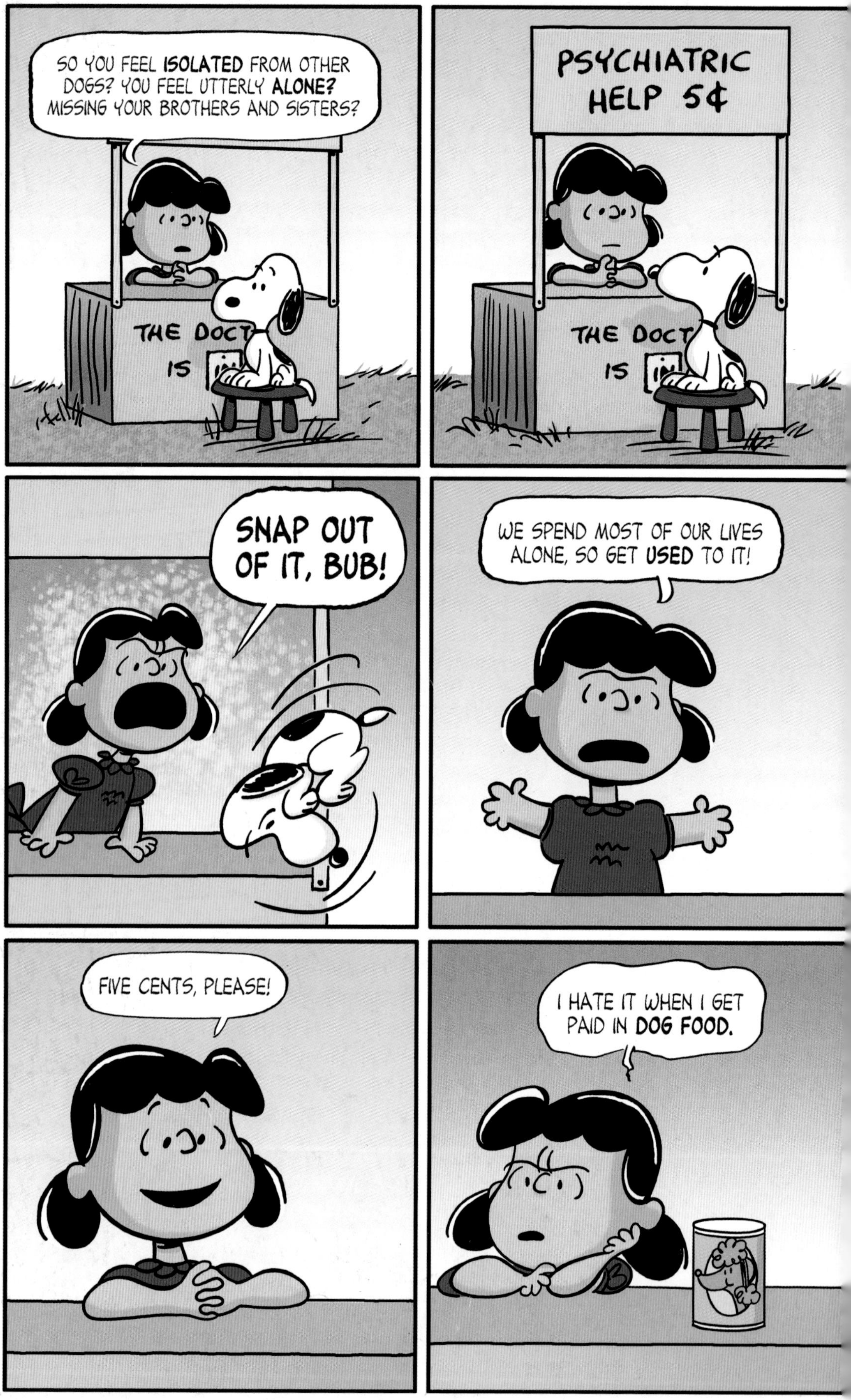
SO YOU FEEL **ISOLATED** FROM OTHER DOGS? YOU FEEL UTTERLY **ALONE?** MISSING YOUR BROTHERS AND SISTERS?
THE DOCT
IS
PSYCHIATRIC HELP 5¢
THE DOCT
IS
SNAP OUT OF IT, BUB!
WE SPEND MOST OF OUR LIVES ALONE, SO GET **USED** TO IT!
FIVE CENTS, PLEASE!
I HATE IT WHEN I GET PAID IN **DOG FOOD.**

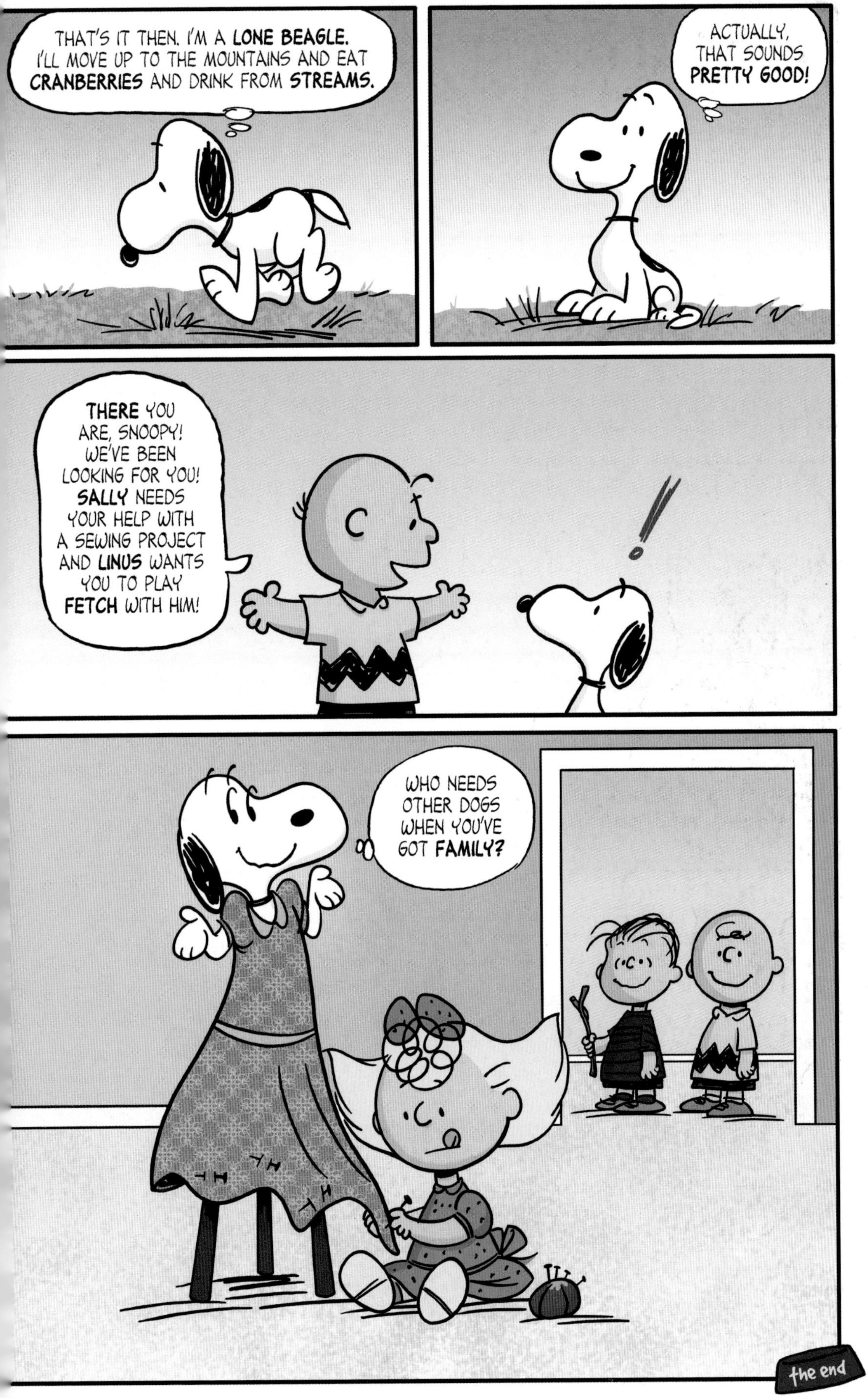
THAT'S IT THEN. I'M A **LONE BEAGLE.** I'LL MOVE UP TO THE MOUNTAINS AND EAT **CRANBERRIES** AND DRINK FROM **STREAMS.**
ACTUALLY, THAT SOUNDS **PRETTY GOOD!**
THERE YOU ARE, SNOOPY! WE'VE BEEN LOOKING FOR YOU! **SALLY** NEEDS YOUR HELP WITH A SEWING PROJECT AND **LINUS** WANTS YOU TO PLAY **FETCH** WITH HIM!
!
WHO NEEDS OTHER DOGS WHEN YOU'VE GOT **FAMILY?**
the end

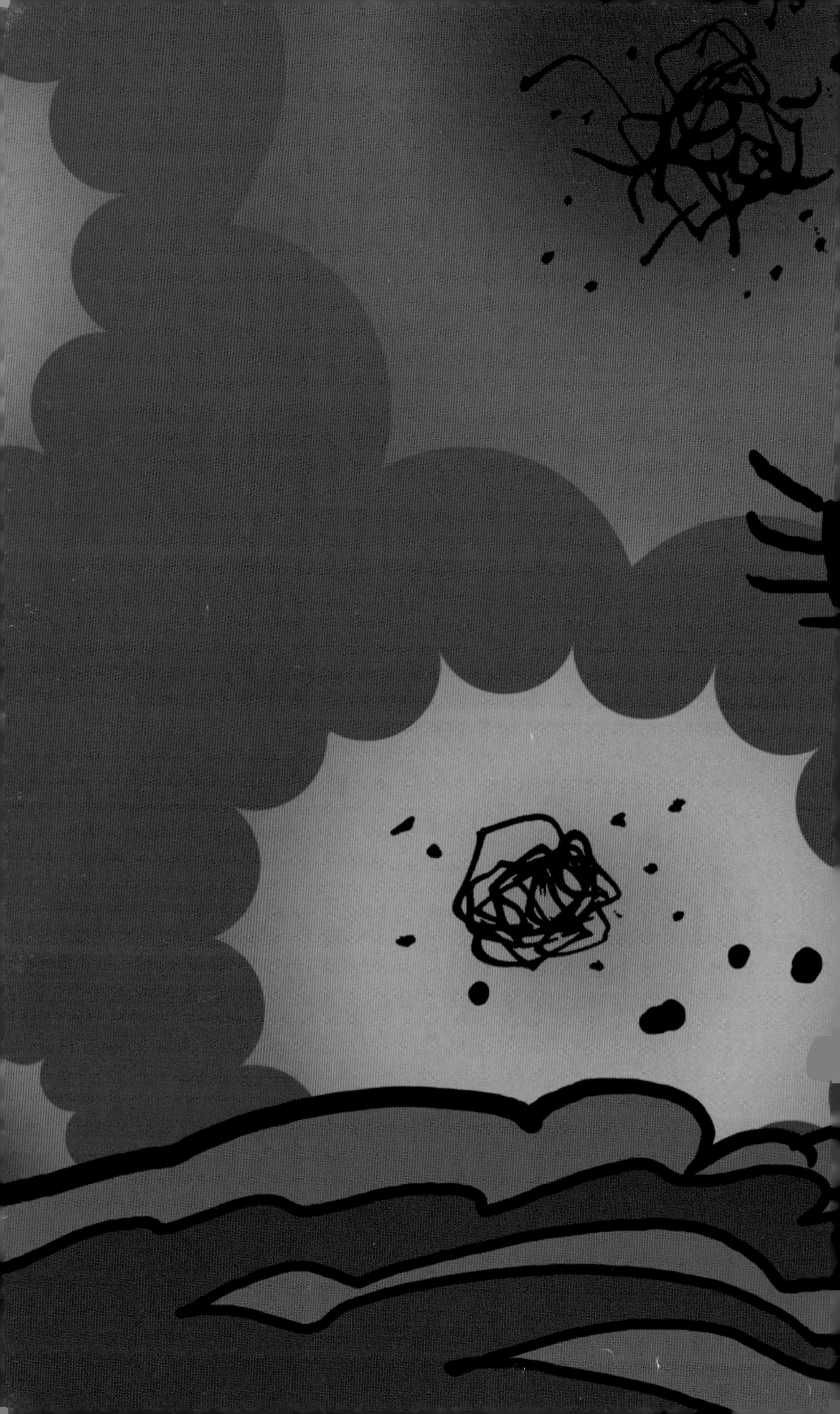

Cover Gallery

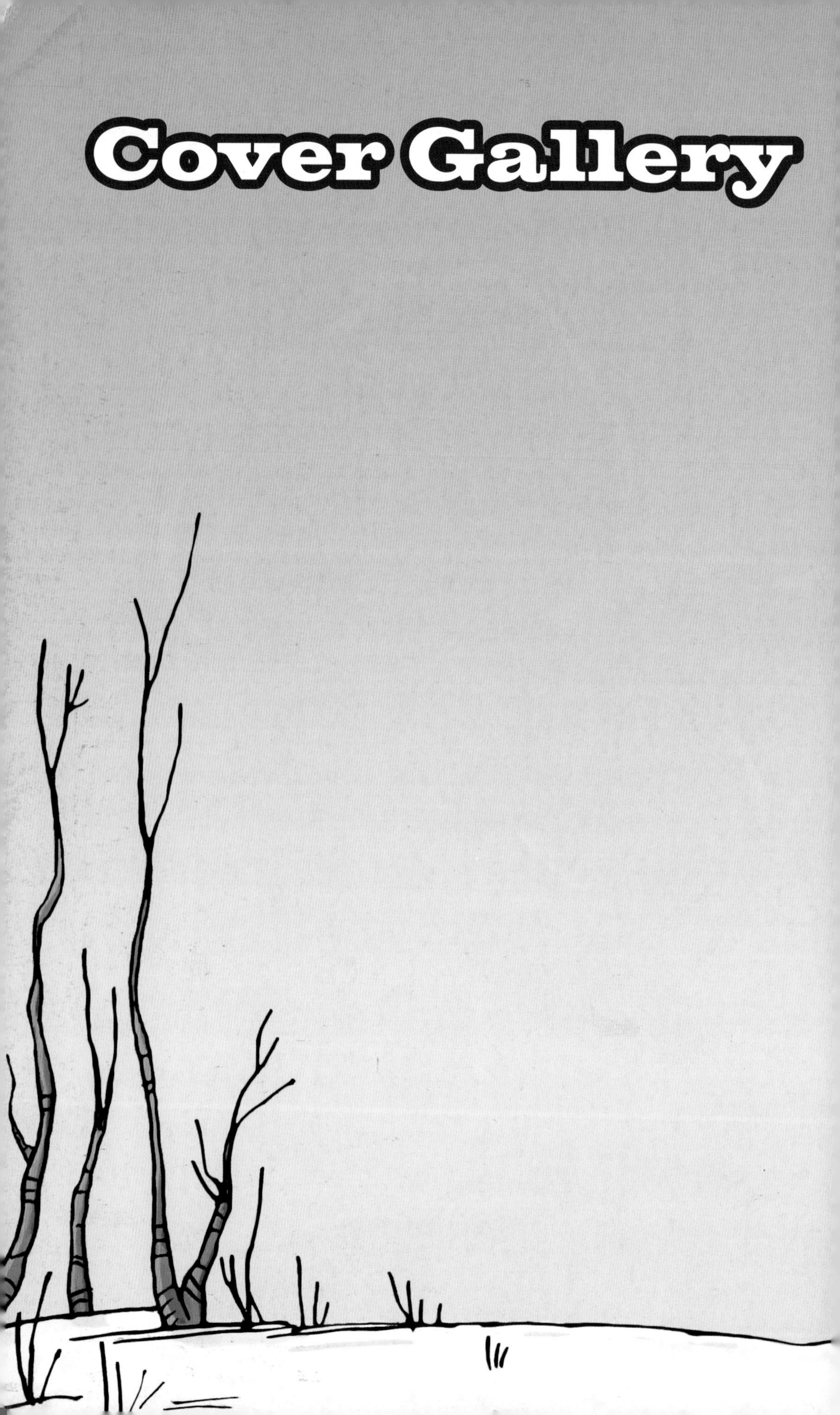

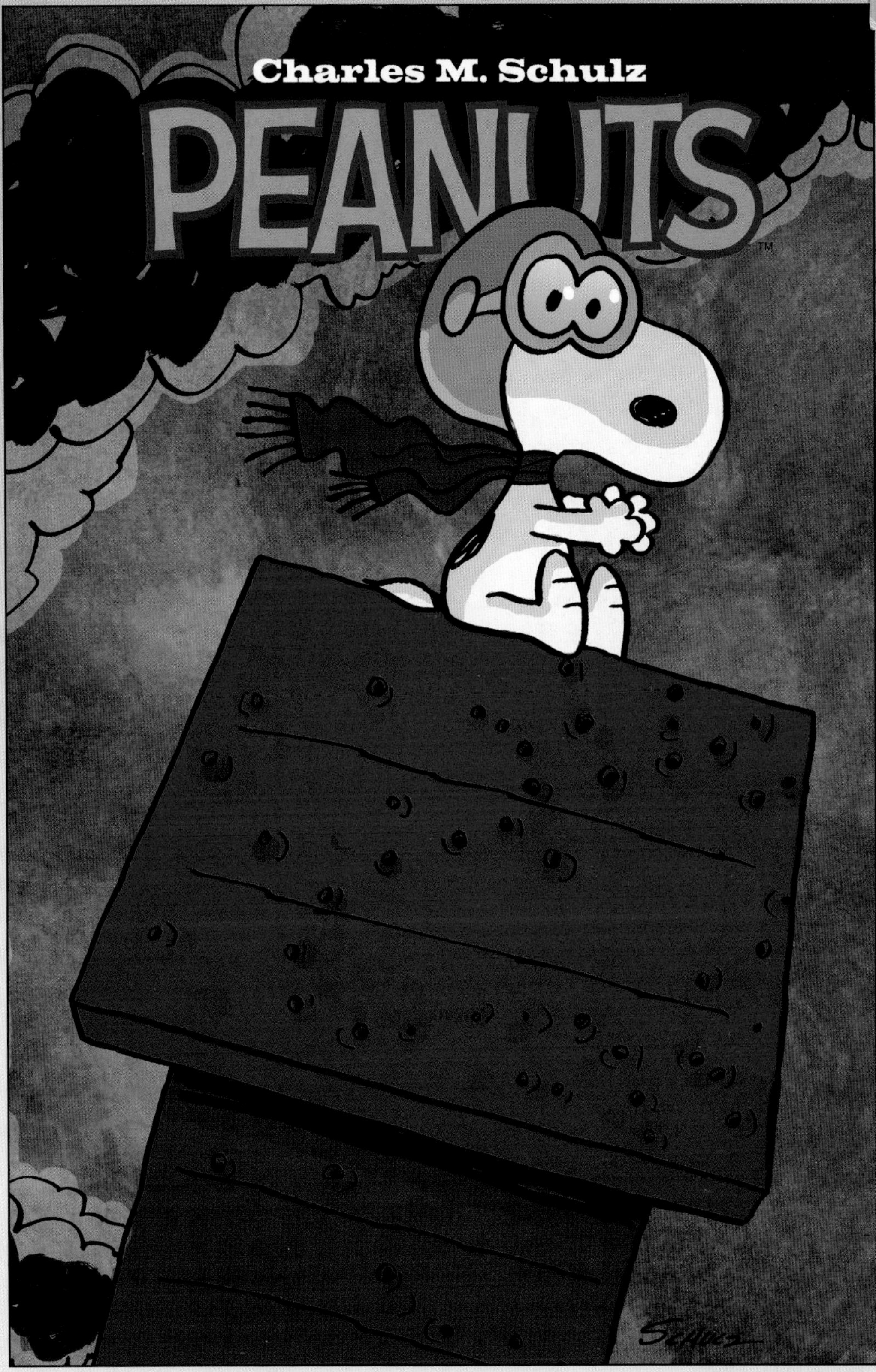
Charles M. Schulz
PEANUTS
TM

Pencils by Vicki Scott
Inks by Paige Braddock
Colors by Art Roche
Design by Iain R. Morris

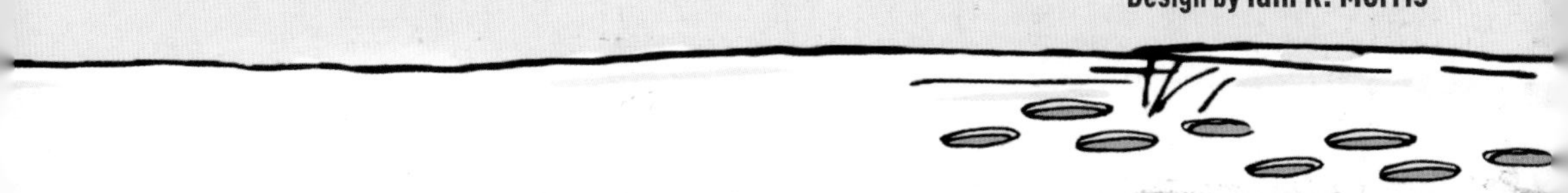

Peanuts Volume 2 #6

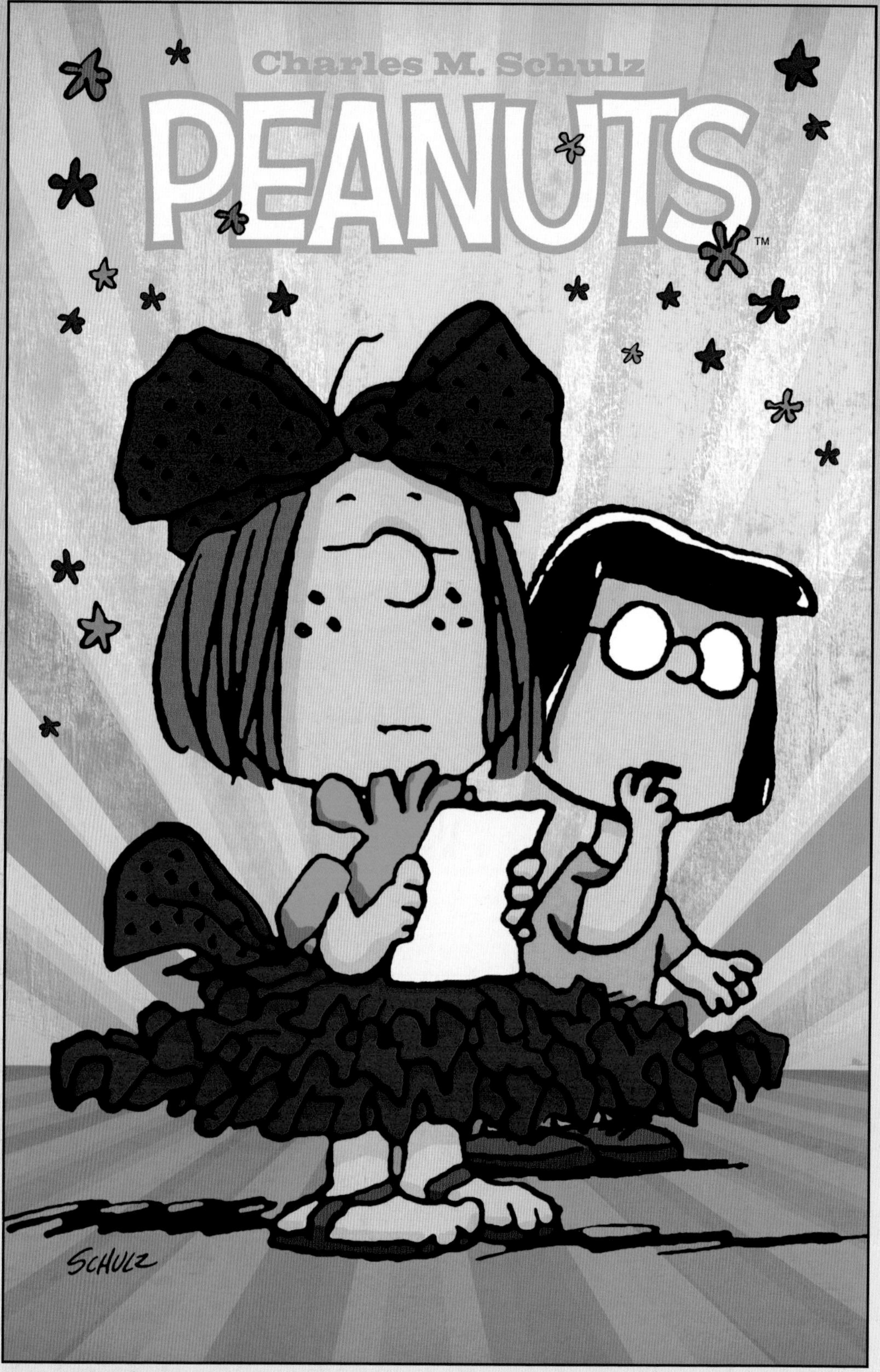

Charles M. Schulz
PEANUTS
SCHULZ

by Charles M. Schulz
Design by Iain R. Morris

Peanuts Volume 2 #6 ECCC Exclusive Cover

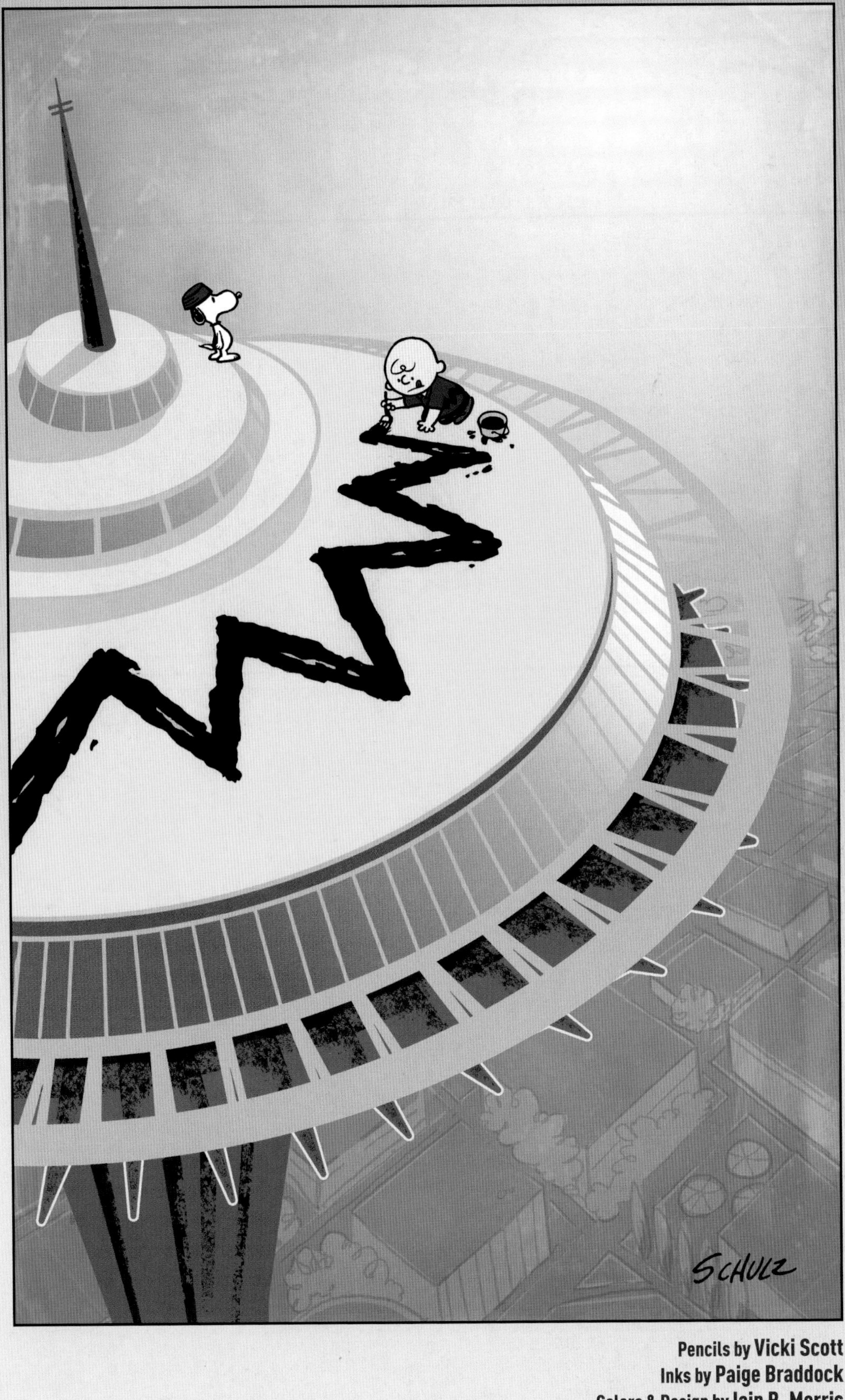
SCHULZ

Pencils by **Vicki Scott**
Inks by **Paige Braddock**
Colors & Design by **Iain R. Morris**

Peanuts Volume 2 #7

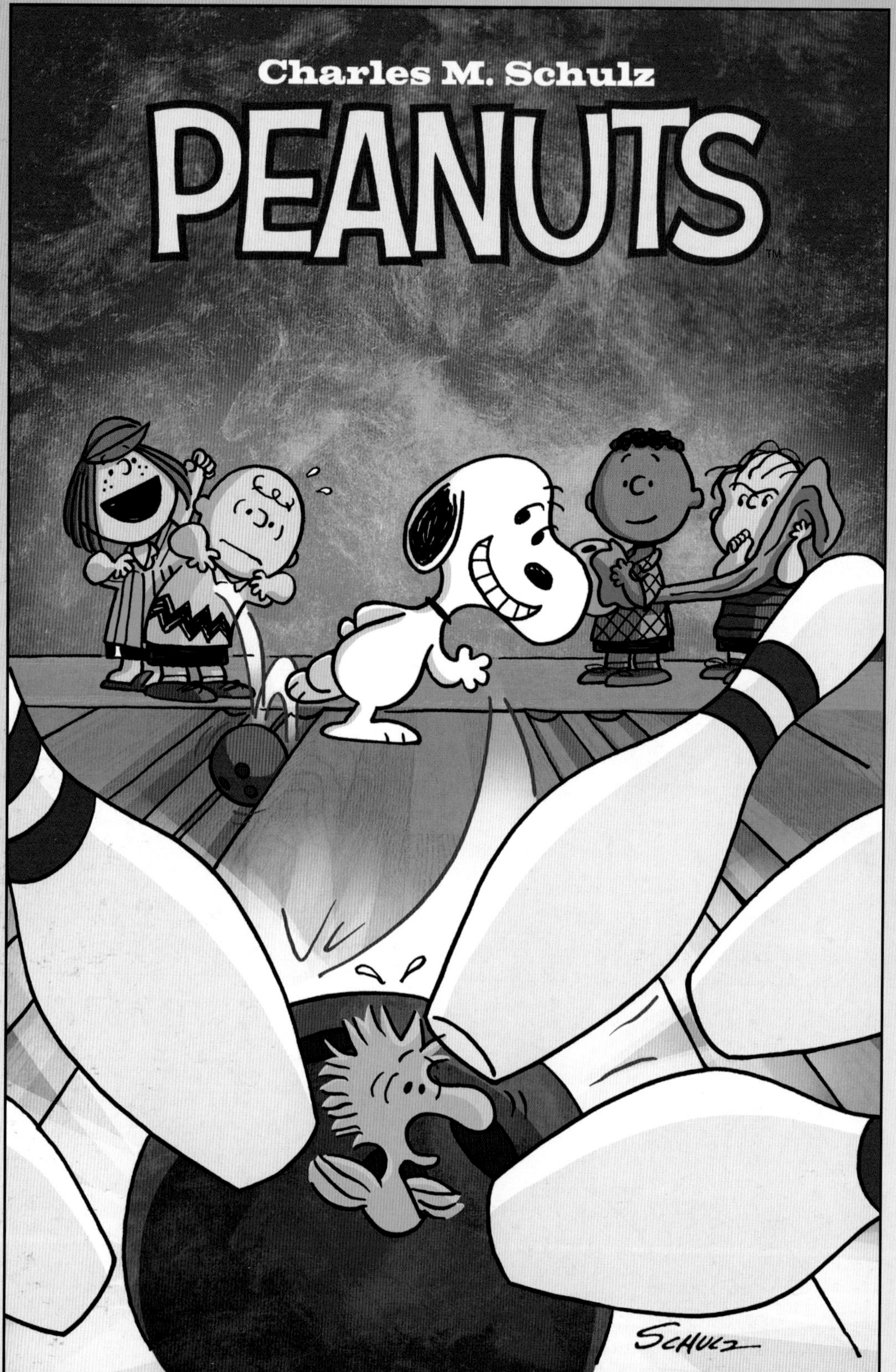
Charles M. Schulz
PEANUTS
SCHULZ

Pencils by Vicki Scott
Inks by Paige Braddock
Colors by Nina Kester

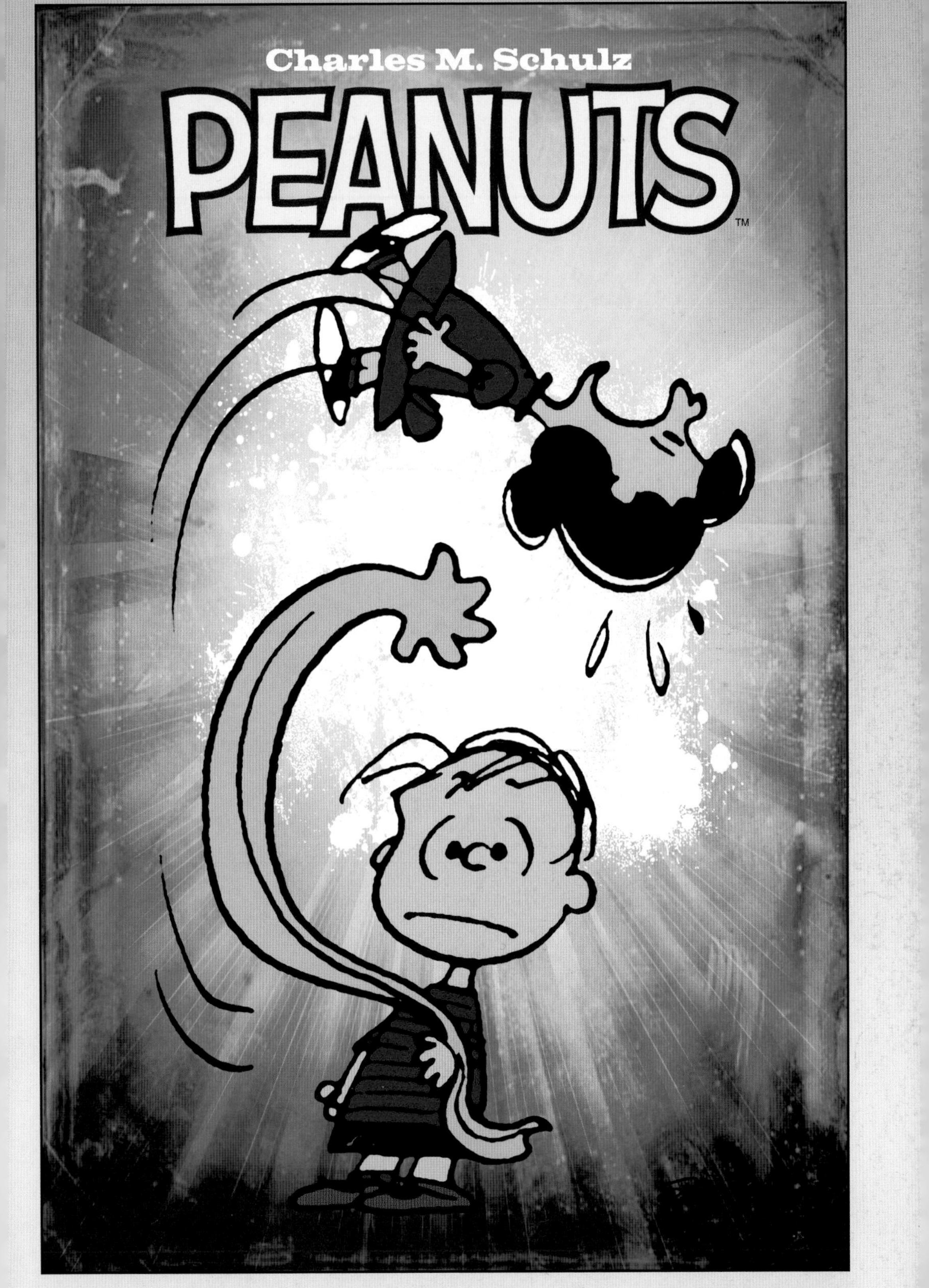
Charles M. Schulz
PEANUTS
TM

Art by Charles M. Schulz
Design by Iain R. Morris

Peanuts Volume 2 #5 Flying Ace
First Appearance Cover

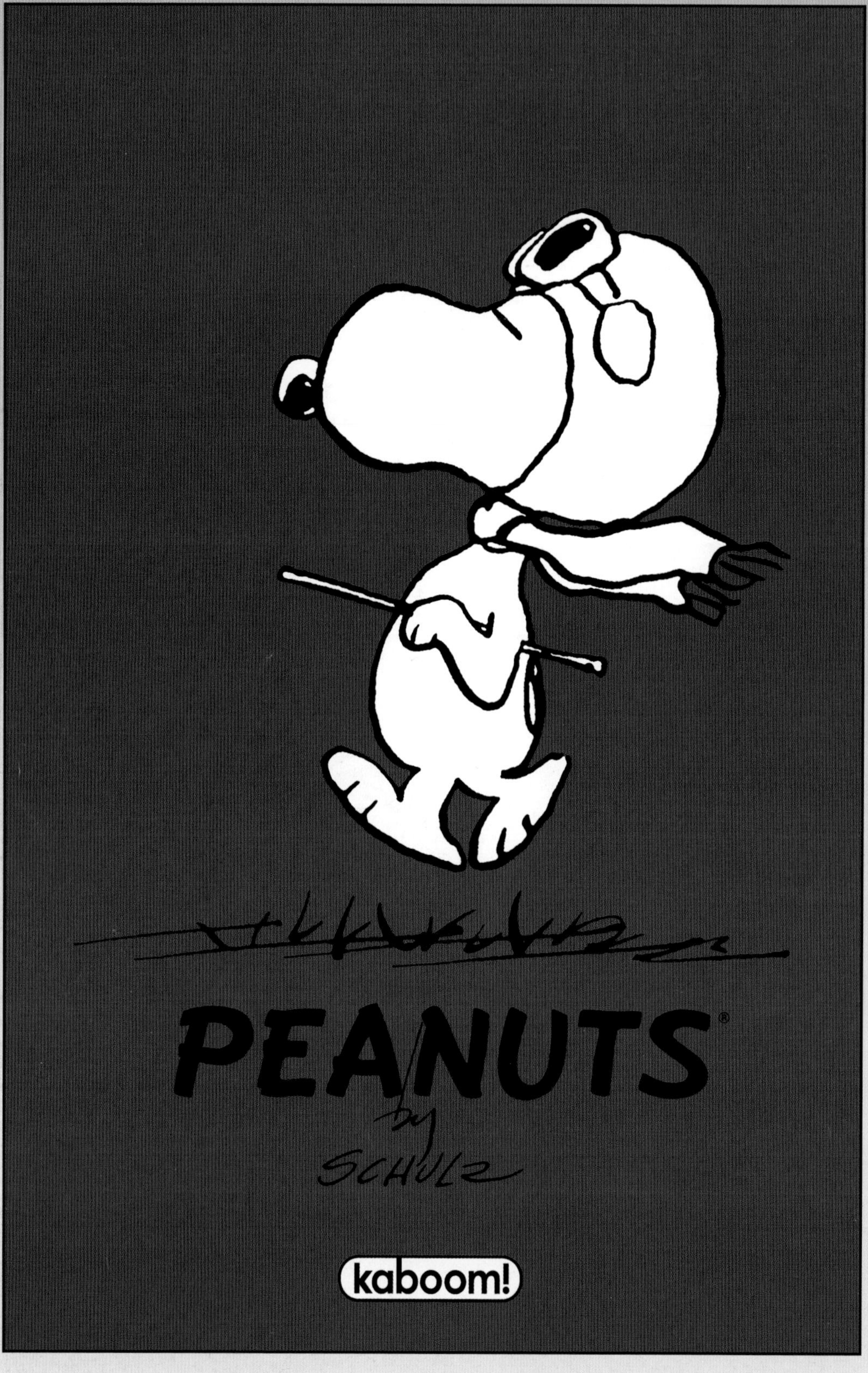
PEANUTS®
by SCHULZ
kaboom!

PEANUTS

by SCHULZ

PEANUTS
by SCHULZ
PILOTS! EMPTY YOUR POCKETS HERE!
GOOD MORNING, GROUND CREW!
HERE'S THE WORLD WAR I FLYING ACE POSING BESIDE HIS "SOPWITH CAMEL"...
CONTACT!
IT'S THE DAWN PATROL! WE'RE OUT TO HUNT DOWN THE RED BARON!
I CROSS OVER THE ENEMY LINES...I CAN SEE THE NETWORK OF TRENCHES BELOW...
SUDDENLY A "FOKKER TRIPLANE" APPEARS OUT OF THE CLOUDS! IT'S THE RED BARON!!
DIVING DOWN OUT OF THE SUN, ANTI-AIRCRAFT FIRE EXPLODING ALL AROUND ME, I CATCH HIM IN MY SIGHTS! I...
RAT A TAT TAT TAT TAT TAT TAT!
AAUGH!
MAYBE I CAN GET A JOB WITH A GOOD COMMERCIAL AIRLINE...
SCHULZ

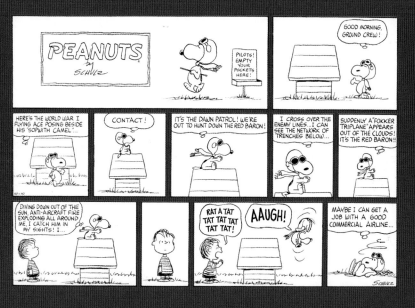

FLYING ACE
FIRST APPEARANCE
OCTOBER 10, 1965

kaboom!

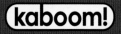

SELECT SERIES III
ISSUE FIVE

Art by **Charles M. Schulz**
Design by **Emily Chang**

Peanuts Volume 2 #6 Marcie
First Appearance Cover

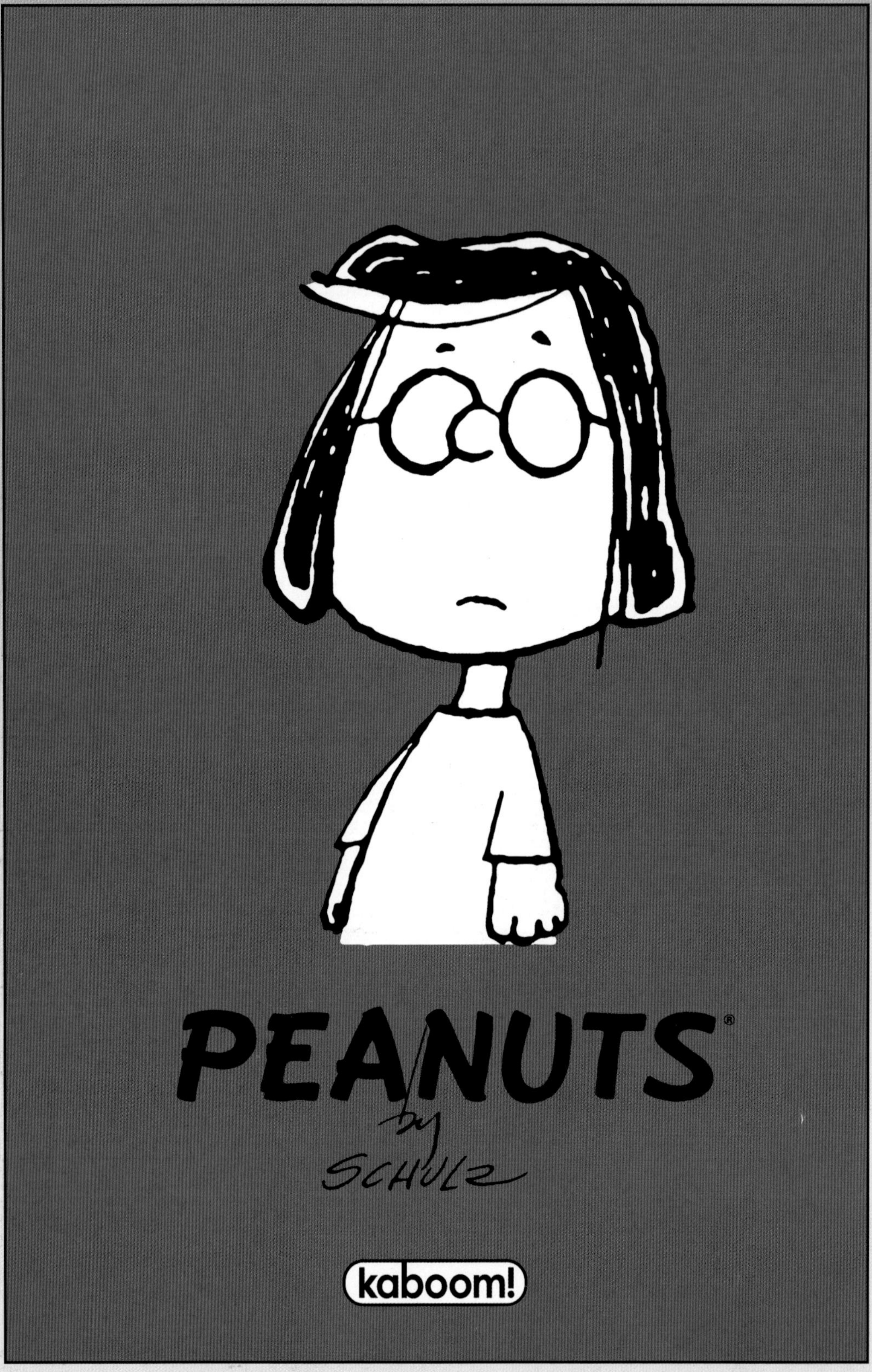
PEANUTS®
by SCHULZ
kaboom!

PEANUTS

by SCHULZ

RAIN! GOOD GRIEF!
HOW CAN YOU HAVE FUN AT CAMP WITH DORKY WEATHER LIKE THIS? I WONDER HOW CHUCK IS DOING?
SIR, WHAT TIME IS LUNCH?
DON'T CALL ME "SIR"! WHAT KIND OF A DORKY KID ARE YOU?
DORKY?
7-20
SCHULZ

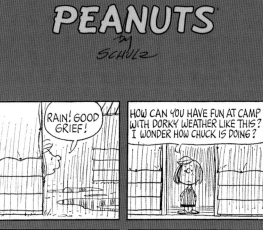

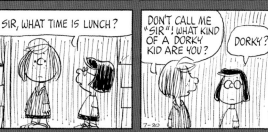

MARCIE

FIRST APPEARANCE

JUNE 18, 1968

kaboom!

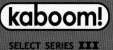

SELECT SERIES III

ISSUE SIX

Art by Charles M. Schulz

Design by Emily Chang

Peanuts Volume 2 #7 Franklin
First Appearance Cover

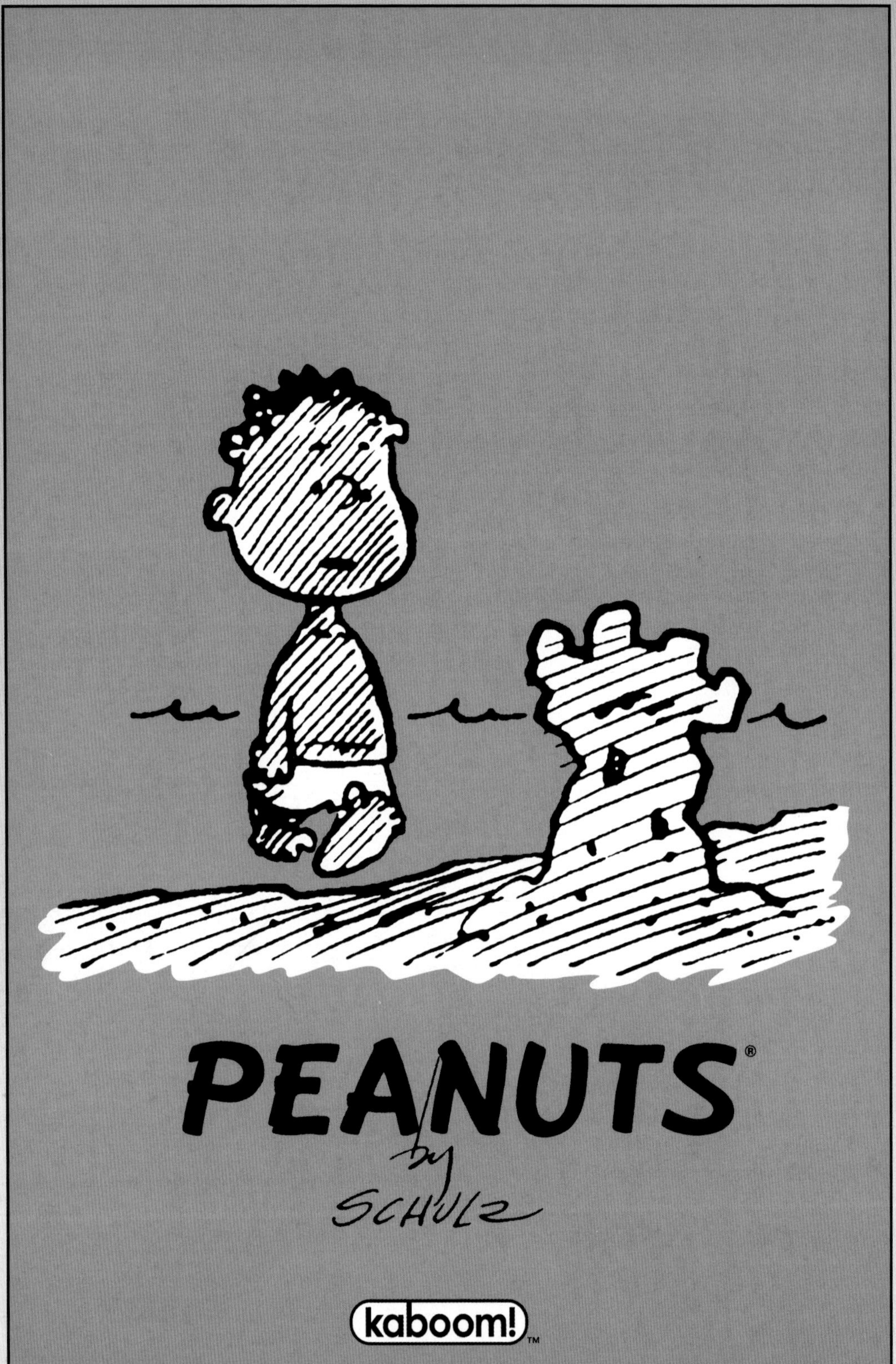
PEANUTS®
by
SCHULZ
kaboom!™

PEANUTS

by SCHULZ

IS THIS YOUR BEACH BALL?
HEY! YEAH! THANK YOU VERY MUCH!
I WAS SWIMMING OUT THERE, AND IT CAME FLOATING BY..
7-31
MY SILLY SISTER THREW IT INTO THE WATER
I SEE YOU'RE MAKING A SAND CASTLE..
IT LOOKS KIND OF CROOKED
I GUESS MAYBE IT IS.. WHERE I COME FROM, I'M NOT FAMOUS FOR DOING THINGS RIGHT...
SCHULZ

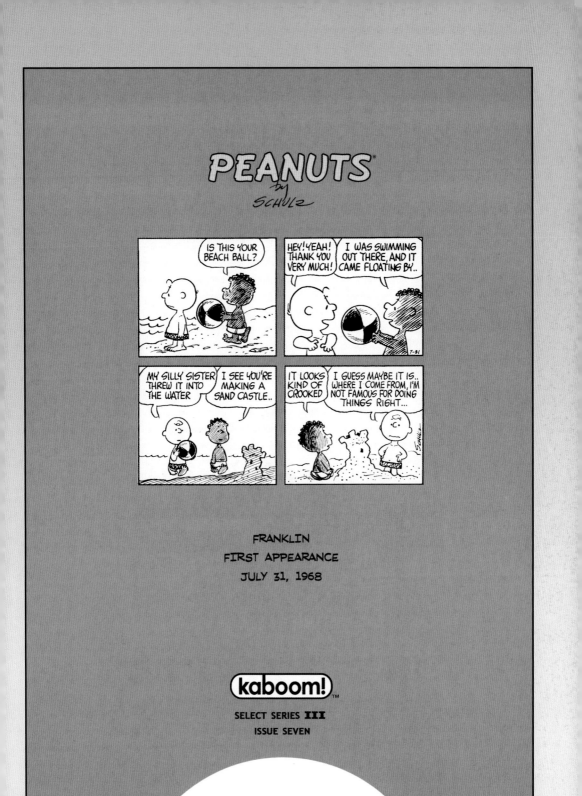

FRANKLIN

FIRST APPEARANCE

JULY 31, 1968

kaboom!™

SELECT SERIES III

ISSUE SEVEN

Art by Charles M. Schulz

Design by Emily Chang

Peanuts Volume 2 #8 Sally First Appearance Cover

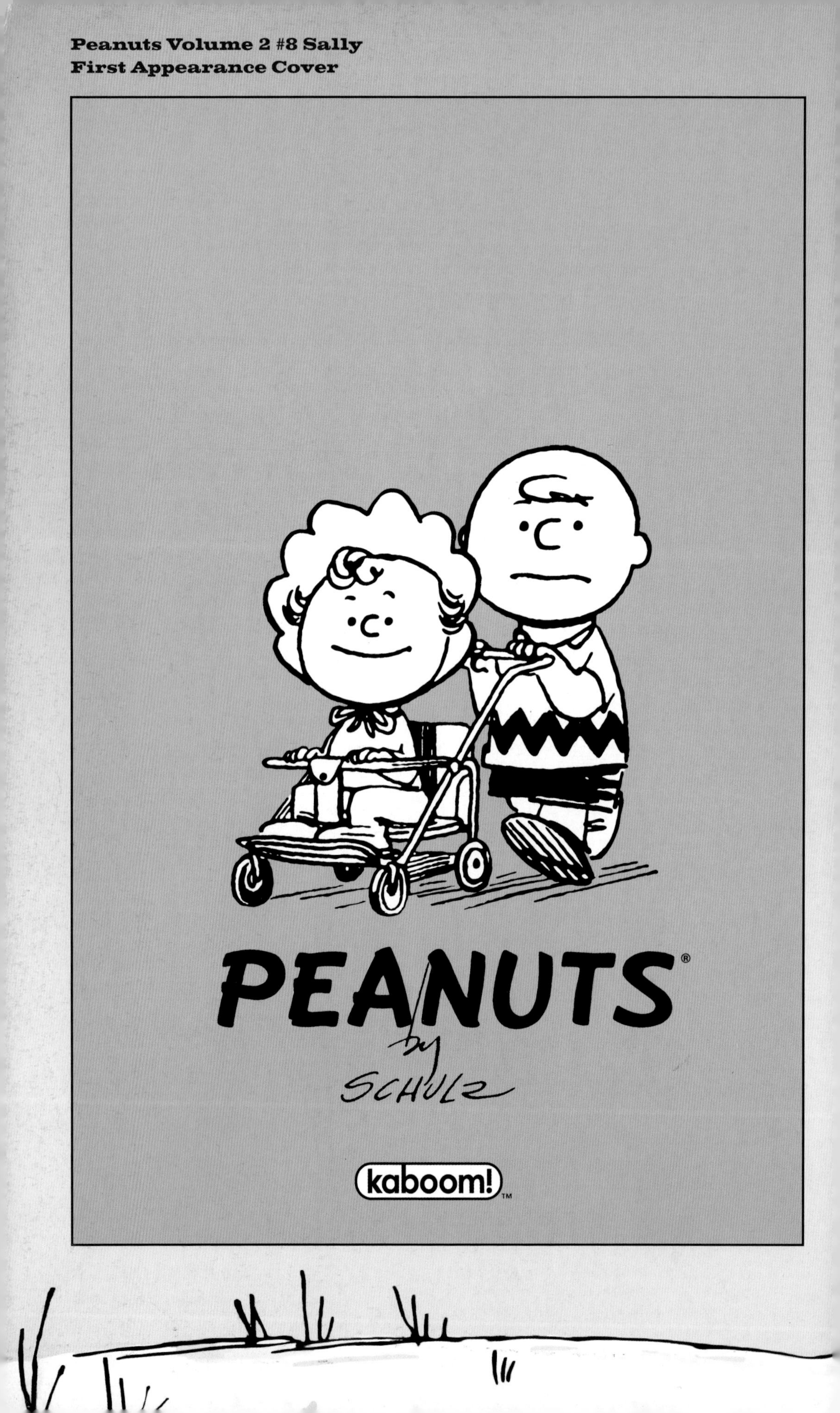
PEANUTS®
by SCHULZ
kaboom!™

PEANUTS by SCHULZ

PEANUTS
WHERE'S ALL YOUR STUFF, CHARLIE BROWN? WHERE'S YOUR GLOVE AND YOUR BAT AND EVERYTHING?
I CAN'T PLAY TODAY!
?
WADDYA MEAN, YOU CAN'T PLAY TODAY?!
JUST WHAT I SAID... I CAN'T PLAY TODAY! THERE'S SOMETHING ELSE I HAVE TO DO!!
BUT YOU'VE **GOTTA** PLAY, CHARLIE BROWN.. YOU'RE OUR **MANAGER**!
YOU MAY BE A **LOUSY** MANAGER, BUT YOU'RE STILL OUR MANAGER!
WE **NEED** YOU!
I CAN'T HELP IT...
YOU GOTTA PLAY, CHARLIE BROWN!
YOU GOTTA! YOU GOTTA!
I JUST DON'T UNDERSTAND IT!
I UNDER-STAND IT!
YOU UNDERSTAND IT? SINCE WHEN DID **YOU** BECOME SO UNDERSTANDING?
IT'S NOT A MATTER OF UNDERSTANDING
SIGH
IT'S SIMPLY THE AGE-OLD STORY!
SCHULZ

SALLY

FIRST APPEARANCE

AUGUST 23, 1959

kaboom!™

SELECT SERIES III

ISSUE EIGHT

Art by Charles M. Schulz

Design by Emily Chang

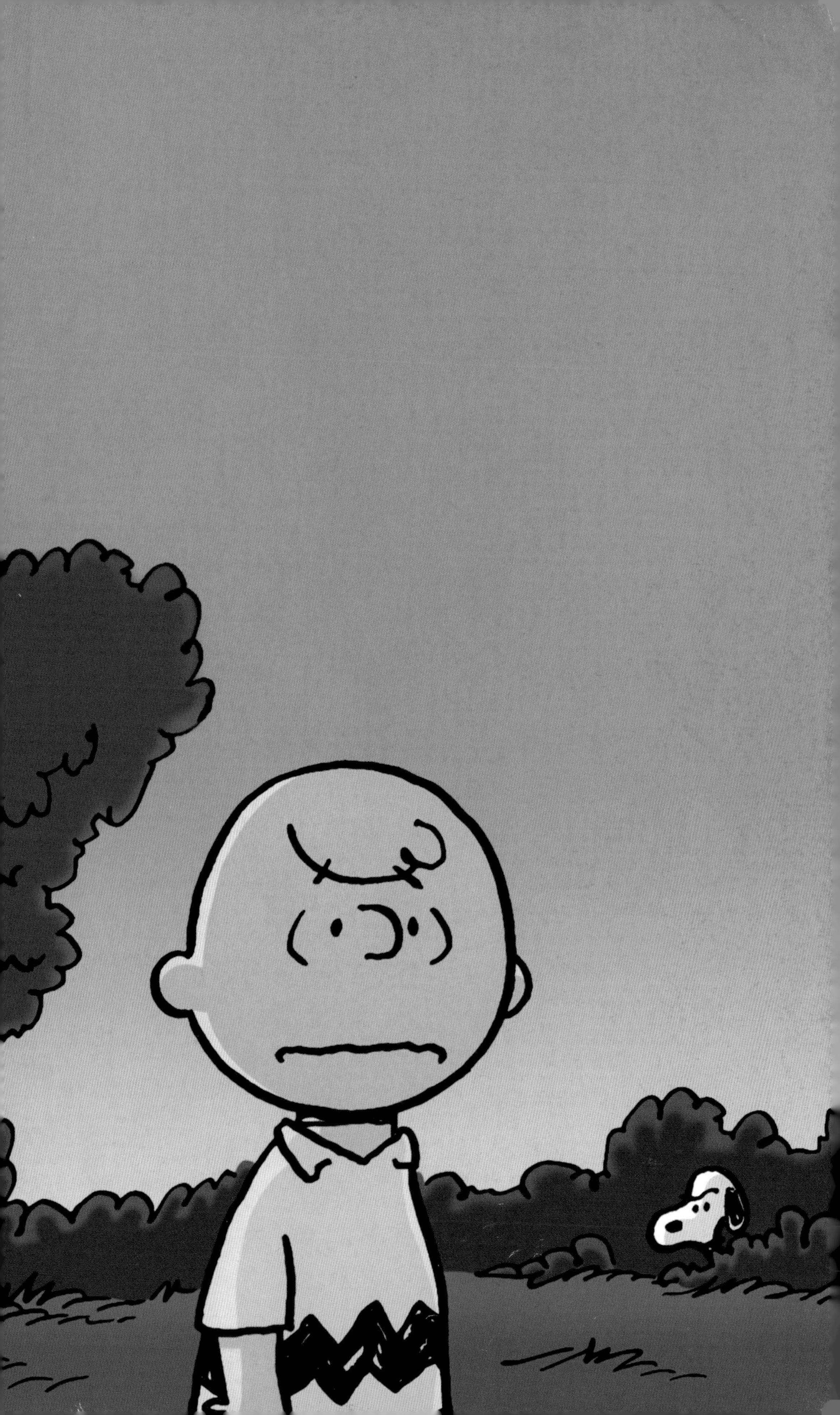

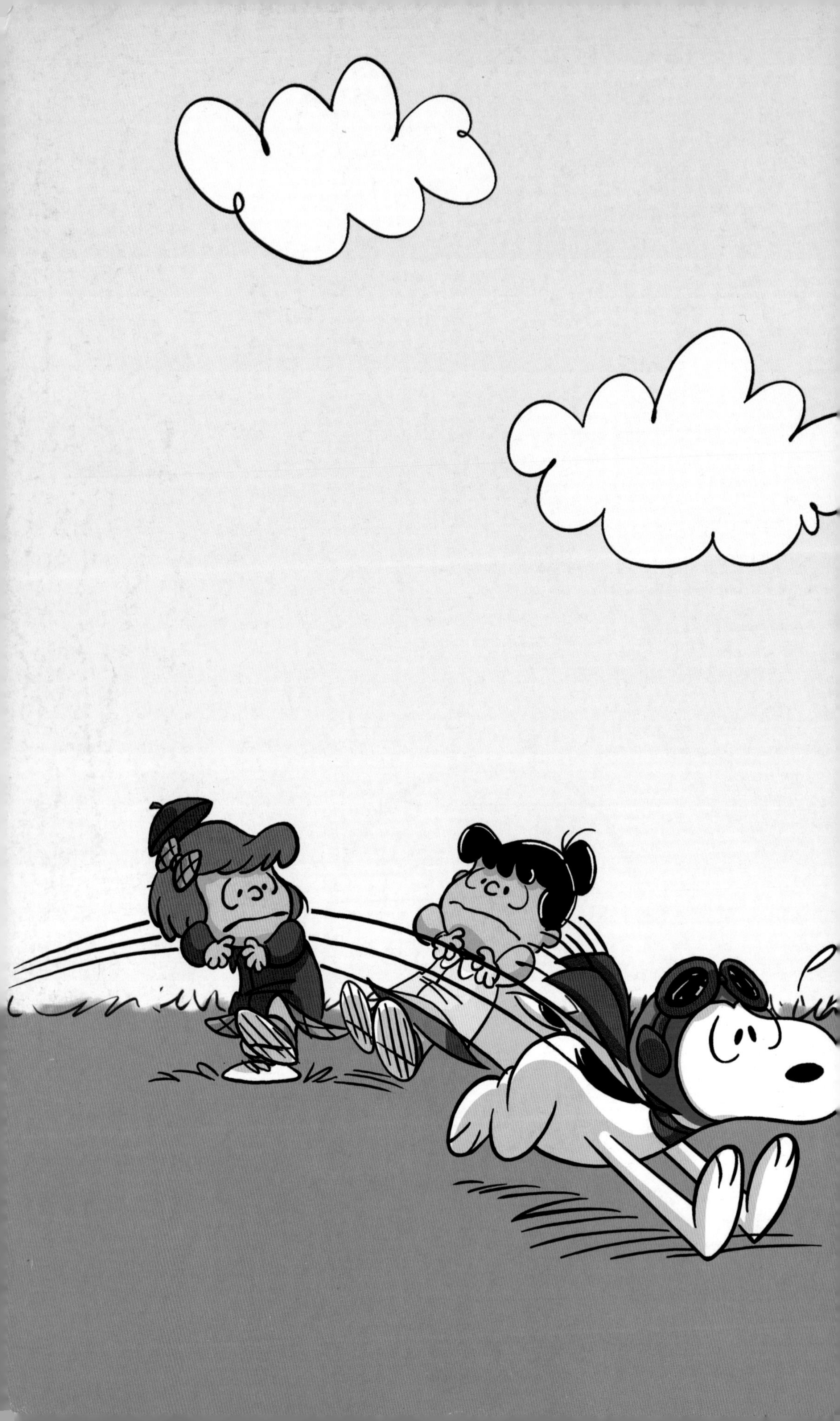

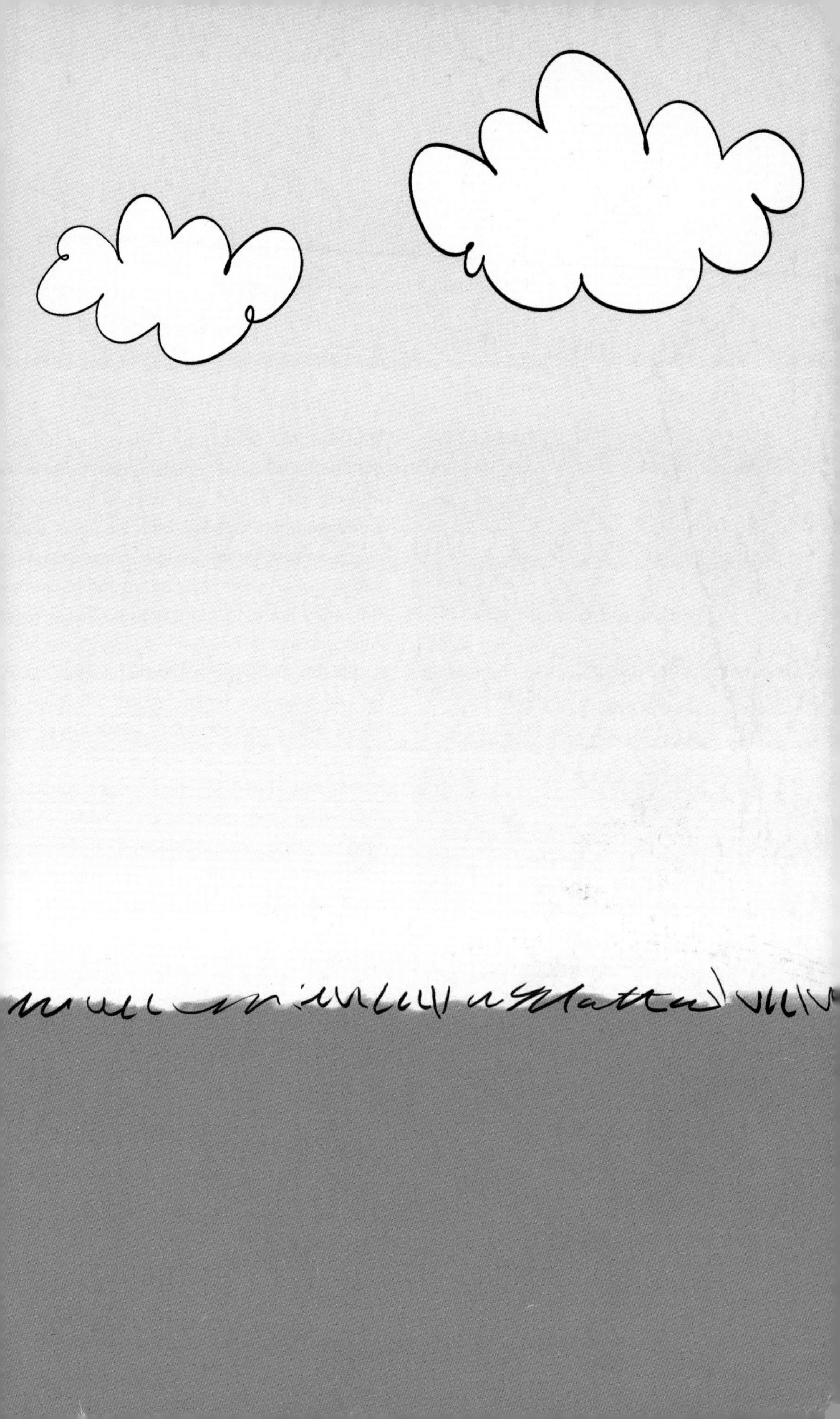

Charles M. Schulz once described himself as "born to draw comic strips." Born in Minneapolis, at just two days old, an uncle nicknamed him "Sparky" after the horse Spark Plug from the "Barney Google" comic strip, and throughout his youth, he and his father shared a Sunday morning ritual reading the funnies. After serving in the Army during World War II, Schulz's first big break came in 1947 when he sold a cartoon feature called "Li'l Folks" to the *St. Paul Pioneer Press*. In 1950, Schulz met with United Feature Syndicate, and on October 2 of that year, PEANUTS, named by the syndicate, debuted in seven newspapers. Charles Schulz died in Santa Rosa, California, in February 2000—just hours before his last original strip was to appear in Sunday papers.